Ali McKenzie

FROM THE FUTURE, WITH LOVE

Acorn Independent Press

My thanks and appreciation to Carmella for her ongoing support. Also to Debbie, David and Dave, for all sharing a small but important part of my literary adventure.

Chapter One

*'Simone was my sibling substitute,
I didn't need a real one.'*

How odd that the hands of a clock always move with the same speed, and yet for one person, time passes quickly and for another, far too slowly. Robyn fixed her gaze on the second hand, trying to puzzle the concept when she should really have been worrying about the English test paper on the desk in front of her.

Simone had made her promise to stay in the exam room until the bitter end and try her hardest. Oh well, half a promise kept at least, she was still here, wasn't she? Frowning, she re-read the scribbled paragraphs, which hadn't taken long to compose. 'Robyn Marie Harley', at least she'd written her name correctly and underlined it for confirmation. Daydreams and doodles had filled the rest of the allotted two hours, which had determined to pass as reluctantly as possible. The other students were writing frantically, worried that they would run out of the same precious few minutes.

Robyn drummed her fingers silently and looked at the clock again. Only another minute had passed, maybe her perspective was actually altering the passing of time. She frowned at the ridiculous notion and glancing around the hall her eyes rested on the desk to her right, Simone's desk, or at least it should have been.

Simone Harmon. Alphabetically, they'd been sat together in the reception class of the local primary school and had become best friends from those early days. After a week, the young pupils no longer had to sit in a particular order and so moved noisily around the classroom, finding new and exciting children to talk to. But Simone and Robyn had stuck together, daring anyone to sit between them.

Nine minutes to go, down to single figures. A burst of pleasure generated her first smile of the afternoon. Eyeing the paper critically, she wrote two more lines before crossing them out and shoving the whole thing as far away from her as the small desk allowed.

Everything seemed pointless since the accident in January. Or more accurately, four years before that when Robyn's parents, looking for answers as to why they couldn't conceive another child, found out that David Harley had testicular cancer.

A combination of high-dose chemotherapy, radiotherapy and surgery couldn't save the intelligent, fun-loving, forty-two-year-old loving husband and father. Within a few months after his death, Robyn had begun to lose her mother as well, not by such an obvious cause, but one that was just as devastating – alcohol.

Simone, her parents and younger brother Joey, became the surrogate family she needed, as she helplessly watched her mother's self-induced, spiralling decline into the abyss. At least that was Robyn's take on it. Not quite sixteen, she couldn't understand why her surviving parent was not the rock she'd always been, particularly now, when she needed her most.

Bitter words were flung between mother and daughter, ending with Robyn's hurtful taunt that her father would have been ashamed. From that moment on, they avoided each other, passing like silent shadows in a house that had once been filled with happiness and laughter.

Two minutes left, and she wasn't the only one fidgeting now. Even Richard Saunders, the boy who lived opposite, and who had got an unconditional uni offer, as had Simone, was packing his stuff away. Robyn caught his eye and gave a rare smile, he was okay really. His family had offered help after the death of her father. As with everyone else, they'd soon made an excuse to drift and stay away once Josie's drinking had made them feel awkward. In Richard's case, his own mother had drifted even further, following an affair with a work colleague. Robyn wondered how things might have been different for all of them.

Schoolwork, as well as everything else, had suffered. Scraping just enough decent grades in her 'A' levels, Robyn had got into the same local University as Simone by the skin of her teeth. Thank God for clearing! Without the support and guidance from her parents, she didn't have the slightest idea what she wanted to do and blindly followed her friend. A degree in English Literature was bound to land her a decent job, Simone's mother had enthused.

'Time's up,' a voice came from the front. 'Put your pens down, all papers stay on the desks in front of you. Leave as quietly and quickly as possible.'

Robyn felt nothing as she marched out of the hall, the university and off-campus, knowing she would never return. This wasn't what she wanted, it had taken the accident to bring that home once and for all. Perhaps there was a way of convincing Simone, who would beg her to take re-sits, that there was a much better alternative, for both of them.

'Do you want a lift home, Robyn?'

An old Land Rover pulled up and she grinned at the driver. 'No thanks, Rich, I'm doing a bit of shopping first.'

'Okay, see you around,' He stuck his hand out and waved before driving off.

He's become rather *available* lately, Robyn thought as alarm bells started to ring. God, no, far too posh, they'd never suit at all. While he was at private school playing Rugby in the under 15's league, she and Simone were going through a rebellious token '*goth*' phase. She chuckled remembering years eight and nine in St. John's Academy.

The head teacher had done his best to ban makeup of any kind and was not impressed to see yet another new group of white faced, black-eyed teens, milling about the playgrounds like the living dead.

The time had also seemed right to follow like sheep and get a tattoo. One day after school, she and Simone had visited the house of a friend. For £10, the father had asked no questions and Robyn sported a ring of pink daisies that circled her navel, whilst Simone feeling braver, had her name in traditional Chinese characters on the underside of her right wrist. It was the only time the girls had seen both sets of parents united in a temper that took almost a week to die down.

With both of them being blonde, and Simone steadfastly refusing to dye her hair, the staunch black-haired, clique soon tired of them. After a last-ditch attempt by Robyn, involving the cheapest and blackest dye she could find, the whole goth thing lost its appeal. She was left with a ruined mass of black, grey and ginger hair that resembled a Halloween wig. The muffled sounds of her friend's laughter and profuse apologies at finding it so funny rang in her ears, the whole way to the hairdressers.

A drastic restyle into a short bob, as well as colouring the remains a soft caramel brown, was the only way forward. Robyn recalled Richard taking the trouble to cross the road and comment how nice her hair looked. That had been almost five years ago. Now it was back to its natural honey blonde and midway down her back.

None of the curls had regrown, but a natural wave gave it a jaunty lift and bounce that Simone's mum always said she'd pay good money to have.

Simone's hair, a shade lighter again had been almost long enough to sit on. That was before the accident. Now her hair was gone, partly shaved off before she was rushed to the operating theatre after sustaining what appeared to be a life-threatening head injury.

Celebrating the end of an assessment week in January, Robyn had received a drunken phone call from her mother. She'd apparently cut herself badly on broken glass and needed her daughter home immediately. Leaving Simone with a group from their course, Robyn said goodnight and headed off. The next morning, she was woken by a frantic phone call from Mr Harmon saying Simone was in intensive care and to come to the hospital quickly. Her world plunged into darkness once again.

* * *

'Hi Robz, how was it? Don't you dare even think of lying to me.' Simone spoke slowly, her voice slurring at times.

The FaceTime notification had sounded the minute Robyn put her foot in the door. Even from over six hundred miles away, her friend seemed to know her every move. 'God, I can't hide anything from you. Nice hair, by the way, I didn't see it properly last time under that ridiculous beanie.'

'Don't change the subject,' Simone grinned, rubbing her left hand over the thick tight spikes that had almost reached two inches and were finally beginning to flatten slightly. Because her face was small and oval, she looked elfin like, her honey brown eyes sparkled mischievously.

'Crap, if you must know, a complete and utter balls-up.'

Laughter bubbled up and exploded through the airwaves from Aberdeenshire all the way south to Devon. After chatting for a few minutes, Robyn saw Mrs Harmon – Babs as she'd been told to call her – enter Simone's room.

'Hello dear, I think I need to rescue my daughter, although it's wonderful to hear her laugh so much.' She peered closely at Simone's iPhone and Robyn jumped slightly as a large eye seemed to appraise her. 'You're looking too thin and pale, definitely too pale. The sooner you get here in the Highland air the better. Don't drive Robyn, it's too far. Get the train, we'll send you the money. Or even fly, I'm sure Exeter or Bristol fly to Aberdeen.'

Robyn could have cried; the whole of Simone's family was so good to her. 'I can't wait. All being well, I'll be with you by Monday evening. And thanks, Babs, but I want my car.' She didn't tell them that she expected to stay for a very long time; hopefully finding work, as well as helping Simone with her rehabilitation. 'I promise to take it really slowly and I'll stop overnight.' She saw the look of worry on the older woman's face, worry that was echoed in her own mind. Full of self-doubt, even after passing her driving test eight months ago, twenty miles was the furthest she'd driven in one go.

Her father's car had sat unused in the garage until her seventeenth birthday when she'd signed up with the 'Pass with Us' driving school, which actually consisted of just one man in a Smart Fortwo. She'd nearly died from embarrassment driving past Richard who was parking his father's Range Rover. He was obviously trying hard not to laugh, but it soon shut him up when she informed him she'd be having her father's Audi A4 eventually. She hadn't mentioned that she was scared to death of driving it.

Robyn had told Simone she intended to set off the next day, which would give her two nights to break the journey. Daunting didn't even begin to describe how she felt covering over two hundred miles a day on her own.

The last hurdle needed to be jumped with some care. Robyn would be twenty in a few weeks, so didn't need permission. A blessing of sorts would be nice, especially as her mother held the purse strings of the money her father had left her.

Pleasantly surprised to find her in the kitchen, actually preparing a meal, Robyn sat at the table and wondered how her news would be received. Would her mother be disappointed, cross or perhaps not care less, glad to be rid of the responsibility?

'This looks nice, Mum, thanks.' Robyn poked the risotto with suspicion, it certainly wasn't up to the standard of cooking her mother had produced when her father was alive, but it was the best thing to appear on this table for a long time.

They ate in silence, but as soon as Robyn had taken her last mouthful, Josie started to speak. 'I have something to talk to you about.'

'Oh right,' Robyn said, taken aback. Those were pretty much the words she'd been about to use herself. There'd been no inquiry about the exam, of course, her mother wouldn't remember that was today.

'Um, I need to ask you about Richard, are the two of you, *involved* in any way?'

'Richard? As in Richard Saunders, over the road?'

'Yes Robyn, *that* Richard,' her mother said a bit irritably. 'What's so funny?'

'You are,' Robyn spluttered. 'Honestly, Mum, where on earth has this come from? I've never shown the slightest interest in him, or him in me.' *Which you'd know if your face wasn't always stuck to a bottle*, she hated herself for feeling so spiteful.

'Ah well, good. I mean, if you were, that would be fine. He's a nice boy and everything, it's just that I've been seeing Steven for a while now, I needed to know before things get... serious.'

Robyn gaped for a few moments while she tried to form a response. The silence began to grow uncomfortable. 'Steven Saunders, really? I didn't think you could say anything that would surprise me anymore, unless it was to tell me you'd joined A.A.'

Josie looked at her plate, her lip trembling slightly. 'That's cruel, when did you last see a bottle of vodka in the house?'

Robyn's eyes immediately darted to the box of recycled waste in the corner of the kitchen, there were no bottles. 'There's a wine box in the fridge,' she answered quickly.

'Yes, there is, and it's been there for two weeks now. I haven't had more than one glass of wine a day for over two months. But why would you notice that?' Josie asked, more than a little hurt.

'Is that Steven's influence?'

'Well, I'm happy, so yes, it helps. I started really trying my hardest after Simone's accident. I know I wasn't there for you, not when it counted. I let you down again, didn't I?'

The chair scraped back across the floor as Robyn took her dish and walked to the sink, turning her back to hide the awkwardness she felt. This was turning out to be quite an evening. Running the hot water, she squeezed some detergent into the bowl and thought about what her mother had said. It was true, she hadn't seen any empty bottles apart from an odd bottle of wine occasionally, like the other night, when she'd washed up two glasses and thought nothing of it.

The bubbles began to overflow. 'I've been pretty caught up with Sim, I guess I haven't really taken much notice of things here.'

'How did your exam go, it was the last one today, wasn't it?'

Robyn blew out a breath and turned to see her mother watching carefully. She had the same bright blue eyes as her own which could turn almost navy at times, especially if they were filled with unshed tears. 'I thought you'd forgotten, it was awful Mum, I won't be going back.' Robyn started to cry, hating herself for being so weak. 'I've let Dad down, that money he put aside for uni fees, it was all for nothing.'

'My poor darling,' Josie moved fast to give Robyn a hug. 'You should never have done an English degree. History was always your thing; why didn't you look at those courses, or other options, maybe not have gone to uni at all?' *Why didn't I say something instead of thinking I had no right to offer advice?*

Robyn's mouth fell open again. *Mum, why in God's name, didn't you say that last year?* 'You remembered I love history?'

Josie gave a sad smile. 'I never forgot. Really, Robyn, I wasn't always so… tragic.' She carried on as if having to prove to her daughter she knew things about her life. 'You won the history prize in year seven and eight, you got an A in your GCSE and at 'A' level.' She took a breath. 'Darling, you've worked for the last three years at the castle shop, when all your friends, including Simone, had weekend jobs in the mall.'

It was true. The only time she hadn't followed her best friend to work in one of the boutiques was because she enjoyed her job so much at the large fortified manor house. The history of the family went back to medieval times and she knew everything there was to know about the Bonvilles and the Courtenays, plus every other Earl that had been in residence.

'So, what now?' Josie asked.

'I'm leaving tomorrow to visit Sim, we did talk about it. You know I'm going to be gone for quite a while.' It hadn't been said with the flourish Robyn had planned, a sort of 'to hell with you and your sad life'. It was instead spoken quietly and with a new awareness of her mother's feelings, something she hadn't felt the need to consider for a long time.

'I know,' Josie smiled resignedly. 'You have your father's car and I'll transfer some money into your bank account. The rest you won't get until you reach twenty-five, I'm afraid. That was his wish. Come here Robyn, for goodness sake.' She hugged her daughter again this time a few tears did fall. 'Be safe and be happy.'

'You too Mum, maybe Richard and I will become related after all.'

'The brother you never had, the one we couldn't give you.'

'Don't say that. Simone was my sibling substitute, I didn't need a real one,' Robyn smiled.

'You will drive carefully, won't you dear, that's a fast car, even if it is getting on a bit.'

'Not you as well,' Robyn giggled between a few swallowed sobs. 'I passed my test first time, I'll be fine.'

'How many times exactly did you take your theory?' Josie saw her daughter wince. 'Have you even driven over forty miles an hour? They're a lot of motorways from here to Aberdeen.'

'Don't fuss mum.' As she said the words a heavy weight seemed to lift from her shoulders. It was something she hadn't said since her father had died, and she'd been convinced her mother didn't care enough to fuss.

'I'll be fussing a lot more from now on, even if it is by phone.'

'Mum, if things don't work out with Steven, for any reason, don't start drinking again.'

Josie smiled, 'I won't go down that road a second time, don't worry. I'm pretty confident things are going to work out *very* well, you don't need to fuss.' They both laughed.

That night Robyn sat in bed planning her road trip. It would be pointless loading music onto a USB or thinking her phone or MP3 player would fit anywhere. It was going to be down to the car radio and CDs for entertainment. The B&Bs would hopefully be cheap and cheerful if the websites were true to their word. Most importantly, she planned to visit a few places of historical interest on the way.

Three days to reach Stonehaven, a harbour town just south of Aberdeen, with Dunnottar Castle nearby, its origins stemming from the 3rd century. Robyn had already memorised the historical facts, which included a Viking raid, capture by William Wallace and a visit by Mary Queen of Scots. That would be something for her to take full advantage of on the days when Simone was having physio or other treatments Robyn couldn't help with.

Simone's father, Clive Harmon, had made the momentous decision to relocate not long after Simone's accident. Specialised in his field of Mechanical Engineering, he'd been head hunted a year earlier. The family had been reluctant to move at the time and he'd originally turned down the offer. When they asked a second time he'd researched the neuro rehab units, as well as private care available for his daughter, and Babs had put up no objection. Joey was thrilled, as he loved the outdoors and excelled at geography. The mention of the Grampian mountains and Cairngorm's National park, plus all the lochs and islands soon made up for any loyalty felt to the beautiful south-west coastline. He didn't realise at first, not all of these new treasures were right on his doorstep, but his father promised him that over time, they would explore everywhere together. Joey studied the map and made itinerary lists of every place north of the Highland boundary fault line, quite sure his father would keep his word.

Robyn wondered exactly how she would find Simone. She knew her friend well enough to tell she was hiding things when they FaceTimed or chatted on Skype. That was probably because she hadn't wanted to distract her from the exams. From now on, there would be no hiding anything.

She thought back to the accident and the awful sight of Simone lying in intensive care surrounded by her family. Tubes, pumps, drips, and other various machines had been beeping every two minutes, and worst of all was the cardiac monitor, which Robyn could hardly drag her eyes from, as she was so afraid the zigzags might suddenly drop to a flat-line.

It was only when the nurses began to make eye contact and smile more at the family, did they believe that Simone was actually going to recover from her awful trauma, if being paralysed down her right side could be called a recovery. Still, considering the outcome had looked very bleak at the beginning, it had taken a while to accept that a miracle had occurred and Simone really had escaped death.

She drew her knees up and turned to the wall, rethinking all this now, was not ideal, she needed a good night's sleep. Words such as cerebral perfusion pressure, oedema, haematoma, and intracranial hypertension had played like a mantra, every time she'd closed her eyes for those first few weeks. Even now, she'd occasionally wake in the darkness and hear the haunting incantation.

If she ever found out who the hit and run driver was, she'd kill him, absolutely – with no mercy whatsoever.

* * *

Armed with a bucket and windscreen wash, Robyn was surprised to see the garage open. It was far too early for her mother to be up, it was too early for herself really, but knowing the car had been put away in a bit of a state when she'd driven home from work last week, she fully intended to give it a clean.

Her colleagues in the gift shop had been sorry to hear she was handing in her notice, thinking it was extremely brave of her to be driving all the way to Aberdeen alone. Robyn had allowed herself one last walk around the castle grounds, thinking that maybe one day, if she did return to Devon, she could get a job here in a different capacity and use her knowledge of local history.

'Morning, Robyn. This was going to be a surprise.' Richard greeted her with a cheerful grin.

The white Audi was gleaming, she could see from the hand-held vacuum cleaner laying on the back seat that the inside had been valeted as well. '*Oh, my God*,' she squeaked. 'You star, you must have got up at like, six o'clock. Thank you, Rich.' She was overwhelmed, they weren't really friendly enough for him to do something as nice as this. Then it dawned, on her. 'Did your dad have a talk with you last night or did you already know?'

'I sort of knew,' he nodded. 'Are you okay with it?'

'It'll take a bit of getting used to, someone in Mum's life other than Dad, but yeah, I'm fine. And you?'

He held up the cleaning cloths. 'I wouldn't be doing this otherwise, would I? From what Dad said, he's pretty serious, but the divorce needs sorting first.' He vigorously scrubbed at some dried mud on the front headlamp. 'I've never seen him as relaxed as he's been the last few months.'

'I still don't get what it has to do with you cleaning my car.'

'That's as much down to Simone as it is to the fact you could potentially be my stepsister one day soon.' He gave an embarrassed grin. 'I shouldn't really have said that.'

'Has Simone asked you to keep an eye on me?' Robyn started to laugh.

'Something like that, we've been Skyping quite a bit. She likes regular updates.'

No wonder Rich had been offering lifts more often. He was always conveniently driving by if it was raining or getting late. She never took the Audi onto campus, as the parking was expensive and she was afraid of the bays, they all looked so narrow. Maybe she should have traded it in for a small hatchback, something she could have driven without having an anxiety attack.

'Morning, darling,' Josie joined them. 'Hello, Richard. Thanks for this and everything else you did yesterday.'

'Wait a minute, everything else! What *else* exactly?' Robyn looked at them both accusingly.

'Well,' Josie began. 'Richard took it for MOT and service and the satnav's been updated, it hasn't been done since we bought the car ten years ago.'

'Full tank of diesel,' Richard interrupted. 'Don't forget it's not a petrol engine.' He saw her cringe; fully aware Robyn had made a costly mistake when she'd filled the car for the first time. 'Two new tyres and an idiot's guide on how to change a flat. Hopefully, you shouldn't have to do that 'cos Josie's signed you up for roadside recovery.'

Robyn thought of her mean comments at the supper table the night before. 'I'm sorry Mum,' she muttered quietly.

Josie smiled. 'Come in now, I have a big cooked breakfast with your name on it. Will you join us, Richard?'

'I'm tempted, but you two should have some privacy for your goodbyes. Tell Simone 'hi' and say that I'll definitely take her up on her offer to come up in October,' he winked.

Robyn followed her mother inside and sat down to the smell of sausages and bacon that was rising from the grill. First Skyping, now a visit, what was going on with those two?

Chapter Two

'If it doesn't feel right, it probably isn't.'

The comforting green road signs of the familiar A-road suddenly morphed into blue. Robyn's heart gave a jolt; she was driving on a motorway for the first time ever. Why, oh why, hadn't she taken up Clive's offer of some accompanied driving after her test? They would have done motorway stuff and some reverse and parallel parking. To top it all there were suddenly two lanes to her left. Where the hell had they come from, she was in the inside lane a moment ago? Looking ahead she could see one fizzled out and the other carried straight on to an exit. All Robyn had to do was sit tight and she'd be back on the inside in no time. *I can do this*, another hundred metres and the M5 was back to three lanes again. *Thank you, God.*

The car went like a dream, although at sixty miles an hour, fourth gear wasn't ideal. Once or twice Robyn had hit seventy and bravely put it in fifth, but it had worried her so much she took her foot off the accelerator and changed back down to fourth again. *Are you laughing at me, Dad? I bet if you were alive you'd be warning me about all sorts of stuff. But then I wouldn't have the Audi — Mum would never have started drinking — she wouldn't have cut her hand that night — Simone wouldn't have been walking home alone… Christ, don't go there!*

After another slight wobble passing Bristol, when she nearly exited the motorway to head for London instead of staying Northbound, Robyn finally started to relax a little and began to enjoy herself. Richard had worked out some alternative routes for her and left diagrams and instructions of what she needed to programme into the satnav. He'd even put an up-to-date road map on the front passenger seat, in case the technology let her down. If that happened, she'd be done for.

At a little after 2 pm, she pulled into Warwick Castle's large car park. It was slightly out of her way, but Robyn had visited once before with her parents, an eighth birthday treat. Today brought back bittersweet memories of her father reading the information on each suit of armour while her mother worried about where they would eat their picnic in the drizzle. Messing about in the dungeons, Robyn had really believed they'd be locked up if she dropped litter or misbehaved. Happy times that, along with her first set of Horrible History books, had kick-started her love of anything from the Dark Ages through to the Victorian era.

Today's bright blue skies were too good an opportunity to miss. Providing she didn't stay for longer than three hours, she could hug the A roads and find her first B&B just outside Stafford in time for the included evening meal. After a quick message to Simone, she set off around the grounds exploring every corner, before climbing what seemed like thousands of never-ending spiral stairs to the highest tower, and once there, sent her friend a quick selfie to prove it.

Simone heard the notification beep and reached out with her left hand to read the message. She'd got this off to a fine art now, but as with most things, it was slow. Since her rehab had begun with a vengeance and she'd started on the long road to independence, her daily routine took an age to accomplish. Acceptance was hard at times, although still preferable to calling for help every five minutes.

'Is that from Robz?' Joey asked, throwing his Nintendo onto the sofa. 'Where is she now?'

'See for yourself,' Simone replied, turning the phone so her brother could see. There was a picture of Robyn grinning whilst trying to point over her shoulder at grey stone battlements and a view that stretched away into the background.

'Cool, she'll never get here if she stops at every castle she passes,' he laughed.

'Yeah, it wouldn't surprise me if we don't see her until the end of next week.'

Robyn had been vague about her travel plans, only indicating that she'd planned a few visits en route. It was Richard that had filled in more details last night as he was printing off notes and places of interest nearer to the roads that her friend would actually be travelling on. What a dear he was. If her plan came to fruition, he'd be the lure to return Robyn home and continue with her degree.

Simone was unaware of the events shaping up nicely between Josie Harley and Steven Saunders. She also didn't know that Richard's continued enthusiasm in Skyping her regularly had nothing to do with Robyn, other than friendly concern. The real object of his interest was Simone herself and always had been.

She messaged back quickly about the dangers of trying new sexual positions on the ramparts. Then asked her brother to hold the phone, being careful not to let him read it, so they could send back their own selfie pulling silly faces.

Robyn almost missed her step, giggling, as she read the message twice. She chose to ignore an irritated harrumph from an old woman climbing slowly down behind her, who commented, loudly, about youngsters with phones not looking where they were going. Nothing on earth could spoil this experience, and discovering the dungeons still held precious memories from over ten years ago made the afternoon even more magical.

The buzz she got from the castle visit, along with the picture from Sim, which had lifted her spirits sky high, took her all the way to Rose Cottage, her first overnight stop. Realising she'd successfully navigated her way past Birmingham without a single mishap, she approached the parking area at the rear of the B&B with renewed confidence.

On first inspection, it appeared full. The thought of having to turn in the limited room offered by the small cobbled yard, or worse still, reverse back into the tiny lane that wound its way down the side of the cottage were both definite impossibilities. The familiar butterflies of anxiety started to beat their wings. Inching forward, she spotted a potential gap. The problem was the car on one side, flush against the far wall was a black Mercedes S-Class and the registration was new. Robyn sucked in a breath, that had to be worth £70k, surely? On the other side and hogging the white line, was a small red hatchback. Muttering a few choice words about inconsiderate parking, Robyn swung the car hard left and manoeuvred into the smallest space in the world, aware that she'd parked at an angle but no longer caring.

Sitting for a moment, to let the cold sweat on her forehead evaporate, the next challenge was going to be getting out. Cautiously opening the door, she had all of six inches to squeeze past the shiny black sleek body of the impressive saloon. Holding her breath, and hoping it would magically make her a few inches' slimmer, she shimmied past the boot of both cars, looking critically at the black glossy paintwork for the slightest mark she may have caused. The windows were blacked out and she had to resist the urge to press her face against them and try and peer in.

Robyn's eyes darted around to see if anyone had witnessed her inelegant exit. Relieved that they hadn't, she sprung the boot of the Audi and retrieved a small purple overnight bag. The large suitcase could stay where it was until she reached Stonehaven. About to lock up, she gave a small scream of frustration; her phone was still inside. Inching her way back, she grabbed the phone, glaring at it before moving crab-like between the cars, yet again. Either the owners were making too much money if they could afford a car like this, or someone had mistaken Rose Cottage for Rosing Manor, the large country hotel a mile down the road. Leaving the horrors of the car park behind, Robyn walked purposely toward the door marked reception, unaware that three pairs of eyes had been watching from a window above, two with amusement and one with sheer incredulity.

'You'll never guess what Sim. There's a film crew staying here, I'm parked next to one of their cars.'

'How exciting, let me know if you talk to them over dinner. What are they filming? Maybe you could muscle in as an extra.'

Robyn was curled up on the bed prepared to have a long cosy chat, but she could tell her friend was struggling this evening and hadn't suggested FaceTiming, which wasn't a good sign. 'Simone, you're tired, aren't you? You should tell me.'

'I just love hearing from you Robz, your day sounded wonderful...' she replied, her voice petering out a little wistfully.

'Go and 'ave a lay down me luvver,' said Robyn, putting on a thick Devon accent, and she felt gratified to hear a tired chuckle. 'If they offer me a starring role, you'll be the first to know.'

The dining area was cluttered and almost as difficult to navigate as the carpark. The owner, an extraordinarily tall and thin spinster of the parish called Miss Easterly, had squeezed all types of chintz throws and cushions on or over every available seat. The thick orange velvet curtains were oppressive and masked the evening sunlight, which attempted to shine through the small panelled windows. Dried bunches of flowers and grasses would have been acceptable, had they not been forced into ugly vases as the centrepieces on each table.

The website photo must have been taken from the passage with a wide-angled lens, Robyn calculated after being directed to share a table with a middle-aged couple. The food at least made up for the décor; thick slices of beef and the best roast potatoes she'd ever tasted.

'Cooked in lard,' the woman opposite commented, a little disdainfully.

There were nine people eating and another three places laid. Miss Easterly frowned and toyed with the reserved sign, every time she walked past the empty table. 'Just rude,' she muttered to herself. 'They could have let me know they didn't want dinner.' Robyn caught the eye of the gentleman opposite, who gave her a conspiratorial wink.

Between courses, the level of chattering grew and after making a polite introduction to her fellow table partners, Robyn was more than a little surprised to find out they were, in fact, the film crew. It was actually only a local news story, concerning the discovery of a large hole suspected to be an old mineshaft. Very interesting but not at all what she'd been led to believe by Miss Easterly when she'd checked in. According to her, some kind of epic film remake was about to happen on the doorstep.

This would be a good time to mention the parking situation and assure them that she'd move her car straight after breakfast. Somehow, she couldn't picture either of them driving that fabulous black Merc. About to confess all before saying goodnight, she clamped her mouth shut as the woman mentioned checking out at 9 am the following morning. Planning an early breakfast, Robyn would be gone well before that.

'A house is not a home without a cat.' 'If you want the best seat, ask the cat.' 'Man or Cat? No contest.' And so it went on. Robyn felt compelled to read every ridiculous plaque she passed on her way to the lounge, which unsurprisingly turned out to be a bitter disappointment. Worse than the dining room, if that was possible, and stuffed with even more flowery cushions that stank of cats. Two fluffy white Persians spread across the sofa, and the other chairs had remnants of cat hair. Robyn looked down at her black skirt, her token effort at dressing for dinner and began to exit the room in favour of a long hot bath and an early night.

A loud pained meow nearly gave her a heart attack. She'd stepped on the tail of an elderly balding ginger tom. Feeling guilty, she attempted to give him a stroke, adding her own yell as the bad-tempered snaggle-toothed feline took a fierce swipe at her hand, drawing blood.

At least her bedroom was less cluttered and the old-fashioned lion-foot bath had looked most inviting, earlier. Robyn turned the key and glanced up as she heard a door opening further along the corridor. A quick glimpse of a rather fine set of masculine shoulders caused a stirring of regret that she hadn't had an opportunity to see this man during dinner. *The empty places must have been for them.* In those few seconds, she'd clocked his height and build, both of which were impressive, and the way his black hair curled neatly on the collar of his dark shirt hadn't gone unnoticed. *He could be fifty for all I know and gay.* The second voice coming from the room had definitely been masculine. Raised voices and some maniacal laughter caused her to stick her head back out a fraction. *Definitely not an old man's ass*, she thought appreciatively. Not able to hear what was being said, and aware she could be caught eavesdropping at any moment, she entered her room, slamming the door a little more sharply than intended.

* * *

8.30 am. Robyn groaned as the numbers came into focus. She'd planned to be leaving at this time, not waking up. After an extra quick wash, she threw everything together and headed down for breakfast. Her hand began to sting, reminding her of the cat scratch and she guiltily looked at the smear of dried blood on the wall outside her room. She must have held the door frame while she spied on her rather alluring neighbour. A handy alcohol wipe blended the remnants into the pink flowery wallpaper.

Even with the embarrassment of the parking, she couldn't leave without a hearty breakfast, hoping not to have to eat again until the evening. Concealing a bread roll and a banana in her bag for later, she walked to the reception where Miss Easterly was preparing the bill. At least there was no discrepancy with the cost. It was just as stated on the website and Robyn had to admit the price was very reasonable.

The final and most unpleasant discovery were the abundant climbing red and pink roses that surrounded the front door. Having only used the side entrance from the car park, these had only been viewed quickly as she drove past before turning into the narrow lane. Up close, Robyn could see the arch was far too uniform and the flowers were in fact plastic. She gave a snort of disgust and pocketed her phone, having planned to take a few close-up pictures of what had appeared to be magnificent roses in full bloom.

Rather than walk back through the cottage, she followed the lane around to the car park, but just as she was about to turn in, the black Mercedes exited, forcing her against the hedge. From the front, she could make out the driver and another man in the passenger seat, neither of which were her dining companions, nor the man in the corridor. The car drew parallel and moved past her so slowly it almost came to a halt. Due to the dark windows, she could see nothing but sensed she was being stared at from whoever was in the back. It left an uncomfortable feeling long after the car had turned out of the lane and sped away.

She studied the empty gap and gave a sigh of contentment at having the luxury of walking straight to the driver's door. Today's planned itinerary included a quick visit to the 11th century Peveril Castle, and she would later cross the border to reach her overnight stop, just north of Gretna Green. With the CDs in a box next to her, all in order, she turned the music up. Programming the satnav and completely disregarding Richard's advice about listening to the local radio stations to check for any holdups she pulled out of the parking bay. Driving away, she saw the news couple loading some equipment into the boot of the badly parked small red hatchback and chuckled all the way to the main road.

Robyn left the castle ruins and spent far too long in the village of Castleton, browsing books about William Peveril, the favoured knight of William the Conqueror, and then dawdling by the river, the concept of time escaped her once again. Church bells rang and a glimpse of a bride exiting a white Rolls brought her swiftly back to reality. 2 pm. How on earth had that happened? Running way behind schedule now, Robyn hurried to her car, forgetting to reset the satnav.

It didn't take long to come to the conclusion that she was lost. Fairly sure that the car was still travelling north, Robyn kept her eyes open for a lay-by. All she needed to do was put in the postcode of *'After the Blacksmith'*, her nominated overnight stop.

'That's a strange name,' she'd said to Richard, the morning he'd given her the postcodes and directions.

'It's the over the anvil thing, isn't it,' he replied, seeing her blank expression. 'You know, eloping to Gretna Green?'

'Oh yes, of course, that makes sense,' she grinned. 'Married by a blacksmith over his anvil, not even a priest or anything. They really did do it like that you know.'

'And then went and had a shag in the After the Blacksmith. I hope for your sake they've changed the sheets.'

'Erugh, I think I preferred you when you didn't have the stepbrother-in-waiting excuse to be so familiar.' She gave him a hug and wondered for the first time what it might have been like to have grown up with a sibling like Richard. Please let this work between mum and Steven, she'd thought. I really want him for a brother.

The new postcode was in, the accelerator flat on the floor, the engine screaming, but the car wouldn't move. Robyn switched everything off and went to investigate. The inside rear tyre was stuck over the edge of a small gully, well and truly wedged. Worse still, she wasn't getting any signal on her phone. 'Shit, shit, shit,' she shouted. 'Now what?'

Letting the handbrake off, Robyn used all her strength to try and push the rear of the car. When it felt like it may roll back, she screamed loudly and threw herself to one side just as she heard a car approaching.

It was the first one in ages and she needed help, but aware she was in a vulnerable position, Robyn wondered what should she do. How had she gotten so far off the beaten track? A large black... Mercedes. Surely not. Robyn strained to read the number plate; this was too weird, far too much of a coincidence. Grabbing her phone, she gabbled into it, pretending someone was on the other end. 'Drive past, please keep going,' she muttered.

It was not to be. The car came to stop, the driver's door opened and a youngish man with short dark brown hair, followed by the front seat passenger, walked towards her.

'Can we help?'

Robyn's mouth had gone dry and she couldn't get any words out. Totally incapable of speech, she gave a shrug.

'Maybe we should take a look,' the second man grinned. 'I'm Adam by the way.' He came far too close and offered his hand. 'He's Tarro,' he indicated to his companion who had gone to take a look at the offending wheel.

'Okay,' she said nervously, taking a step back and offering a clammy hand in return. Robyn detested limp handshakes but was more than aware that's exactly what she'd given him. His hair was a lighter brown, not so short. His dark eyes seemed to twinkle and he carried on grinning whilst his companion began to look irritated. *What was it Dad always used to say? 'If it doesn't feel right, it probably isn't.'* She began to tremble and her chest felt tight.

'Come on Adam, we need to roll the car backwards.'

'Why backwards?' she asked suspiciously.

'Because we can knock down some of this grass verge, and the tyre should go forward over it.' He spoke slowly as if explaining to a child, glaring while he did so.

'Tarro's right,' Adam said, still grinning. 'Is the handbrake off?'

Robyn could only nod, they must know she'd been the one parked next to them at Rose Cottage. Maybe there had been a scratch on their paintwork after all and they'd followed to teach her some sort of lesson? She glanced at their car and caught her breath when she saw a third man sat in the back looking straight at her. He had black hair; the man from last night? The other two were discussing the position of the tyre, one grinning, one frowning.

The one called Tarro said something and went to the boot of the Mercedes, returning with a small shovel. Robyn's eyes opened wide, she moved slowly toward the driver's seat, ready to jump in and lock the doors if necessary. A few minutes later, after they'd dug around the tyre and not threatened to bash her over the head, she relaxed a little.

'We'll give it a push,' Adam shouted from the rear. 'If that doesn't work, you'll have to try driving, *very* slowly.' He waited for some kind of response. '*Well?*'

'Err, yeah okay, should I help as well?'

'No, you're alright, stay put.' They started pushing and it didn't take long before all four tyres sat firmly on the flat ground.

Robyn smiled at last. 'Thanks, thank you *very* much.'

'You're welcome,' Adam said. 'We'll make sure you drive off okay.' Tarro gave a terse nod and headed back to the driver's seat of the Mercedes.

Robyn had only just studied the map before she'd realised the car was stuck, so knew the next few miles of road were country lanes and didn't like the thought of them following her through. 'I'm actually going to stay here for a while, don't wait for me.'

Adam raised his eyebrows and give a short laugh before joining his companions.

As they pulled away, Tarro's window was down. He nodded and gave a tight smile. The man in the back leant forward, still staring, what was his problem? The minute they were out of sight, she flipped down the vanity mirror – did she have something on her face? Why had he looked at her so intently?

Two more miles, then she'd be back to civilisation. Her phone lit up. Good, there must be a signal here; at least Simone would get her last text. Robyn crawled around each bend, the lane was becoming even narrower and a thin trail of grass had started to grow up the middle. At one point, her wing mirrors were almost touching the hedges on both sides. Somewhere there must be a switch to fold them in. She started fumbling beneath the steering wheel, nearly hitting the back of the black Mercedes, which had appeared out of nowhere, blocking the narrow lane completely.

This was it then! They'd driven to a quieter place, knowing she would show up. Adam, the smiling assassin, would be waiting to pounce the moment she got out. Tarro would be hidden a little further along, in case she ran, ready to bash her with the shovel. And the other one? He was probably pulling some slim knife from his boot. She checked that the doors were locked and looked at her phone, no signal again. Robyn had never been so scared, genuinely believing she'd driven into a trap. She was far too anxious to think logically and decided to stay put with the doors locked. She would die of suffocation before letting them in... five minutes later, as nothing had moved in front, she cautiously opened the door.

Perhaps they'd just gone for a walk or were having a joint pee somewhere? Whatever the reason, she couldn't sit here all day. It was already late afternoon and it would take hours still, to reach Gretna Green.

The car was empty. She double checked the back seat and walked for a few minutes up the lane before turning around. Not a sign, no gate no entrance, just thick hedge. Where could they be? People didn't just disappear. The front left side of the Mercedes was smashed, she hadn't noticed walking past on the driver's side. They'd had an accident; someone could be hurt. Checking the back seat one final time, she slammed the door shut and felt something sticky on her hand. *Blood*, that wasn't good, and after closer examination, there was some on the inside window as well. Had they started walking? If so, how far had they got, and how far should she go to look for them?

It was then that she noticed a dip in the hedge, near the boot of her own car. Moving it forward a few feet, she investigated and found she could force her way through into the field behind. Ripening wheat, and by the looks of the broken stalks, someone had recently trampled through it. Unsure she was doing the right thing, but thinking of the blood on her hand, she hurried along the recently made trail until it led her to... the black-haired man, who was obviously hurt.

Robyn held her breath. She could see blood on the side of his head before even kneeling down. All she could think about was Simone's awful head injury. 'Can you hear me? I think you should be on your side,' Robyn said gently, hearing a muffled groan in response to her questions. 'I'm going to see if the other two are okay. I'm sure they've gone to get help. Maybe there's a farmhouse further on?' She tried to reassure him, wondering why the trail led towards the centre of the wheatfield. 'Did you hit your head on the window?'

'Yes,' he managed to wriggle himself so he lay flat on his back and look straight at her. Eyes dark as bitter chocolate burned into blue for a few seconds. 'My anchor,' he said, before losing focus and closing them.

Myanka, who or what the hell was that?

Chapter Three

'I had stew tonight, twenty-first-century stew.
It was delicious.'

Simone dropped the squeezy ball and watched as it rolled away across the grass. She would have much preferred to exercise the fingers of her right hand by typing on her laptop, but that alone wouldn't strengthen the muscles apparently. Or was it something to do with co-ordination, or maybe the joints? She sighed and looked detachedly at the next set of instructions on her list. Make a fist, five finger spread, pinch thumb and forefinger together, and so it went on. She glanced at the clock, it was nearly 4 pm. Robyn should be at the B&B now, why hadn't she texted?

A blood clot on her brain following the head injury over five months ago had caused this hemiparesis, the consultant had explained. The first few weeks in the hospital were a blur and Simone had difficulty remembering much of it. When she'd been allowed to go home, her parents had gone completely overboard, talking about the wonderful rehabilitation in Aberdeen. What the hell was wrong with them. They didn't need to emigrate to Scotland for rehab, she'd already been told a full recovery was expected. It would just take time.

Babs Harmon had sat quietly with her daughter, explaining that the offer of a new job had a lot to do with it. Her father was having problems coming to terms with everything. He'd promised to pick his daughter up on the night of the accident, but after going out for a meal and drinking too much, he phoned Simone telling her to get a taxi.

Simone's argument, that it was her own decision to walk home, didn't help. Clive was eaten up with guilt and he couldn't bear to think the person responsible for the hit and run could be someone he knew, possibly worked with, or had shared a drink with, in his local. It was a small village and the chances of an unknown driver happening to pass through at that time of night were slim.

A notification beep at last. Simone carefully wrapped the fingers of her right hand around the phone, holding it claw-like, as her left hand pressed the buttons.

'got lost ffs. car stuck in ditch. creepy guys helped me. getting to gretna late. don't freak. all ok. xx'

Simone re-read the message carefully, quite sure that a lot was left unsaid. Robyn would have been frantic if all that had happened; she knew her friend didn't cope well when forces transpired against her. What did she mean by late? And more to the point, *what* creepy guys? Trying not to worry, she opened her laptop to see if Richard was on Skype. He wasn't, but now her phone had slid off her lap and was out of reach.

There had been many times tears of frustration threatened over her inability to manage the simplest of things. Her mother had given her a bell to ring. The very sight of it disgusted her, a constant confirmation of her incapability and feebleness. Bad enough having to ring it if she needed the bathroom. The first few times, the whole family had rushed to help. Simone loved them for caring, but could have screamed at their desperate eagerness to do something. 'For Christ sake, do you all want to watch me pee,' she'd shouted one day, feeling terribly guilty when her father and brother dejectedly slunk away.

Her father's face had taken on a permanent look of eternal remorse. Sometime soon she was going to have to address these issues, but didn't seem to have the emotional stamina yet to deal with his misplaced guilt hang-up.

Perhaps Richard could bring his visit forward, why wait until October? Her dad would have to buck up a bit with two guests in the house. A few weeks to have Robyn all to herself and then he could be the voice of reason, tempting her back to uni. Simone's conscience started to prickle with doubts. Was she just pushing because it's what she would have done? Was that really the best choice for her friend? Maybe a year out could be a godsend. Robyn could rethink, perhaps study history instead and move here permanently. Or was that selfish, wanting to keep her?

Just south of the main town, their house overlooked a beautiful stretch of coastline. The top of Dunnottar Castle was also visible in the distance. Robyn would love it. A train ran frequently into Aberdeen or the drive was just over half an hour. Simone sighed, Robyn had always followed where she'd led. It wasn't done on purpose, they'd always wanted to do the same things, it was just that she'd been the natural leader.

Her mother's big project, after getting her daughter well, was converting a large barn on the edge of their property. Holiday flats she'd said. Well, why not provide a flat for Robyn and even herself if she were back on her 'legs' by then. Simone started to smile and dream about what might be. It was time to really listen to what Robyn wanted. She'd play it by ear, but the more she thought about it, the more this seemed the perfect solution.

It certainly didn't fit with the plan of Richard tempting her back home. He could come anyway; it would be nice to see him. Surprisingly, his calls and chats had become important and she sometimes found herself thinking of excuses to contact him, just to hear his voice. She frowned. If Robyn stayed, then the whole idea of the matchmaking was pointless. What would be would be. She started slowly typing a message, bringing forward the proposed visit to the middle of August.

* * *

Robyn rocked back on her heels and wondered what on earth to do next. *Myanka?* A friend? Girlfriend? Wife? or the name of a place maybe? She gently went through his pockets looking for some sort of ID. Apart from the odd moan, he kept his eyes closed and didn't attempt to speak again.

Who went around with empty pockets? There was nothing, not a key, phone, or even a wallet. A few plastic discs, that looked like blank poker chips, that was all. 'I'm leaving you for just a moment.' She said, bringing her mouth down to his ear and speaking softly. 'I want to see if I can find your friends.' She saw a flicker of his eyelids, he must have understood. 'Don't try and move. I'll be right back.'

Following the flattened trail of wheat, she expected it to go straight through the field and lead to another road or hopefully some houses. Its abrupt end was more than a little unnerving. The flattened patch just stopped. There was absolutely no way the men could have gone any further in this direction. Robyn started to feel a bit spooked, this was getting beyond weird. Why wouldn't they carry on through the field if they were looking for civilisation? She retraced her steps and knelt back down. 'I've got some water in my car, I'll go and get it.' As she started to get up again, his hand reached for hers and his eyes opened wide in surprise.

Robyn followed where he was looking. 'Sorry, my hand's sticky, it's your blood I think. It was on the door handle of your car.'

'Very good,' he croaked.

She shook her head, putting the odd behaviour down to his accident. 'Do you think you can walk back down to the road? Or do you want to wait here while I go and get help?'

He sat up slowly, touched his forehead and gave a slight wince. 'I can try.'

Taking it slowly, they eventually reached the hedge. Robyn moved from under his shoulder and pulled some of the springy bush back to reveal the narrow lane. She opened the back door of the Audi and sat him down without swinging his legs in.

'Stay like that. I need to move the Merc; the road widens a little up ahead. I'm going to see if I can tuck it away, so we can get past.' If she couldn't, Robyn knew she'd have to get hold of the police somehow. Without waiting for a response, she sat in the driver's seat of the black Mercedes, where even the air smelled expensive. Something stuck out of what looked like an ignition, and after pumping a few pedals, not having the slightest idea what she was doing, the engine purred into life. The place Robyn had noticed earlier was deep enough to let another car through. Breathing a sigh of relief, she hurried back.

'I'll pull out, so you can sit in the front.' She watched him stand patiently until there was room to get to the passenger's side. 'If we're going to be travelling together, I'm Robyn.' She waited for the offer of a name. 'What should I call you,' she asked impatiently.

'Shay,' he muttered, accepting her help into the front seat. 'Or Shayden, Lomax. Did you say you have some water?'

She handed him a bottle. 'Here's a couple of Paracetamol and some wipes.' She finished cleaning her own hands and gave him the packet. *Shay sounds*

Irish, so does Myanka. Tarro's a bit weird, it could be a nickname.

'Where are we going, Robyn?'

She jumped and saw the corners of his lips twitch a little. 'Sorry, I was miles away. Gretna Green,' she smiled. 'Tomorrow I have a long drive to Aberdeen, what about your friends? You'll have to let them know somehow.'

'Don't worry, they can always find me.' He went quiet when he saw her look at him strangely.'

After a few miles, Robyn pulled into a lay-by and checked her phone. 'Signal,' she whooped. 'Thank God.' She phoned the B&B, explaining she'd be arriving late and asked for another single room, or adjoining if possible. The only option available was a twin, whilst having real reservations, the whole point of helping Shay was to keep a close eye on him. Not sure it was a smart move; she was worried about his head injury. He'd absolutely refused to go to A&E, even after listening politely to her warning about not being alone for at least twenty-four hours. She glanced across at her quiet passenger. There was *something* about him; he wasn't a danger, she felt sure of it. 'I'll take the twin please,' she said with more confidence than she felt.

It was nearly 4 pm, at least three hours behind schedule now. After quickly sending another text to Simone, just saying she was running late, but no problems, she set off again, finally hitting the M6 that would take them around Carlisle and all the way to Gretna. After the Blacksmith wasn't much further, according to Richard's instructions. She chuckled remembering the conversation about the anvil. She certainly hadn't been expecting to arrive and share a room with a virtual stranger. Two hundred years ago, she'd have left the next day either married or if not, a ruined woman.

Robyn wasn't stupid, a bit gullible at times perhaps, but she was quite aware the situation was risky. This was exactly the reason she wouldn't speak to Simone until the next day. Her friend would be so worried, it would probably cause a relapse. Had it been anything other than a head injury, it wouldn't have affected her so much and she'd have dumped Shay at the nearest hospital and left him to it. Unfortunately, looking at the cut and purpling bruise above his eye, all she could think about was the tubes and beeping machines. If he was well in the morning, she'd offer to drop him somewhere, or he could stay another night and contact his friends. Whatever happened then, she would have done her best.

Having someone sat next to her, worked wonders for Robyn's confidence at the wheel. The massive hold up for roadworks, just north of Carlisle, knocked them back again and while sitting in the long queue, she heard Richard's voice in her head. '*Don't just listen to CDs, check the local radio station. Do it frequently Robyn, it'll tell you about accidents and roadworks.*' 'Bloody clever dick,' she muttered, frowning at the long snake of slow moving single-line traffic ahead.

'Pardon,' Shay said, opening his eyes.

'Nothing, go back to sleep. Actually, no, *don't* sleep, I think you're meant to keep awake.'

'Really, for how long?' he turned to look out of the window and gave a small smile.

'Err, six hours,' it sounded about right, but she didn't have a clue really. Better they talk so she could suss him out before they shared a room together. 'Where do you live and who's Myanka? You can use my laptop later, if you need to contact somebody, as long as we have Wi-Fi.'

'You are very kind. I don't know anyone called Myanka.'

'Are you sure? You were calling her. I thought you may be Irish, err, I mean the names Shay and Myanka? You don't have an accent, though, not an Irish one at any rate.' *Christ, I sound like an arse.*

'How far north are you travelling tomorrow?' He purposely answered her question with another.

'Just south of Aberdeen, and you?'

'Me too, err, I mean a bit further.' The further north he could travel with her, the better. 'Could we possibly share the expense?'

Robyn started chewing her lip, she knew he carried no money, perhaps all his stuff was back in the other car and he'd forgotten. His clothes looked expensive, and as for the Merc...

'I'm sorry, I shouldn't have asked, you don't know me. Forget I said anything. Really, I'm grateful for the help so far.'

'Do you mind if I think about it? You're right Shay, we don't know each other; this is a bit weird for me to be honest.' The traffic started moving, the lanes opened up, and impatient drivers in a hurry to get home shot past her on both sides. 'Oh fuck.' Completely trapped in the middle lane, Robyn put her foot down and hoped for the best.

Shay took one look and thought a slight bump to his head may be the least of his problems. He didn't say another word, realising that she needed to watch the road and had a bad habit of looking away every time she engaged in conversation.

It was 9 pm when they finally arrived at the small hotel. The plump and jolly Mrs Mason was the complete opposite of their previous landlady. She showed them the room, on the ground floor and said a pan of stew was simmering. She'd dish it up right away if that was alright.

Shay looked a bit pale and sunk onto the bed. 'I think I'll stay here, you go and eat.'

Robyn looked at him carefully. 'I don't think so, you weren't at breakfast, and you weren't at dinner last night. When exactly *did* you last eat?'

He looked surprised. 'I haven't eaten today, you're right.'

'Hmm, too busy following me, which we'll discuss tomorrow before I decide if I'm going to take you any further.' Everything began to hit home now that they were actually in the room they would be sharing for a whole night. Her eyes narrowed slightly, but it was too late now. Hopefully, her instincts were right on this occasion. 'I don't want a sick person to worry about and I certainly don't want a stalker either. Come and eat some stew.' She left the room without waiting for a response and felt a moment of satisfaction when she heard his footsteps echo on the parquet flooring as he followed behind.

Two bowls full of lamb, carrot and barley stew later, Shay mopped up the last of the gravy with thick slices of caraway bread. 'Peasant food,' he said appreciatively.

Robyn started to laugh, watching him push the biggest chunks of meat to one side.

'Finished my dears?' asked Mrs Mason, popping her head in. 'Did you enjoy the dumplings? My husband likes a dumpling, says a stew's not right without a dumpling.'

Robyn cringed, Mrs Mason was a chatterbox and she wasn't in the mood. Tiredness was beginning to sweep through her body. The bed had felt wonderful for all of the two minutes she'd sat on it.

'Here's a plate of shortbread, you can take it to your room if you like. I'm sorry everything's a bit... traditional, that's what my guests expect.'

'It was lovely thank you, Mrs Mason,' Shay said, getting up and patting his stomach. 'A wonderful stew with your finest dumplings, worth every penny.'

The rotund landlady backed away, giggling like a schoolgirl. Shay certainly had personal charm in abundance, Robyn noted. It was a pity he didn't appear to have a wallet to match. Who was going to pay for all this in the morning?

Shay quietly got out of bed in the early hours and checking Robyn was asleep, made his way outside. Relieved to see Adam waiting, he told him, 'I need currency, quite a bit. I'm hoping to stay around Robyn for a while.'

'Robyn, is it?' Adam grinned.

'Where's Tarro, sorting the car?'

'It's done,' Adam gestured to the road where the shiny black Mercedes was parked. 'We weren't sure whether to intervene this afternoon.'

'You saw everything?' he asked, giving Tarro a quick wave.

Adam handed him some medicine and nodded. 'At one point, she was standing right in the middle of the portal with us, and with your blood on her hands. It caused quite an eddy.' He grinned. 'Anything else you need for now?'

'Perhaps a money belt, something I can say I was wearing under my clothes. She went through my pockets,' he explained.

'I wouldn't mind her going through my pockets.' Adam grinned. 'What a waste, touching up Mr Cool. Still, you must like her company, you've already anchored her, so you could just leave now.'

'I need to know where the anchor's going to settle if it's to be of use to us. Anyhow, our job is hard enough at times. It doesn't hurt to take a little pleasure in what we do, does it? I like to get to know people. It's not just about DNA, we're meant to observe and learn. A bit like you did with that girl who told you she was a friend of a friend of someone who knew Nell Gwyn. At least I won't become contaminated.'

Adam grinned even wider and started to chuckle. 'It was worth a spell in the decontamination room and she was a very strong anchor. I only had to step through the portal and I could sense her.'

'Not for long. She was dead three months later, a *very* handy window!'

'Tarro can beat that, he had one for all of a week in 1805, the anchor decided to fight a duel remember?' He watched Shay laugh and thought that he didn't do it often enough. 'Careful, you're beginning to sound like us. Those suppressed emotions may start to let go and take flight, then what would happen?'

'I'd be fixed again, as you very well know. Talking of which, take Tarro in for a check, he scowled the whole time you were helping to move Robyn's car. He lost his temper last night and once again, just before he hit the hedge.'

'You're right, he was getting very worked up in those narrow lanes. I'll bring the paper money and belt into your room later. Don't take any medicine here, I'll drop a pain reliever and healing pad into the belt.'

'She's given me two lots of Paracetamol, which I've managed to throw away. I had stew tonight, twenty-first-century stew. It was delicious, well the dumplings were. I tried to pick out the flesh. It's hard to avoid meat and dairy. I know I'll suffer for it later.'

'Hopefully not too badly,' Adam agreed sympathetically. 'I'll drop a couple of emetics in as well, sorry mate, but if you've been eating meat, better safe than sorry. Seriously, Shay, we need to concentrate on why we're here. Some established anchors, as far north as possible, would be helpful. We've none up there at all in this time period. At least you have one now, that's something.'

'Be careful not to wake her when you drop that stuff off and don't forget to take Tarro to the lab.' Shay watched his friends drive away and crept back to the room. Robyn was asleep, her fair hair fanned out over the pillow and long lashes curled from under closed eyelids. Blue eyes, the best kind; it was worth coming to the past just to see them. Nothing else to worry about except a change of underwear! Hopefully, she hadn't checked the boot when she moved their car. He could pretend his bag had been there.

* * *

The money belt was sticking out from under his neatly folded clothes. He had some cash, that was a relief. She'd woken twice to check on him during the night. One time she thought he was standing by the window, but it had been a trick of the light, that or the resident ghost. Considering this building was only thirty-five years old, that was most unlikely. While he slept, it was her turn to study him. The sunlight was pushing its way between the partially opened curtains and fell across his nicely tanned skin. Thick, tousled black hair, curled beneath his ears. Robyn edged a little closer, listening to the even breathing. His lips were parted slightly, well-defined, not too pouty. A kiss came uninvited to mind and she pushed it away, concentrating instead on how he'd look if he let go and gave a truly spontaneous smile. Up until now, he'd been polite and smiled plenty of times. But they were small, thin offerings, nothing that caused his eyes to light up, or crease his face with laughter lines. Perhaps because his head still hurt, she thought, leaning further over his bed.

Shay was awake and had been as soon as the shower had turned on, twenty minutes ago. He could tell she was hovering over him, probably checking his wound, as she'd done twice before. It would be nearly healed now, thanks to the pad he'd already used and disposed of, how was he going to explain that? At one point Robyn had crept across to his bed, just as Adam was locating Tarro. The three of them were anchored and could move quickly, but it would have taken some explaining if his friend had been caught red-handed in the middle of the room. He felt her cool touch as her fingers started to gently brush his hair to one side, and he opened his eyes.

'Oh, you're awake. I just wanted to see how the bruising was looking,' she said defensively. 'You need to get up now anyway. Sorry, but it's a long way, you can always doze in the back seat if you want.'

'I can come with you then? Are you sure, Robyn?'

'Err yeah, I guess.' She'd meant to give it a bit more thought over breakfast, but it was said now. 'Are you feeling better?'

'Much better, thanks. I do need to find a shop somewhere if you can spare the time?'

'A shop, what for?'

'Toothbrush, underwear, a couple of t-shirts. My bag was in the boot of the Mercedes.'

'The boot,' Robyn groaned. 'I'm so sorry, I didn't even think of looking. We'll pass through plenty of villages, don't worry. You can err use my shower gel. If you need any more Paracetamol, they're in the Deadly Hallows makeup bag.' He was looking at her blankly. 'The triangle and circle design.' She swept her arm down over the Gryffindor pyjamas she was wearing. 'Harry Potter.' *Is he from another planet?*

'Yes, the wizard, I know who he is,' Shay said abruptly, moving quickly to the bathroom before the conversation got any more awkward.

Robyn took the opportunity to dress quickly and pack her bag. He could travel with her, as far as Stonehaven, but she wanted some answers. And she owed Simone a call...

Chapter Four

*'If I accept even half of what I'm seeing, does
that make me insane?'*

Robyn left Simone a long voicemail, explaining that she
was driving all day apart from one last stop, near Perth,
and all being well, would arrive in time for supper.

She hoped her friend wouldn't worry and was
thankful she didn't have to account for everything now.
It would be so much easier to explain in person after the
event.

Mrs Mason had helpfully pointed out some local
shops on Richard's map, where they could purchase a
few supplies. Much to Robyn's annoyance, all talk to do
with the map was directed at Shay, as if she wasn't there
at all. It's my bloody car, she wanted to scream, and my
map, she thought childishly.

'I've shown your boyfriend where you can do your
shopping dear, but it's Sunday, so the larger stores open
a bit later.'

'Well, we can't hang around here,' she snapped. 'We'll
find somewhere on the way and don't suggest Glasgow,'
she glared at Shay as if it was his fault. 'I'll be leaving
the motorway before that.' Flouncing back in her seat
and scowling at the back of the retreating Mrs Mason,
Robyn shoved her empty plate away.

'I guessed that Robyn, I don't need a big town.' He
looked a bit bemused. 'Has she upset you, assuming
we're in some kind of relationship?'

'No, let's get out of here.' She was cross at being
ignored and patronised, embarrassed over the comment
about her 'boyfriend' and then cross at herself for being

embarrassed. *If you were my boyfriend I certainly wouldn't have booked a room with twin beds.*

'Are you sure you're okay?' He watched her blue eyes, flash with, what exactly – anger, passion? Something fluttered inside him, she was already causing his suppressed emotions to act unpredictably. It was bad enough that Tarro was unstable, they couldn't afford two of them to be out of balance.

'I'm fine, really. Are you ready to go?'

Shay paid the bill, insisting it was the least he could do. Then, after making an excuse to pop back to their room, promptly threw up last night's stew into the toilet. Somehow, he'd have to get away with eating as little as possible today. There'd been no comment from Robyn when he'd only had a cup of black coffee and one hash brown, for breakfast. But that was because she'd been in a mood. Mrs Mason had looked most affronted when she picked up his plate and the 'Full English' had remained essentially untouched. One sausage had been speared and dropped stealthily onto Robyn's plate. He wondered how she managed to eat such large quantities of food and stay looking so healthy. That was, after all, one of the reasons he was here in the twenty-first century, to find out.

The roads were virtually empty and the local radio station played quietly in the background. With no roadworks or accidents reported anywhere along her planned route, Robyn's mood lifted quickly. A few surreptitious glances in her passenger's direction had her curiosity winning the battle over the companionable silence she was presently enjoying. 'Why exactly are you travelling north?'

The question came out of the blue. Shay had been lulled into a false sense of security for the last ten miles. Content to immerse himself in the passing scenery or study Robyn, who's constantly changing facial expressions gave all her thoughts away, which he found delightful. Now he needed to sit up, concentrate and give credible answers. 'I'm visiting old battle sites,' he said carefully. 'There're quite a few in the Highlands, not far from where you're heading. Culloden, for example, in 1746, Alford in 1645, Barra, err, in 1308, I think, and plenty of others.

'Are you a historian, or is it just a hobby?' She perked up instantly, any remains of her sulk having now completely vanished.

'A bit of both. How about you, why are you travelling to Aberdeen? You have a regional accent; the south-west of England, I think.'

'Oh dear, do I sound like a farmer?' she laughed.

'Not at all, it has a very soft lilt, barely detectable... it suits you,' he added. 'So, come on, why the long drive?'

Robyn found herself explaining everything, from Simone's accident to her abysmal end of year exam, her mother's alcohol problem and her father's death. By the time she'd finished, encouraged by nods and supportive noises, they were on the road to Perth and it was time for a stop of some kind. She'd totally forgotten about looking out for a shop and still hadn't learned anything about her travelling companion, other than his interest in historical battles.

'I was planning a visit to Scone Palace. It's probably another forty minutes or so, we can have lunch there and I think you'll enjoy it, especially now you've told me you have an interest in history. Do you know,' she continued animatedly, 'Macbeth was crowned, on the original site? They still had the stone of destiny then. Just imagine, being part of all that.'

With a horrified expression, Shay grabbed the steering wheel and shouted '*BRAKE*'.

'Oh shit,' Robyn screamed, her heart started to pound when she looked ahead. There were traffic lights looming and she'd nearly ploughed them into the back of the car in front.

'Let's stop here first, for a short break. You've been driving for nearly three hours.' *And probably only looking straight ahead for one of them.* His ploy of keeping her talking, so he wouldn't have to, had worked, but at considerable cost to his nerves. Thankfully, as soon as they passed the lights, Robyn pulled off the main road, and as luck would have it, into a small village that sported an assortment of shops. 'A coffee and maybe a cake, I think,' he said taking charge. 'We can still visit the Palace,' he added as she was about to protest.

A teashop with cupcakes in the window was too tempting to ignore. Robyn was still shaken, so failed to notice Shay only ate about a half of his. They browsed the shops, both buying a few bits. Shay got his underwear and toothbrush, while Robyn had a covert glance to see if he preferred boxers or briefs.

When they returned to the car Shay offered to drive, ignoring the chewing gum and toffee wrappers that decorated the dash. Robyn grudgingly accepted as the traffic light incident had given her a scare. They drove for the next half an hour, both lost in their own thoughts. After crossing the river Tay, they arrived at Scone Palace shortly after 1 pm.

Shay paid again and also bought a guidebook which Robyn was thrilled about. 'I don't normally buy these. They always seem so expensive when I can look everything up online. Um, feel free to do your own thing, we can meet back at the car.'

Shay nodded but stayed by her side, which for some reason, made her very happy. After walking around together, pointing out things of particular interest and reading the information about the displays, Robyn began to feel more than a little comfortable in his company, to the extent that she may even miss him when they parted later that day.

The gardens were every bit as impressive as the inside. Sipping cold drinks, and sharing a salad sandwich, they walked through the star maze, found the market cross and stopped at the graveyard.

'This arch was the entrance to the old town,' Robyn read. 'The whole village was here, in these actual grounds.' She closed her eyes. 'Can you imagine what it must have been like, the people, the smells, the clothes? I go to places, burial sites, ruins and I pretend I'm really there, at the actual time.' She opened her eyes and saw that Shay was staring, almost mesmerised. 'Come on,' she laughed, breaking the spell, 'You're the odd one, not me.'

He raised an eyebrow, 'You think *I'm* odd?'

'Errm, in a good way,' she grinned. They sat down on a bench admiring the view of the castle and the tiny chapel that marked the ancient crowning place of the Kings of Scotland. 'It's your turn to talk,' she turned and met his eyes. He didn't try to look away which she took as a positive sign. 'I want a promise from you.'

He nodded, 'If I can.'

'I only want to hear the truth, If you can't answer, that's fair enough... I suppose I'll just have to draw my own conclusions.'

'Very well, Robyn,' Shay sighed. He used hundreds of anchors, but only a handful knew the barest facts. If anyone repeated the things he'd told them they would most likely end up in a lunatic asylum, or worse. Would Robyn accept him? He hoped so, it was all a little bit too soon for revelations of such magnitude. If it went horribly wrong, he'd lose, not only his first anchor here, but someone he was forming an attachment to for the first time ever, and not solely from the DNA connection.

'First of all, how come you happened to be on the same road when I got stuck in the ditch? I was lost, it was well off the beaten track.'

'We were travelling north,' he stopped. How could he tell her that Tarro had been through every car in the car park and found her maps? They needed anchors where there were no portals. She was going in the right direction, it was as simple as that. 'Um, I err...'

'Christ we're going to be here all afternoon. Did you follow me? Yes or no?'

'Yes,' he replied and heard her gasp. 'Not for any untoward reason, nothing sinister,' he tried to reassure her. 'I'm afraid, what I'm about to tell you will sound like I'm taking advantage of your love of history, especially after what you said earlier about imagining yourself in... another time.'

'How did you do it? I'd been driving for hours. I was lost and you just came out of nowhere.' Her face fell. 'Please tell me you didn't put some kind of tracking device under my car?'

She was so full of questions, they were pouring out before he'd a chance to answer properly. 'Robyn, please listen carefully to what I'm going to say. I can prove it to some extent.' He took her hand, preparing to transport straight to the portal and out of her life if necessary. Expecting to feel the familiar attachment he felt with all his anchors he was surprised this was much stronger. She'd absorbed his blood as well, that was the difference. By the shocked look on her face, she was feeling it too.

'What's that?' she tried to snatch her hand back, but he didn't let go.

'That's a connection, *our* connection to be exact.'

'I don't think I like it, what's happening?'

She's going to panic. Shay made the decision to tell her something quickly, at least then she could laugh or get angry. Anything to stop her from being so scared.

If he had to disappear and abandon this particular anchor, he would. It had happened often enough when he'd miscalculated before materialising. 'I live not far from here, as I told you yesterday, just... not in this time. I'm from the future and we need help, that's why I'm here.' He watched her mouth open and close. Her hand tugged, but he kept it firmly held. Then her brow creased and her eyes narrowed.

'Give me my hand back *right* now,' she said quietly through clenched teeth. 'If this is your idea of a joke, it's *not* funny.' If it wasn't for the vibration in her hand, Robyn probably would have just laughed, or pretended to be seriously interested and played along. But she was outraged that he'd stoop to such a pathetic story and worse still, she couldn't fathom how he was doing the electric current thing. This was all complete madness. Shay seemed so sane, wasn't that the most dangerous kind?

People were milling around, he couldn't risk disappearing and reappearing in front of them. 'Walk over to those trees with me, *please*?' He had to haul her from the bench, but the fact that she was going with him, albeit reluctantly, was promising. For all her protestations, Robyn was far too curious to walk away; he'd known that yesterday when she'd helped him; it was the reason he was sure she'd be receptive to his explanation and demonstration. 'Stand there,' he said, backing her up against a large oak that sheltered them from the main path. 'This isn't a trick. I'm going to let go of your hand, watch carefully and then count slowly to twenty.'

Robyn felt the current in her hand fade and the next moment he was gone. Forgetting about counting, she gave a small shriek and ran around the tree. 'Shay?' she called, a feeling of cold dread beginning to settle around her. No sooner had it done so, the electrical vibration began again, this time travelling up her arms.

'Did you count?' he asked quietly.

'Bloody hell,' she brought her hands to her mouth. 'Where the fuck did you go?'

He checked again to make sure no one was nearby. 'I want to show you, but we won't be able to get back here if you're with me. 'I'll get Adam, don't go away.'

'Get *Adam*? Don't go away!' Robyn repeated. Her knees were so weak, she wouldn't be going anywhere. Within a couple of minutes, she felt the tingle in her body, then he was there again. Amidst her anxiety, fear, and dare she admit it, excitement, she was aware of the relief that flowed through her on his return.

Adam smiled, amused by the whole thing. 'Hi Robyn, good to see you again, enjoying the demonstration?' He showed no concern whatsoever for her shocked state. 'Shay really shouldn't be doing this, he'll be in *so* much trouble.'

'Are you okay?' Shay asked, ignoring his friend.

'If I accept even half of what I'm seeing, does that make me insane? And why is it I don't seem to have a problem with you?'

'It's the connection I've already forged with our blood,' Shay said gently. 'And it's a good thing to have an open mind. You're going to need it for this next bit, are you ready?'

She nodded, looking at Adam in disbelief, expecting to be taken to some camouflaged hiding place. This time the static pulse didn't stop and when she looked around, she was in the middle of the wheatfield. The flattened trail from the day before stretching out in front of them.

Shay caught her as she began to fall in a faint. He took them straight back to the oak and from there, to the nearest bench. 'Are you alright? I'm sorry, I wanted you to see... to understand.'

'Understand *what*? I need to sit for a minute, then you have to tell me everything.' A short while later, Robyn woke with her head against Shay's chest and his arm around her. Strangely, she didn't want to ruin the moment, but catching a glimpse of his watch jolted her back to the present. 'Oh no, I didn't mean to doze off, what time is it?'

'Don't worry, you only slept for twenty minutes, shall we walk to the car?'

'Yes, I think you better drive again, if you don't mind. Where did Adam go?'

'Back to Tarro, we're all anchors for each other.'

'So, you'll be joining them when we get to Stonehaven?'

'Yes, but I can come back to you anytime.' He saw her smile and felt pleased. She was having quite an effect on his emotions.

'So, that was a portal in the field and I'm an anchor. Is that what you're saying? Hang on… how am I an anchor?'

'The wheatfield is the furthest portal north in this particular time period,' Shay explained for the third time. 'We can come through a portal and then lock on to an anchor, and yes that's you. Well, you're an anchor for me, but not for Adam and Tarro. I have lots of anchors, most don't know, but a few like you'… *There are no others like you*, the thought came so unexpectedly it left him reeling.

'A few like me, what?' Robyn asked impatiently.

Shay smiled. 'A few, I sort of have an interest in and follow their progress. They don't know of course.'

He's anchored to others, other women. She felt an irrational streak of something that felt like jealousy.

'I've never told any of them what I've told you today, sometimes the essentials but only because I was compromised and had to give an explanation. You're the first person I've ever shown, honestly Robyn. I'm not sure why, but I felt the need. Tarro and Adam are good friends, they won't repeat anything that would get me in trouble, but even so, they don't wholly approve.'

I'm the only one he's ever shown. 'Umm... what exactly *is* a portal?'

'Portals are openings to other times.'

'Hmm, I meant is it like a mist or a whirlwind? Do you feel yourself moving? I didn't take it in just now, I was too shocked. It's very complicated.'

'A slight movement, perhaps a vortex would be the closest thing, but really it's like stepping through a doorway. We can hover if the coast isn't clear to step out. The first night we saw you, trying to park your car,' he tried to disguise a snort of laughter by disguising it as a cough, 'we knew you'd be a useful anchor. Tarro found your route plans, all the way to Aberdeen, it was a wonderful opportunity for us. There are no portals in this part at all, that's why we need transport.'

'Hence the Merc, hang on a sec, that bastard broke into my car?' *I can hardly be shocked by that I suppose.* 'Is this anchor stuff something to do with what you said about a connection, with our blood?'

'The blood on the wall outside of your room.' He saw her glance at her hand, the cat scratch had been deep and a long thin dried scab still remained.

'I didn't see it till the morning. I tried to clean it off.'

He nodded. 'As soon as you slam... closed the door, I absorbed all I could. I'm sorry Robyn, mostly our anchors are never aware. We try not to materialise in front of them. It's the reason I didn't help Adam and Tarro with your car. It was better that you didn't see me, now of course, that's immaterial. When you helped me after the accident, your hands were covered in my blood, it made the link very strong.'

'I nearly didn't stop, when I saw your car. Everything was telling me to do the sensible thing, reverse back down the lane and call for help. I couldn't though,' She began to laugh. 'I mean I really couldn't as in physically reverse all that way, plus I wanted to find out of course.'

He started to laugh. 'Tarro wanted to get me through the portal, but I'd already sensed you. I think you must have just come into the field at that exact moment.'

'You *sensed* me, just from that little bit of blood?'

He nodded. 'It's to do with the absorption of DNA into small implants we have. And now I've absorbed my own blood back from your hands, and it's... sort of amalgamated I think. It's never happened like this before, our connection is very strong Robyn.'

It was hard to take all this in, but after what she'd witnessed, she found herself believing everything he was saying. 'How many anchors do you have?'

'Hundreds, over the different time periods. You're the only one for here and now,' he smiled. Shay was pleased to see she seemed engrossed but he realised it could be a terrible mistake to share so much information. Unusually, he was having trouble controlling himself and now that he'd started, he wanted her to know everything. 'Sometimes anchors aren't necessary at all because we have so many portals to choose from, but occasionally like here, we don't have any at all. Then we rely on people like you to help us move around quickly.' He saw her pull a face. 'I'm not very good at expressing things. Adam could explain all this much better.'

'So, if you're in the portal how far away can you *feel* your anchor?'

'That depends on how healthy they are, from the wheatfield, I guess... three to get to the north coast, perhaps two, it all depends.'

'Okay, let's say I go along with this story of yours.' She started chewing her lip, barely noticing where they were. A signpost for Stracathro caught her eye but it didn't register. 'Why do you do it? And how far in the future do you come from?'

Caution finally won the emotional battle. 'Perhaps we could meet again soon and I'll explain more?'

'Oh no, you're not getting away with it that easily.'

'I don't want to get away with anything. I really want to see you again.'

The car flew over a bridge and Robyn sat up, paying attention for the first time to their actual journey. 'That was the River North Esk, we're nearly there. Shay, pull over. Damn it, I'm not ready to let you go.'

Robyn got out of the car and stretched, watching Shay follow her lead. 'Answer my questions,' she said, looking straight at him, not allowing any break in eye contact. 'Where exactly do you come from and more importantly when?'

'My home isn't that far, I told you that; it's the Yorkshire Dales, actually.'

Subconsciously, Robyn relaxed when she heard this. Perhaps it was the reassurance of hearing something familiar. Had he said some futuristic sounding name, which she'd been expecting, like District 18-A or Area K, it might have been different. 'A Yorkshire lad, eh?' She leant her hip against the bonnet.

Shay chuckled, 'I suppose I am.'

'You said something earlier about needing help, what exactly?'

'Too many questions. I'll answer one more and then you'll have to agree to see me again if you want to find out the rest.'

She frowned. What did she want to know the most? 'When will I see you next?'

'You'll want some time with your friend, how about two days from now? I'll be aware of when you're alone. And that, my dear Robyn, was your last question.'

'What? *No*, that's not fair.' Despite everything, she started to laugh. 'Just you wait, I'll have a list of questions written down ready next time.'

'I'd expect no less. We're about ten minutes away, shall we say goodbye here?'

Her face fell. 'Yes, I suppose so. One quick thing, that electric static stuff I felt?'

'*Yes?*' He gave an exaggerated sigh.

'Why didn't I feel it other times, when we've touched?'

'That's simple. The electrical implants, the ones I mentioned earlier, are activated when I'm moving through a portal or towards an anchor.' He took a step towards her and dropped a small kiss on her cheek. 'You'll always know if I come to you that way.'

'There was no bag in the boot of the Mercedes was there? And you certainly didn't need to buy boxers. What happens, a quick whizz through the portal for a change of clothes?'

'Not always. I can get back to the portal anytime, but with a shortage of anchors, we have to be prepared to travel... that was another question you just sneaked in.' She was looking confused and a bit sad. He was genuinely going to miss her. A connection wasn't the same as an emotion, he shouldn't be feeling like this. The sensible thing would be to find new anchors and forget Robyn. She was waking up feelings in him he thought he'd never experience and for once, he wasn't about to do the sensible thing.

'Two days then,' she said softly, walking towards the car. He didn't answer and without having to look, she could feel he was gone.

Chapter Five

*'We'll rectify the marshmallow shortage
tomorrow.'*

'At last, I was *so* worried, why didn't you answer any
of my calls?' Simone sat in a reclining chair in the front
room, looking alternately relieved, happy and furious.
'Never mind, come here this instant.'

Robyn flew across the room and wrapped her in
an enormous hug, muttering profuse apologies and
babbling out a revised version of how the whole 'Shay'
thing came about. She explained about the tyre being
stuck, then finding him hurt and their car smashed, and
finally, her decision to give him a lift. For now, the time
travel stuff would have to remain a secret; possibly the
first she'd ever kept from her best friend.

'*Robyn*, the tyre! that was the creepy guys you texted
me about for God's sake. You shared a room with
one of them, a *complete* stranger, *anything* could have
happened. You should have taken him to the nearest
hospital. If you felt that bad about it, maybe hung
around to find out the outcome, but *nothing* more.'

The events sounded even more foolish when someone
repeated them, or rather ranted them back. She couldn't
admit she was drawn to him through the power of
blood. In fact, she couldn't justify any of it. 'I had a gut
feeling Sim. I just knew he was a good bloke, as it turned
out I was right.'

'Well, where's he staying. What's he doing now?'

Robyn sighed, 'He's up here visiting ancient Scottish
battle sites, staying somewhere in the area. I'm meeting
him the day after tomorrow. Enough about Shay, how
the bloody hell are *you*?'

Simone laughed. 'Don't think Mr tall dark and handsome is finished with. I've got loads more questions, but they can wait for now. Watch this.' She picked up her squeezy ball, did all her finger exercises and enunciated her vowels almost perfectly, with only a slight slur on the 'U' being a giveaway.

'That's so good. Sim, you're going to make a full recovery, I know it. Can we go for a walk tomorrow? I mean in your chair; can I push you around?'

'You can but we'll need to keep to flat ground. We can go into town and have an ice cream at the harbour, that sort of thing. Or if you're not castled out, there's Dunnottar. We may need the car for that. It is walkable, but maybe not if you're doing all the pushing.'

'Do you have any therapy scheduled?'

'I demanded tomorrow off,' she grinned. 'As soon as we moved here Dad looked into private care.' She frowned. 'I wish he hadn't, the NHS was absolutely fine. Still, Maggie and Peter, my therapists, are very flexible and the majority of it is done here in the house. I go to hydrotherapy three times a week. They fetch me and we're back within two hours usually.'

'What can I do to help, are there any activities or exercises?'

'Loads – physio, occupational stuff, electrical stimulation, but they do it all,' She saw Robyn's face fall. 'That's what they're paid for Robz. Just you being here is the best tonic I could ever hope for, you'll give me such a boost. By the time you go back to uni in September, I may even be weight bearing.' The silence screamed back what Simone already suspected. Robyn didn't want to go back. Her heart gave a leap of joy, even though her head told her to convince her friend otherwise.

Later that evening, Babs showed Robyn to the spare room but suggested she may like to share with Simone, just for tonight, if she wasn't too tired. 'I come in at least once to check her, but I'll try not to disturb you, dear.'

'Don't be silly Babs, I don't mind. I can do the checking, tell me what to do.'

Babs shook her head. 'I'd feel happier if you'd help in other ways. Simone needs assistance to the bathroom sometimes or just to reposition slightly. Really, I don't do so much for her anymore. I wake automatically, though, which I have done since the accident. I can't settle again if I don't see her. You understand, don't you?' she asked anxiously.

'Of course, I understand. But she needn't feel embarrassed about anything, certainly not in front of me.' Robyn said emphatically.

'She will, though, that's the point. Simone hates ringing the bell for help. Now that we're all so hopeful for a full recovery, she gets impatient for it. I'll leave you to unpack in here while I go and sort the airbed.'

Robyn nodded and sank wearily on the small double divan. 'I'm trading you in for a blow-up model tonight,' she laughed and flopped backwards onto the soft duvet. Where was Shay when she needed him? Perhaps he could whisk them six months into the future and Simone would be well again. Come to think of it, where exactly was he really? Further north, or back in his own time with Tarro or Adam? One of them would stay here as an anchor until they had some others. That was her understanding of how it all worked at any rate. She felt an inexplicable longing. Was it only this morning they'd woken in the same bedroom and only a little over twenty-four hours since they'd actually started travelling together? It seemed so much longer. *I miss him, how pathetic is that?* She blamed tiredness on her erratic thoughts. *For God's sake, there's no such thing as love at first sight. This must be the side effect of being a damn anchor, he didn't warn me about that bit.*

Balancing two steaming mugs of hot chocolate, a can of curly cream and a packet of hundreds and thousands, because there were no marshmallows, Robyn sat carefully on the side of Simone's bed. 'Made with proper hot milk, courtesy of your mum.' She saw her friend dubiously eyeing the packet of little sweets. 'That was a necessary substitute, I'm afraid.'

Simone took the chocolate, which looked more like a Mr Whippy from the enthusiastic amount of cream that Robyn had already squirted. 'We'll rectify the marshmallow shortage tomorrow.' In no time, they both had white moustaches and the packet of hundreds and thousands had split, the tiny sweets colourfully decorating the duvet. The girls were giggling so much they hardly noticed Simone's laptop screen change. 'Oh, it's Richard,' she said, quickly answering the Skype call and asking Robyn to turn it so that he could see them both.

'Well, that answers my first question,' he grinned. 'Robyn obviously got there okay and looking at the state of you both, I think I'll just say hello, goodbye and leave you to it.'

Simone laughed. 'Before you disappear, did you have a think about August?'

'It's easy from this end. I'll fly from Exeter, as long I'm not too fussy about the times. It's reasonable enough. Are you sure your parents are okay having me and Robyn at the same time?'

'Of course,' Simone hadn't even asked; she'd sort that later. 'Robyn will be able to show you around while I'm having my therapy.'

What? That was the first Robyn had heard about it. Richard might be a nice guy, but that didn't mean she wanted to be stuck with him. If she wasn't keeping Simone company, the plan was to look for a job, although that plan had changed slightly. She now wanted to spend more time with Shay as well. She had no intention of letting her time traveller slip through her fingers.

'No offence,' the voice from the laptop broke her thoughts, 'but I'm going to be seeing plenty of her in September. I'll bring Robyn's set reading for her to get on with. Josie said it was left in the bedroom.' He gave a smirk, 'If she's even coming back to uni, that is.'

'What's with the '*she*', I'm right here thank you very much! Anyway, that suits me fine, I'll be job hunting and I don't need my future stepbrother cramping my style.'

'Style? haha, I don't think so. Anyway, Dad's taking full advantage of your absence, things are moving fast down here in the parental romance department. I've hardly seen him for the last three days.'

Robyn realised she'd totally forgotten to mention anything about her mother and Steven Saunders. She looked apologetically at Simone, whose mouth was opening and closing like a fish caught on a line.

'Are you okay, Sim?' Rich asked, looking concerned. 'Sorry, I thought Robyn had already told you. I'll leave her to explain it. The job hunting is news to me, although I'm not altogether surprised. Well done Robz, give your best friend a seizure, why don't you?'

'Shut up big mouth, say goodbye to Sim, 'cos I'm closing the *bloody* lid.' She allowed him time to say a quick goodnight and he promised to talk again in a couple of days.

'Your *stepbrother*?' Simone spluttered, all kinds of thoughts swirled around her head, not least that Richard was still coming up regardless, and he wasn't taking the opportunity she'd thrown at him to spend time alone with Robyn.

'Sorry about that, I only found out the day before I left home. How did I forget to tell you?'

'How indeed? Tall dark strangers clouding your thoughts, obviously. Bloody hell, it's like only the best bit of gossip for months, your mum and Rich's dad. I can't believe it, is she on the wagon then?'

'Not completely teetotal, I don't know what that really means. Is she still an alcoholic?'

Simone gave a lopsided shrug. 'I don't know either but it's got to be better than it was, right? Richard Saunders for a *stepbrother*. I thought maybe there was something going on between the two of you.'

'About that, what the hell were you playing at? Trying to set us up, even inviting him *here*. You definitely need to work harder on that recovery, you've got far too much time on your hands my *luvver*.'

Simone started to laugh. Her family had tried hard to chivvy her along, but no one said it like Robyn. Only Joey came close at times. 'Well, I'm trying *bird*,' she threw in her own West Country word, adding the soft drawl.

The girls continued to chat, even whilst Simone constantly yawned. She swore blind she wasn't tired and winkled out a bit more information about Shay, how he was apparently a Yorkshire lad, yet with no hint of an accent. If anything, according to Robyn, he sounded like the product of a public school. Carefully watching her friend's non-verbal expressions as she described the man, Simone filled in the blanks, of which she was sure there were plenty, and drew her own conclusion. Robz liked him, as in '*liked*' him. Sometime after the lights went out and the moon cast a thin pearly glow through the gap in the curtains, her voice drifted across the darkened room. 'Did he kiss you?'

Robyn thought about answering, but turned over instead, leaving her friend guessing and gave a quiet chuckle at the frustrated snort.

* * *

The next morning Babs, backed up by Clive, put a dampener on the girls' castle plans by explaining to Robyn she would never manage to both push a wheelchair and help Simone in and out of the car on her own. By all means, go for a walk, but what about finding and using toilets etc.

'The harbour is quite far enough,' she said in her 'sensible' voice. 'It's nearly a mile. By the time you walk there, have a coffee or ice cream and make your way back, that'll be plenty, you'll see.'

Robyn reluctantly agreed. Truthfully, she'd been a little shocked seeing Simone. Her friend had painted a very different picture when talking on the phone, always cheerfully saying how well she was doing. It wasn't that her recovery was going badly, she was meeting and surpassing all the goals her therapists' set, it was more Robyn's realisation that she'd had no idea what to expect. The plans of exploring Aberdeen and the surrounding area together, with Robyn happily pushing Simone around, were not a reality that was likely to happen anytime soon.

'I know she's fed up with us,' Babs continued, 'but Clive or I need to take you if a car's involved. We can always split up and give you two time alone. I'm sorry dear, don't be downhearted. We'll speak to Maggie and Peter tomorrow, I'm sure they can make a few suggestions.'

'I'm not going to be your jailer, Robz,' Simone said sadly. 'I want you to explore the whole area while you're here, go out and do what you want and then come back at the end of the day and tell me everything. We'll go out this morning and after lunch, laze around in the garden until tea. Tomorrow, you go and meet your mysterious man and after that, we'll see what happens, okay?'

She had to agree and they could always do trips with Babs and Clive as well. The last thing Simone needed was to feel like a millstone, so plastering on a big smile, she nodded.

An hour later when they were ready to finally venture out, Babs hooked a bag full of 'just in case' items to the back of the chair. 'Watch the sun girls, it's very hot today, you'll burn if you're not careful.' She shook her head at the thin strapped little tops they were both wearing.

'*Goodbye* Mother,' Simone said irritably. 'Christ, get us out of here now Robz, and don't worry about that bag of stuff, I never need any of it.' She sat back and chatted as they walked slowly along the winding coastal path, soon arriving at the harbour.

'That was never a mile?' Robyn was pleased that they'd got there quicker than she'd expected. Even though they'd taken the walk at an easy pace, it made her more confident about going slightly further next time.

'Mum exaggerates, even if she was right about us going off in the car. I got a bit carried away. I can do a lot more than she gives me credit for though.' She stopped to point out the best way down, where they could avoid any steps. 'It's busy here, the holiday season's well and truly started and the schools haven't even kicked out yet.'

'Same at home, that's what we get for living near the beaches I suppose.'

'I would never want to be too far from the sea,' Simone said. 'When we first arrived, I was so pissed off with the whole having to move thing, I thought I'd hate it, but the house and views soon won me over. I just wish I could...'

Robyn didn't need to hear what was left unsaid. Once again, she was nearly blinded by a burning rage at the thought of a driver that had caused so much devastation to her friend and driven off as if nothing had happened. She turned and gave Simone a bright smile. 'Right then, where do they sell the best ice cream?'

It was amazing that in such a busy town, teeming with sightseers, how many locals noticed Simone and came to greet her. She rolled her eyes at Robyn but managed a brief smile in response to the enquiries.

'Blimey Sim, is it the wheelchair or the fact that your family are considered the 'newbies' here?'

'A bit of both, I think the chair wins it,' she grimaced slightly. 'If we'd moved into the new builds they may not be so fussed. We're obviously accepted because the house is well established and no threat to the green belt. Dad got us quite a substantial home. There's a cellar you haven't seen, outbuildings and over a half acre of field. Did you see the old stone barns from your bedroom window?'

'Yeah, a whole line of them by the look of it, where the field starts to slope.'

'Mum's hoping to convert them into holiday lets or something. She's full of it, ask her if you have a spare three hours, she'll tell you all about her plans. The drawings will come out, so be warned.' The girls giggled. 'You know Robz, if you decided not to go back to uni, I think you'd enjoy a year or so up here.'

'I've already decided,' said Robyn, nibbling her flake and looking at the small sailing dinghies. One was heading through the harbour entrance. The sea was so calm, the tranquil scene could have been a painting on a wall somewhere.

'Have you considered becoming a temporary Scot then?'

It was impossible to miss the hint of hopefulness in the question. 'Well, I hate the sound of bagpipes, second only to the accordion, and tartan *really* isn't my thing.'

She gave a teasing grin. 'But I do love shortbread and go a little weak at the knees when I hear the accent. If I can find something to do, I'd love to stay for a while. I'll have to pay your parents some rent, of course.'

Simone felt happier than she had for months. They wouldn't want rent; well, not for a while at any rate, but she knew Robyn would feel the need to contribute. 'Don't look for anything right away, you deserve a holiday and I want to spend time with you. Sorry, that's a bit selfish, isn't it?'

'Not at all, it was always about you Sim, or about us, I should say.' She beamed at her friend and finished the rest of her flake in one mouthful. Lurking at the back of her mind was another reason to stay in this area. She was an anchor. If she travelled all the way back to Devon, would he still need her?

* * *

The three-car pile-up happened on the A road, not far from the Culloden Monument. Two people were pronounced dead at the scene and another two admitted to hospital. In the ensuing chaos following, nobody noticed two men who looked like they were helping but were actually collecting DNA samples. Adam only gave a moment's pause to the young boy who was dying before his eyes. He couldn't change what was happening now, but it may make a difference to his own time. Shay had seen it all before, and much worse. Filling his own pots and discs with blood and bone marrow, he glanced across the moor. They were too low to see the monument. He'd stood in its very place more than once. On April 16th 1746 to be exact, when he'd blended in, kept his head down and did much the same as he was doing right now. What would Robyn think of him, would she be repulsed and fail to understand why he wouldn't help to save a life? How much more could he get away with telling her? His friends had already taken him to task, reminding him what he shouldn't be saying.

'Are you done?' Adam asked, looking towards the waiting car. 'We need to get these back while they're fresh and make sure that Tarro's checked over. I've got another two anchors now, thanks to this. Not quite sure where they live, hopefully locally.'

Shay nodded. 'You two go on from here, I'll take the car back to Stonehaven first. We'll pick it up when I come through to Robyn next time.' He didn't miss the look his friend gave him before walking off.

'Help me,' a weak voice called from the side of the road. 'Are you a doctor?'

'No, but the ambulance is on its way.' He knew this lady was going to be okay.

'I'm frightened, my leg hurts and I can't see my grandson.'

How many calls for help would he have to ignore? These people were long dead for him, but he was still here today, talking to them. It was the same with Robyn, the minute he stepped through the portal and arrived in his own time, she would have been dead for over two thousand years. Yet, right at this minute, all he wanted was to see her vibrant smiling face; she couldn't be more 'alive'. Not long, he told himself. Twenty-four hours for her, but for him, the time it took to move the car, go home and check to see what other jobs were required. That could be hours or a few days. It wasn't just Tarro that needed rebalancing, he hadn't experienced some of the feelings that were surfacing in him since adolescence, and Shay wasn't about to let them be suppressed, not quite yet at any rate. So, it was work as usual for now and nothing out of the ordinary that would incur unwanted attention from anyone at home. His relationship, if it became that, would be a secret, that only he, Adam and Tarro shared.

The woman was still crying. She'd be okay, not her grandson though. He couldn't think about all the different outcomes, if he did he'd go mad.

It was often easier to collect fresher samples at minor accident scenes than huge battles or massive tragic events, such as avalanches, earthquakes or tsunamis. It was also easier for the research-based historians to pinpoint victims. However, the range of DNA from all the time periods needed in the lab seemed to be never-ending and, as only a small percentage of it remained unspoilt passing through the portal, he and others like him would most likely be doing this grisly work for many years to come.

***

Robyn grabbed a sandwich, walked through the fields, across the coastal route and down the cliff path to the nearby bay. It was fairly busy and there was absolutely no chance of finding a rock to hide behind, a cave or anywhere else she could be alone when Shay arrived. Why hadn't they arranged a time or even a two-hour slot? This was worse than waiting in all day for a delivery. Maybe it would be better to go back to the house, it seemed pretty pointless hanging about on a crowded beach. As time ticked on and there were no tingles or others signs, she walked slowly back the way she'd come.

The empty barns stood beckoning for exploration, and making a quick detour to the far side of the field, Robyn was pleasantly surprised at the condition they were in. The roof tiles appeared intact on two of them. It may be a different story in the rain, but there was no sign of any damp. The third was more of a shell with no roof at all to speak of. She could see the house quite clearly from this one. If she went back to the first barn and closed the door, there'd be total privacy. I'll give him an hour, she thought, climbing the ladder to what presumably used to be a storage area. 'Do you hear me? One hour.'

The upper loading doors let in shafts of sunlight between the loose planks, and she pushed the east facing ones slightly ajar to look at the view of the sea. A tingling sensation started in her fingers and moved up her arms. 'Hello, Shay,' she turned around and he was there. Fighting an overwhelming desire to run into his arms, Robyn made herself walk slowly and reaching him, leant forward slightly to rest her head against his chest. 'I missed you.' She felt one of his arms come lightly around her waist, the other stayed at his side, almost as if he wasn't sure what he wanted to do.

'I missed you too.'

Chapter Six

*'They've taken the very element that
makes you human.'*

They sat together on the wooden floored upper level of the barn. Robyn told him all about Simone, the different therapies she was undergoing and her own decision to stay in Scotland and look for a permanent job. Every so often she'd sneak in a question or comment about the future, hoping he wouldn't notice. He always did and pretended to study the horizon until the conversation returned to the safer more mundane topics, such as how many mini-marshmallows you could fit in a mug of hot chocolate. 'We're still doing the truth thing, aren't we?' she asked

Shay looked dismayed when she pulled a folded sheet of A4 paper from the pocket of her shorts. 'The truth thing, um, yes of course. Just don't expect me to answer everything I suspect you're about to ask.'

'I'll start with something easy, where were you yesterday?'

'My yesterday, or your yesterday?'

'Oh,' his question immediately threw her, it wasn't even a question on the list. 'I'm not sure I understand.' She snuggled a little closer, pleased that he didn't immediately edge away, as he had the first couple of times.

'As far as *you're* concerned, I was on the outskirts of Culloden Moor yesterday.' He looked down at the top of her head, which was now resting on his arm. Her bodily contact made him feel both wary and strangely protective, he'd no idea why. She looked interested and he wondered what reaction the next part of his answer would receive. 'For me, my yesterday was at home, as were the five days before that.' She was chewing her lip again. 'You saw me two days ago, but I'm actually six days older than I was then. Do you understand?'

'Bloody hell, that was meant to be an easy question. Hang on, Culloden you say, yesterday? There was a bad accident somewhere near there, two people died, it was on the local news last night. Did you see it? It wasn't anything to do with Tarro's driving, was it?'

'No, we didn't witness the actual crash just the aftermath.'

'That must have been awful, a child was killed, can you imagine?' There was only a slight pause before the list was referred to again. 'Okay. Question number one. How far ahead in the future do you come from and why exactly did you come to this time, and is it possible for anyone to do it?' She rattled off what she'd written like a newsreader using an autocue, and then looked up at him expectantly.

'That's one question? This,' he said, grabbing the sheet of paper, screwing it into a tight ball and stuffing it firmly back inside her pocket, 'is not going to work.' Silencing her spluttering indignations, he put a finger over her lips but wasn't prepared for the feel of a small lick.

Robyn watched him pull his hand back as if it had been burnt. She just couldn't help herself. Didn't he know how she felt being so close to him, to have skin on skin contact like that, especially touching her lips? How was she meant to ignore *that*?

Shay felt a stab of something in his gut, he felt it mildly every time he saw her and knew it was completely different from any other anchor he'd ever had, and it was burning away the whole time she sat next to him. *What was the damn question?* He was having trouble concentrating. 'Roughly two and a half thousand years.

We're looking for answers in the past, literally in all the different time zones, and yes, in theory, anyone can do it.' That would open the floodgates. For better or worse, there was no going back.

Desperate to ask something more personal, she focused on this latest revelation, somewhat bemused by the fact he kept looking at his finger. 'Two and a half thousand *years*, really? What do you mean by answers? You said something like that before. You need help, what's wrong with you?'

'Basically, we're dying out, our numbers are decreasing at an alarming rate.' He looked straight ahead and forced himself to continue, even when he felt her hand grab clumsily for his. 'It won't be in my lifetime, probably not for a few generations, but it *will* happen if we can't reverse what's been done. A high number of our children aren't developing properly after puberty,' *that's if they even reach it*. 'One thing we have learnt about the past, Robyn, is not to ignore the signs. You asked why now?' He brought her hand to his lips and kissed it, enjoying the continued feeling of what he thought must be the stirrings of desire. 'The most damage was done in a relatively short space of time, between around the last half of the twentieth century and the beginning of the twenty-third. The repercussions, unfortunately, set a pattern for the future.'

'What did we *do*, what went *wrong*? Is it the greenhouse effect or climate change?' she looked around frantically. 'It's fracking, isn't it? Tell us and then we can put things right, go to the government, *make* them listen.'

'It doesn't work like that. This is the past, or *my* past to be exact. It's happened, it can't be changed. Don't chew your lip, Robyn.' He watched his fingers make their way to her mouth, brushing her lips as if he'd no control over his hands. 'Our immune systems can't cope, it affects the birth rate and the way our children grow. We have um...' *Oh God, her lips.* 'We have every piece of technology you could imagine, but we can't sort this out. Robyn, I can't...'

Ignoring the fact that he'd just told her off and acknowledging that his thumb felt so good pressing against her lower lip, she needed to know everything and something told her this might be the best chance of him telling her more than he perhaps meant too. 'Keep going Shay, tell me the rest.'

'The way we control our emotions are all messed up as well. You've seen a little of how Adam and Tarro appear; one happy, overly so, the other constantly irritable. It could just as easily be Adam flying into a rage and Tarro being the jokey smiling one. They have an overdeveloped emotional ladder, that's how we refer to it anyway. I, on the other hand, was able to have my emotions suppressed at a young age. I'm within the middle rungs, so to speak, or at least I was.' He saw her shocked expression and went quiet. His fingers dropped down, only to be snatched back into her hand as she held on tightly, giving him an encouraging squeeze.

'My God, they've taken the very element that makes you human.'

'Not taken, *suppressed*. When I was a child I had to have frequent tweaks and modifications. We're not emotionless, that was never the intention. It's just to shorten the two ends of the ladder so to speak. I'm struggling to explain this.' He glanced around the barn, watching the sunbeams dance with the dust motes, then looked through the open hatch at the ocean, knowing if he turned to her, the same blue would be reflected in her eyes. Why were there no blue-eyed people in his time? No one had an answer to that.

'The idea, which started a few hundred years before I was born, was to find the optimum scale for emotions, so there would be no jealous rages, for example, or hysterical outbursts where people could act irrationally. We are checked as soon as we are born to see which category we fall in. Seventy percent of us, like me, can be 'fine-tuned'. Then there are others, such as Adam and Tarro. They have to be monitored closely and will never be able to control themselves fully. It may sound barbaric but believe me, things were much worse before, at least our scientists are trying to reverse it now.'

'But to mess with people's feelings, it's not dissimilar to how they treated the mentally ill in the early 1900s, they took out part of their brain!'

'We can all look at the past, make judgements and wonder why and what the hell they did!'

'I guess when you put it like that. Do you think they will ever repair the damage and give you back what's rightfully yours, the right to make mistakes or fall madly in love? Can you love Shay?'

'Yes of course... maybe not the way *you* would define love. I have feelings, I'm very fond of people. I find familiarity comforting. Does that make sense?'

'It's a start. Do you have anyone special in your time, a wife or girlfriend?'

Shay shook his head. 'We should leave it there for today. I'll see you again, though.' He stood up effortlessly, pulling Robyn with him.

'Are you running away? Are you going home to be reset like a computer?'

'I should, but I don't want to.'

'Then don't and don't leave me yet, Simone expects me to be out all afternoon. Please Shay, stay a bit longer.'

'I find it hard to say no to you, that's a new thing for me,' he said with resignation.

'That's not an emotional thing, don't worry. It's how all nice men should feel around the girl they like,' she teased.

'Very well then, a little bit longer. They moved to the open hatch, enjoying the gentle easterly breeze. Robyn sat on the edge and dangled her legs over, coaxing him to do the same.

'Will your children inherit your ability to be suppressed?'

'Emotional parents *usually* have emotional offspring, stable ones have... well, like me. So yes, probably.'

'What about trying to mix the parentage a bit more?'

'That doesn't work, we seem to be the dominant gene and we don't want to breed out all the highly emotional people, they may be the answer. In fact, a lot of us envy them.'

'Hmm, it's not really a gene, though is it? Suppression means it's still there somewhere. Shay, I love history, I'm passionate about it. What's it all for, though, if the future is so fucked up?'

'I'm sorry you're upset, come here.' He pulled her into the crook of his arm and held her tightly against him. 'I'm not sure how much knowledge you can cope with. I shouldn't be telling you any of it. I'd be in serious trouble, so don't mention anything in front of Adam or Tarro.'

He was looking uncomfortable, maybe she could play on that? 'Are you *really* sorry, do you feel sad because you think I'm upset or are you just saying what you think I need to hear?'

Shay paused to think, his brow furrowed slightly. 'I... regret how you feel,' he said slowly.

'Regret, oh well, that's something. Maybe the future isn't full of Mr Spock clones after all.'

'Mr Spock?'

She laughed. 'Don't worry, suppression is better than extinction. '*Extinction of emotions*' sounds like the title of a poem.'

Shay was watching her intently, trying hard not to put his foot in it again.

'Spontaneity,' she beamed. 'Let's see if we can kick-start some desire, that's an excellent emotion to begin with.' Palming his cheeks, Robyn leant forward, brushing his lips softly with her own. *A definite intake of breath there*, she smiled whilst continuing to move her lips. Deepening the kiss, she was determined not to give up now that she'd felt a long-awaited response. He kissed her back and the dark eyes that looked hungrily into her own were dilated. 'Did you like that?' He nodded his head. 'Want to do it again?'

'You're looking at me as if you think I've never kissed a girl before.'

'Oh no, I can tell you have,' she smirked. 'Plenty I'm guessing.'

He burst out laughing, realising he'd had more fun since meeting Robyn than he'd ever had before. 'Just not quite like you, or with such...'

'With such feeling?'

'Yes,' he smiled. 'You seem to have woken something up inside me Robyn.'

'Good, let's see what else we can wake up,' she said mischievously.

It was much later than both of them realised, and as much as Shay would have like to stay kissing and holding Robyn, he was fighting an inner war with feelings that had lain dormant for too long. 'I really must go, before Adam comes looking.'

'Will you come back tomorrow?' she asked.

'Definitely,' he nodded vigorously.

'Will it be your tomorrow?'

'Probably not, I think we're off to Cardiff, eighty years from now.'

'What happened in Card... Ah, you can't tell me I suppose. It must be wonderful to go everywhere and see things, and then you come back and it's the same day, like having multiple lifetimes.'

'It's not like that at all. Say, for instance, you went somewhere with me for a week and returned to this very minute, your body doesn't stop ageing. Physically you'd be a week older.'

'If I went *with* you, does that mean... do you think I could?'

Not having quite lost his wits, he needed some space to think things through. If a mistake was made it could ruin everything. 'Maybe, I don't know; I need to go away and figure this out properly.'

She felt him kiss her again and then he was gone. Hugging the air in front of her, she clung on to the feel of him for as long as possible.

'Sim's in the garden,' Joey sniggered, pouring fruit juice into three glasses. 'I saw you with your new boyfriend.'

Robyn groaned, she'd forgotten a friend's mum dropped him off after school. The rotten little spy had no doubt walked right past them. 'How much to keep quiet?' she frowned, pretending it was a game and enjoying the excuse to give him something.

'*Well*, I did see him snog you.'

'She grabbed him in a tight hug and began tickling till he started to laugh. 'Come on then, what's it going to cost me not to hear it over the dinner table tonight?'

'Dad doesn't get as much time as he'd like to take me places,' he said between giggles. 'It's hard with Sim.'

Robyn stopped the torture and looked hard at Simone's brother. She remembered when he was a tiny baby and Babs had let the girls help bath him. Over the years, she'd read him stories, played football in the garden, paddled in the sea holding his hand tightly, and felt sorry when Simone screamed at him to leave them alone. Joey was the nearest thing she had to a younger sibling of her own. 'It must be difficult to take a back seat so often, eh Joey?'

'Not now you're here with a *car*... school breaks up soon, I don't even mind the boyfriend coming, as long as you don't snog him all the time,' he added cheekily.

Robyn could hear the hopeful note in his voice. Would Shay like to go out with Joey? It might be quite fun to see how he reacted to a twelve-year-old. 'Okay then,' she agreed. 'I'll take you somewhere.'

He grabbed a drink and headed for the front room, looking extremely pleased with himself. Robyn smiled, and picking up the two remaining glasses of orange, made her way through the conservatory to the patio where Simone was waiting.

'At last, I want to hear everything. Apparently, he was snogging your face off.'

'Oh, my God, that little shit. I've just blackmailed him to keep it quiet.'

'You would have told me anyway... *right*?'

Robyn grinned and perched herself on the edge of the sunbed describing in great detail everything she could. There was so much more she couldn't say. Luckily, Simone didn't notice the hesitations, the events of the afternoon were far too juicy.

* * *

Robyn's next few weeks fell into a pattern, as she divided her time between her best friend and the man she was beginning to develop very strong feelings for. They usually met in the barn, avoiding the time that school kicked out, or she'd drive a few miles to a quiet spot. Because she was his anchor, he could always find her. Once they were together, they began to act like any normal couple, walking around the town, finding small cafes for lunch, even if Shay ate very little. Sometimes they caught the train to Aberdeen and visited the many museums and art galleries. Robyn noted the ones she would send her CV to, as this was also on her mind. The outing with Joey was mentioned and he seemed more than happy if it meant they could spend the whole day together. She wondered what excuses he was making to Adam and Tarro about all the time he was away from them. Shay always told her briefly about where he'd been, but never really why. Research was given as his explanation on days when she wouldn't let the subject drop.

Determined to get him to agree to the possibility of her travelling somewhere, she began to slowly break down his already wavering resolve.

After a particularly heated session on a blanket in the barn, when he was at his most vulnerable, she tried again. Robyn had no doubt about her feelings. Shay, on the other hand, had every doubt but was holding on to these precious emotions like they were his lifeblood. As the familiar question broke the silence, he pulled her onto his chest, took one look at her pleading expression and asked, 'Which time period would you like to visit?'

'Do you honestly mean it?' His smiling mouth was right below hers. It was far too tempting to ignore. After kissing him again she rested her head on his shoulder. 'How far back can we go? Or can you take me into the future?'

'I can't take you into the future, Robyn. I don't know if it would be safe for you, we've never experimented with living people. We know that we can't advance further than our own year.'

'Why? Surely that's the most important thing, don't you want to know what happens?'

'The portals don't go forward, it's been tried. Hopefully, the answers are in the past.' He saw her confusion. 'I mean, we can go home to our own time, just not any later. The consensus of opinion is that we're first in the race.'

'Hmm, I suppose someone has to be. What answers, what exactly is it you're looking for?'

He took a deep breath. She'd either accept what he did or find it so macabre that he'd see a look of loathing in her beautiful blue eyes. If that happened he'd go home, get himself 'fixed' and never use her as an anchor again. 'DNA,' he finally said quietly. 'We collect it from all over the world, through the different ages and take it back for our scientists to assess.'

'I don't understand, DNA from the past. How can that be better than what you have?'

Curiosity, so far so good. 'I told you a few weeks back about our problems, if you think back, say, oh I don't know, to the Norman Conquest, for example.' He saw a nod for him to continue, he also noticed her eyes were shining, at the historical reference no doubt. 'Those men and women lived shorter lives than we do, but physically, their bodies were much stronger. At every different place in every different time, humans were adapting to their environments. Take the remote tribes in the rainforests today, they use medicines you've never heard of, but if you plucked one of them out and placed him here, he'd most likely die from common airborne viruses that you're immune to.'

'So, you're doing what? Mixing these samples and trying to engineer something that will cure you?'

'Exactly Robyn, that's *exactly* what we do. The samples don't always remain stable when we take them through the portals, it's an ongoing quest I'm afraid.'

'What in particular do you take back?'

He shifted a little uncomfortably. 'Blood mainly.' He didn't need to mention the odd piece of bone or soft tissue sample from an internal organ, particularly useful if it remained stable during transit. The world population is down by nearly thirty-five percent and the rate's still decreasing. The mistakes of the past are continuing to have a knock-on effect even now. Over the last two thousand years, numbers have surged and dropped, and surged again, all with dramatic effect.' He shouldn't have said all that, but it was so difficult not to when she asked.

'My God, how awful, no wonder you're so worried.' Robyn said catching hold of his hand.

'It's up to the likes of Adam and Tarro and me to keep the labs in constant supply of DNA. The hope is that one day, the definitive mix will be the answer to our prayers.'

There was so much more that she wanted to know about the actual problems he was trying to find a cure for, but his earlier question of where she wanted to go was at the forefront of her thoughts. The Stone Age, the Dark Ages or maybe the first Plantagenet kings, that time was so interesting and the men so chivalrous. Well, maybe not your everyday poor Saxon farmer, he wouldn't really appeal. 'I don't know what time to choose for a visit,' she finally said.

'We're back to that again,' he chuckled, quite glad to have a reprieve from the other conversation. 'How about something simple, maybe fifty years ago?'

'How about *no*, something more exciting, please,' she said, ignoring his arched eyebrow, which was usually sexily distracting. *There may not be a second time, this has to count.* 'Tudor times, somewhere around the late 1500s? I'm sure I can find something to wear.'

'Robyn, the idea is to mingle in a crowd and never, not *ever* draw attention to ourselves. Some piece of modern fabric made up as a fancy-dress costume simply won't do.'

'I'm not stupid, I'd sort an authentic costume.'

'How will you do that?' He shook his head. 'I'll bring you a dress and there will be a few rules. We'll go through them on the day.'

'We're really going,' she squeaked. 'Oh, Shay, thank you.'

'There's only one problem, we'll need another anchor to get back here from the portal. Somehow, I don't think Adam or Tarro would oblige us and I don't want to have to tell them.'

'Simone will do it.' This would be her chance to tell her friend everything. Shay didn't look too sure, was she pushing him too hard? 'You can trust her, I swear. Simone and I have secrets going back fifteen years.' Okay, they weren't quite on a par with time travelling with a super-hot guy from the future, but still. 'I'd really like you to meet Joey as well if we're going to be taking him out, and I suppose Babs and Clive.'

Shay managed a nod, he was looking a little pale and had gone quiet again. The situation was already risky and now someone else was going to be involved. Things were spiralling out of control, was this what happened when emotions weren't kept in check?

'It's too much too soon, isn't it?' she gave him a hug. 'I'm sorry I just want to show you off.'

His arms slid around her waist and he lifted her gently. 'This is hard for me and I'm making some quite rash decisions.'

'Forget I mentioned Simone or her parents, and I can put Joey off for another week at least, or I can take him somewhere on my own.'

Shay relaxed a little. 'I really don't mind taking your friend's brother out. The parents might be tricky; they'll be full of questions.'

'You're right, ever since my dad died and my mum... you know, they sort of took over the caring role. I'm twenty next week, but Babs won't take that into consideration at all.'

'It's your *birthday* next week, what day?'

'The 2nd of August. I suspect Babs already has a day out planned.' She smiled a little regretfully.

'No matter, we can go somewhere together for a day and have you back, pretty much the same time you left.'

'How brilliant,' her eyes shone and she gave him a kiss. 'I can celebrate my birthday for like, forty-eight hours, how cool is that.'

'If you *really* trust Simone tell her, but if you're not sure I'll find an anchor in the nearest hospital. Don't expect to drop into the court of Queen Elizabeth. The closest we get to seeing important historical figures are when they ride through a busy street. We'll go to a typical town very near a portal, Stratford-upon-Avon probably. *I'll* bring the dress and everything else you'll need.'

Shay watched her whoop and dance around the barn, still semi-naked, she was projecting her happiness on to him. Making the illicit trip into a birthday treat seemed to absolve him from any earlier guilt and anxiety. Suddenly, he felt the air around him shift slightly. 'Cover up *quickly*,' he warned. She was fighting with her t-shirt just as Adam materialised.

'Sorry, I didn't realise I needed to announce my arrival.' He grinned at Robyn and turned back to Shay, noting his dark glare and choosing to ignore it. 'Are you sure you know what you're doing?' he mumbled quietly.

'I was just leaving, you didn't have to come and fetch me.' He shrugged and mouthed a silent apology in Robyn's direction.

'Nice tattoo,' Adam said, watching with a smile as Robyn tried in vain to straighten the hem of her top. 'It might help if it wasn't on inside out,' he laughed. 'That's what happens when you have to dress in a hurry.'

'Bloody hell,' she muttered, getting onto the top rung of the ladder. 'I'll see you then,' she said nonchalantly to Shay. If she thought Adam was fooled for one moment, she was very wrong.

Chapter Seven

'You were meant to ask him questions, not tell him about the Scottish play.'

Adam slammed the door of the Mercedes and sat brooding over his next course of action. Tarro was over two thousand years away, getting himself 'fixed', whilst Shay was loved up, which he shouldn't be. The three of them had an unspoken understanding, which included turning a blind eye to minor infringements of the rules. This was new territory, however. Shay was never the one in question and Adam was floundering without the council of his other long-term travelling companion.

A black eye and bruised rib had sealed Tarro's fate a few days ago and his friends had escorted him through the portal and straight to the main lab. The look of betrayal was always difficult to stomach as they left him in the capable hands of the technicians. Now Adam fully recovered from his friend's angry outburst, wanted him back, ASAP. With any luck, he'd be ready and waiting, but if they appeared too keen, questions might be asked. A third Harvester could be delegated which, with Shay off balance, would be disastrous.

The time-traveling groups usually consisted of three or four and a mix of emotional ranges was thought to be best. Any time period required the work of Researchers, Procurers and Harvesters. Adam had worked as a Procurer for a long time, this basically translated as stealing, and he prided himself on being an excellent thief. Shay's point to Robyn about turning up at a village five hundred years ago in a nylon copy of the clothing was sound, as every detail had to be correct. A battlefield could be a bit more forgiving. Usually in chaos, it was not the place the cut of a jacket would be so noticeable. Otherwise, authenticity was the most important thing. Procurers would go first, arriving at night to steal from washing lines, houses or even dead bodies in alleyways. The clothes were thoroughly decontaminated and stored in the large warehouses until the Harvesting and Research teams needed them. Adam, Shay and Tarro did both. In fact, this particular time period was more about research, although if the odd DNA sample became available, an opportunity was never passed by.

Shay dozed in the passenger seat, a dopey smile on his face. Showing signs of pleasure and contentment were common enough, but this was different. Adam knew Shay was actually happy, and that was rare. It was the same with excitement. Shay might give a gasp or open his eyes wide, whereas Adam would leap around, hardly able to contain himself. He couldn't fathom how anyone functioned without the range of emotions he had, even if they did sometimes cause problems. His own views on suppression were best not voiced.

Something more than a brief sexual encounter was going on between his friend and Robyn, that much was obvious. He didn't really worry about what she was being told, even if it was against the rules. At the end of the day, they could pull out, make sure the two never met again and that would be the end of it. Who in the early twenty-first century would believe a young woman's ramblings about a time traveller? It would go the same way as reports about Alien abductions. No, Adam's concerns were purely for his friend, and after making the decision to bide his time for a while longer, he worked on how soon they could reunite with Tarro.

* * *

'Wow, a feast.' Robyn looked appreciatively at the fully laden breakfast table. Usually, a quick cup of tea and slice of toast sufficed, this was something else.

'Happy birthday, Robz,' Simone grinned, not caring for once about making a mess with a hot buttered crumpet. She gave her friend a conspiratorial wink, a reminder that after breakfast, she was going to meet the elusive Shay. Since their conversation two days ago, every emotion possible had swept through her – disbelief, anger, fear, envy, fascination and finally a kind of acceptance, mixed with a longing to be part of it in any small way she could.

Knowing Robyn had a secret to share and suspecting it was to do with the new man in her life, she'd made herself comfortable and looked forward to some '*tasty*' revelations, assuming they were going to involve something funny, naughty or both. A new sex story perhaps or how hot Shay looked without his clothes on. As Robyn talked, it had taken nearly a full minute before registering the words coming from her friend's mouth, and sentences incorporating the words '*anchor*', '*time travel*', not to mention '*portal*', sent an icy cold sensation down her spine because she knew when Robyn was joking, and this was not one of those times.

Simone's mother had been concerned the following morning when her daughter announced she wasn't feeling well and would give hydrotherapy a miss. Robyn felt guilty when she saw the worry it caused and tried to reassure Babs that they had just stayed up talking late into the night. Babs gave a long sigh and asked Robyn be more aware in future.

There was nothing really the matter with Simone. She just had no intention of going anywhere before she'd heard everything again in minute detail.

When Robyn brought up the possibility of becoming an anchor, she was up for it immediately. The plan was, they would go back to Simone's room after breakfast on Robyn's birthday, while Babs would be occupied in the kitchen, sorting a large picnic.

Shay had been told to come straight inside the house to Robyn, which had caused him some concern. If other people were nearby, in the next room, for example, it could be awkward.

In the end, Robyn had given him a precise time and decided Simone's en suite bathroom was the safest place. After giving some blood, her friend could watch them disappear and then hopefully reappear a few seconds later, having been away for the best part of a day.

Getting rid of Joey was the problem. Robyn had caught him a few times hanging around the barn since breaking up from school. It was his home, after all. She'd had to be a lot more circumspect, picking her times to wait for Shay.

Following them back to his sister's room, he looked so hurt when Simone told him to 'Get lost.' Robyn would have promised to take him to the top of Ben Nevis if he'd asked. Fortunately, he didn't.

There was no lock on the bathroom door, so Robyn stood against it, just in case. They had only been there a short while when she felt the familiar tingling and Shay appeared. Simone just managed to stifle a shriek that would have brought her whole family charging in had they heard it.

'Pleased to meet you, Simone.' Shay tried not to stare at the wheelchair. He'd seen plenty of them in his travels, in many different forms, but thought this may actually be the first time he'd ever spoken to somebody having to use one.

She smiled shyly, a little irritated that she felt so overawed. 'Hello Shay, I've been hearing wonderful things about you and what you do. I'm very jealous, nice stockings by the way.' She saw him look a little aghast and tried unsuccessfully to drag her gaze away from his tights. 'Is that a birthday present for Robyn?'

'Err yes, sort of,' Shay turned to hand over the package he was carrying and did a double take, seeing the recipient of his gift bent double and shaking with laughter. 'What's so funny?' He tried to help her to stand straight, not sure what to make of the tears running down her face. She pointed to his pants and there was a squeak from Simone, who from her sitting position, was just at the right eye level to get the best view, she also collapsed into fits of laughter.

'I'm so sorry,' she wiped her eyes. 'You look like you've had some kind of arse implant.'

'Padded breeches, and if you're not going to take this seriously, we won't go! The only place I'll be wearing them will be the barn, for your private amusement.' The twinkle in his eye suggested that could be a much better option. 'May I suggest you get changed quickly.' He retrieved the package from the floor and handed it over.

'My costume,' said Robyn, grabbing it enthusiastically and hastily pulled the wrapping off. 'A chemise, bodice and what's this?' she flapped a soft bit of muslin at him.

'That's a parlet, you wear it just under the gown so you're not showing your lovely tits to everyone.'

'Shay, really,' She saw Simone giggle again and struggled into the underclothes.

'Sorry, I'm in 'twenty-first-century speak' at the moment.' While Robyn continued to dress, he took out a small, flat, round device and checked that Simone was happy to give some blood and become an anchor. She offered him a bit more for his 'DNA stuff', which he accepted gladly. The whole thing was over in seconds and when Robyn checked, there was nothing to see, not even a puncture mark. Shay then pressed the disc to both of his wrists, and a very low humming sound was emitted. 'Now you're my anchor as well.' He smiled at Simone.

The brown light wool gown and white linen cap were the last things to put on, before Shay slipped a wedding ring on her finger, saying they were Thomas and Elizabeth Sturgess if anyone should ask. He fussed around with her hair for a few minutes, tucking the shorter front bits behind her ears, as the length at the back was no problem. They weren't depicting a rich couple, just ordinary country folk visiting friends in the town, so no fancy hairstyle, hats, ruffles or farthingale petticoats were necessary and thankfully, no codpiece. Robyn didn't think she'd survive watching Shay trying to tuck himself into one of those. He gave her a simple grey hooded clock, similar to one he wore, and with that, they were ready to go.

Robyn hugged Simone. 'We'll be back almost before you even know we've gone, apparently.'

'Watch this space,' Shay said with a broad grin, and as they both disappeared Simone couldn't have dragged her eyes away from where they'd just stood if the house had burned down around her.

The wheatfield looked much the same, although it was disconcerting to see a farm worker standing no more than six feet away, oblivious to their presence in the middle of the portal. 'What happens if he wanders into our space?' Robyn asked.

'Nothing, he won't see, hear or sense us at all, we're timeless at the moment.'

'How does the portal know where we want to go?'

'It's called projecting and it takes a lot of practice, but mainly it's to do with the implants. We can stay here all day and I'll explain portals if you want?' he teased.

'Fine, just get on with it.' She kissed the tip of his nose, 'Mr Sturgess'.

Shay smiled and told her to hold on to him tightly, before pressing his wrists together. He'd explained again that there were tiny implants in each wrist, just below the main pulse points, which Robyn hadn't been able to feel. When they touched, the portal was activated. Years back, when time-travel first started, the explorers had been forced to carry quite cumbersome devices. These had evolved over time to minuscule implants that couldn't be lost or damaged. Shay's only reservation about taking Robyn alone was that should something happen to him, she'd be in trouble. Eventually, he'd be noted as missing and his records would show where he'd gone. If a search party was sent out, it wouldn't do Robyn much good, as there'd be no trace of her using the portal. Unless Adam or Tarro guessed what had happened, she'd be stranded in 1571 until she died.

For that reason, he'd already travelled to this very time and place. He knew where his anchor would be, what the weather would be like, that it was a market day, where they could eat lunch and which streets were the safest to walk. He wouldn't tell Robyn he'd planned it so meticulously, not when spontaneity seemed such a big deal for her. In this situation, he wouldn't take any chances.

The arrival portal was a stone's throw from the town, right by the side of a busy road. Every time a cart rolled past, Robyn still found it hard to believe they couldn't be seen. People were walking within a few feet and looked through them as if they were ghosts.

'Are you positive they can't even hear us?' she whispered.

'No don't worry, not while we're in the portal. Unfortunately, it's far too busy to leave it and walk into town from here, which would have been pleasant. We'll use the anchor instead.'

'You have one here? Do they know?'

Shay shook his head. 'I told you only very few know. This one may get a slight tremor in his hand, that's all.'

Robyn waited eagerly to see what would come next. Perhaps some feeling of movement, soaring over the heads of the people below? Certainly, she hadn't expected to just appear behind a bakery, a moment before the back door was thrown open and a man pushed past them to retrieve a sack of flour.

'Oh, my God!' *Blast*, she wasn't meant to say that. It had been on the long list of 'rules' that Shay had given her a few days before. He'd made her promise to adhere to it, so no wonder he was frowning. 'Sorry,' she muttered. 'Is he your anchor?'

'Yes, and be *careful*. You can't walk around exclaiming loudly and swearing every time you spot something or get knocked, or have your toes trod on.' He led her through a back alley that opened up onto a narrow bustling street. There were tall buildings on either side that made it gloomy and the smell was awful. Shallow gutters along the sides of the cobbles were awash with filth. Robyn was glad when they reached the end and it opened onto a large square with a busy market.

'Oh, my G...' She let the words die away and concentrated on keeping her mouth shut.

'If we should get separated, try and find somewhere quiet. The back of any building will do, I'll always be able to find you. Failing that,' he pointed to a crowd surrounding a poor soul screaming in pain. 'Head for the whipping post, I'll meet you there.'

'The w-whipping post.' Robyn turned so quickly, a man wearing what looked like a barrel nearly collided into her. He was closely followed by a jeering mob and the victim looked like he was about to drop with exhaustion. 'What the hell?'

'Robyn keep your *voice* down, I won't tell you again.' His face softened slightly. 'It's called a drunkard's cloak, he was obviously intoxicated and making a nuisance of himself. These are unforgiving times, people are scared of things they don't understand. The penalties for being different or not conforming are savage. That's why you have to be so careful about what you say in their hearing.' He gave her hand a squeeze. 'You don't want to end up pilloried for blasphemy, do you?'

'I won't say another word.' She replied, giving him a tight smile.

'I don't believe that for one minute. Come on I've got some money, let's see what they have for sale.'

'We can buy something *and* take it back?' she asked excitedly, tugging him towards the stalls.

'It depends on what it is,' he laughed. 'Don't get too excited and remember, let me do the talking.'

Robyn bought two silver bracelets, one for herself and one for Simone. If they were never bragged about as being Tudor antiques, or forced under the nose of a specialist in the field, no one would know they were the real thing or think twice. At most, they looked like reproduction costume jewellery. Simone would know it was authentic and that was all that mattered.

Shay was aware he was breaking another rule, but it wasn't as if he was doing it for monetary gain. They weren't meant to bring anything back from the past unless it was for research purposes. A lot of them did, however. Even the most conscientious travellers had their own little hoard of trinkets dating back to ancient roman times and beyond; the odd coin sporting an emperor's head, a tail feather from a dodo, a golden brooch from the lost Aztec civilisation. Shay's personal favourite was a small plate from Pompeii, pre-eruption naturally.

He was seeing everything today through Robyn's eyes. It wasn't that he'd grown blasé about time travelling, it was just that his job had become a necessity and sometimes the actual miracle was lost. Not so, for Robyn; her eyes were rounder than saucers at every sight, sound and smell. He loved watching her reactions and appreciation. She kept smiling at him and whispering her thanks for opening such a world to her. This wouldn't be the only visit; he knew he'd carry on breaking every rule now that he'd started.

They left the noisy market square behind and walked around the quieter areas for a while. 'Henley Street, that rings a bell. I can't think why?'

'Shakespeare, by any chance?' Shay asked.

'Oh, my God.' *Shitting hell, I'm going to get us both in trouble.* 'His birthplace,' she muttered, 'which one?' Shay, frowning again, pointed it out. She tried to place the house amongst the shops selling Christmas decorations and the patisserie that had been opposite when she'd visited a few years ago. 'Look through that window, it's a bit dark but I'm sure there's someone moving about inside. How old would he be?'

'Well, that's most likely a servant, try not to stare. They were quite an affluent family, his father was actually a bailiff, I believe. William would be around six or seven; the thinking is, he attended the local grammar school. When he was older it was a known fact he moved on to King Edward V1 School.' Shay looked around to get his bearings and pointed in the direction of the river. 'Over there somewhere.'

'I don't know what to say, I'm so completely overwhelmed. I'll never be able to thank you for giving me this opportunity.'

'Robyn, don't start crying. That'll draw as much attention as your inappropriate swearing. Let's get some lunch, the food will be quite safe for you to eat, except meat, don't chance it. Don't draw attention to the fact I'm not eating much, okay. In fact, don't speak at all.' He gave her a quick kiss on the top of her head and then rearranged her cap. 'You look quite cute in that, maybe I'll let you keep it,' he smirked.

'If you really want me to play dress up, I can find something much more entertaining,' she replied, giving him a saucy wink.

Shay had sussed out a half-decent inn when he'd previously visited to do his safety checks before bringing Robyn. He also knew that at this exact time on this exact day there would be a nice table available away from the smoky fireplace, which was a little overpowering and quite unnecessary in the middle of April.

A young rosy-cheeked girl offered them a choice of barley or rye bread, dried fish, cheese and onions. She brought two large wooden plates, either ignoring or not believing Shay when he told her he only wanted an ale. Robyn was delighted to be offered cider, and although the bread was a little coarse, the food was surprisingly good.

Everything was going well until a couple entered and stood practically on top of them. Frustrated that there was nowhere to sit, the woman complained loudly. She then proceeded to take out a cat-fur collar she'd just purchased from the market and shake it in the man's face, moaning that it looked suspiciously like 'rat'. Robyn watched as bits of fluff fell onto her food. She turned quickly and just managed to avoid a bash on her nose from the man's rather large, rancid codpiece.

Shay knew what was coming, and as her mouth opened he heard a loud, '*Erugh, gross.*' He quickly offered their table to the couple, insisting they were just leaving. Steering her out by the elbow and dropping a few coins into the hand of the waitress on their way, he managed to deflect from what could have been a close call. Robyn's turn of phrase had caused more than a few heads to turn. 'I know what you're going to say, but this is the way things were,' he said, shuffling her down the steps.

'That was the most disgusting thing I've ever smelt in my whole entire life.' She looked around guiltily. 'Sorry, did we get away with it?'

'Only *just*, if you want to come to other places with me, you're going to have to do better,' he gave a laugh in acceptance of what he'd just committed himself to.

'Really, you'll take me somewhere else, when?'

'Quiet now,' he hissed as they found themselves back on one of the main streets. 'I'll give it some thought wench,' he winked.

'Can we cut through the market again and go down to the river? I don't think I've ever seen it without a bargees' convention taking place. Three times I've been here and on both sides, they were moored nose to tail, or fore and aft, whatever the nautical term is.'

'That sounds about right, come on then, remember to...'

'I know, keep shtum in the market.'

'Christ, I give up.'

'You blasphemer, do you want to end up in the stocks?' she asked smugly.

'You drove me to that woman. I'll blame my naughty wife and you can see what the ducking stool was like.

You'll certainly get an uninterrupted view of the river, all from the comfort of a wooden seat.'

Robyn started to giggle and yet again forgot Shay's warnings. When she slapped him on the arm and leant up to kiss his cheek, a few people nearby started murmuring.

'Forgive us, friends, we art newly wedded and on our '*hony*-moone'.' Shay gave his most engaging smile and Robyn had the good sense to look down at the ground, feigning humility.

'The first month of marriage is the sweetest,' one female voice rose from the crowd.

'I wish thee tenderness and pleasure at each moment,' another said.

There were some ribald comments from the men, with a few compliments to Shay on his bonnie bride. An argument soon broke out over the virtues of a meek and submissive wife over an adventurous and buxom one in the bedroom. As it became more heated, Shay managed to steer Robyn away. Disappearing into the crowded market they left the rabble loudly debating the pros and cons of wedded bliss.

'Did they call it a honeymoon in this time?' she asked quietly

'Apparently so, it was spelt a little differently, so I'm not sure if the pronunciation was the same. That lot didn't seem to notice.'

'No, they were more concerned about my pert breasts and child-bearing hips. Did you hear them? It was outrageous.'

Shay had heard that and quite a bit more, which thankfully Robyn hadn't. 'They're a lot more men around now who have been drinking steadily, so be careful and be on your guard for cut-purses. It may be better if I look after the bracelets, I can tuck them inside my cloak.' He showed her a large cleverly concealed pocket. An added adaptation to make the gathering of DNA samples easier.

Robyn handed them over and a moment later felt the telltale tug of someone pulling on her own pocket. She whipped around, grabbing the wrist of a young and very startled looking boy. 'Well, well, what do we have here?'

'I'm sorry, let me go, they made me,' he nudged his head in the direction of two older boys, who quickly averted their eyes and marched off in the other direction. 'Please Mistress, I won't do it again.'

'Hmm, should I call the constable, Thomas?'

Shay looked at the trembling child. He didn't look like the usual pickpocket, as his clothes were of good quality and he was clean. 'Perhaps our young friend could buyeth three cakes instead,' Shay suggested, giving the boy a coin, 'and sit by the river with us for a few minutes?'

'Oh, aye please, sir,' he said thankfully and rushed over to purchase three honey cakes with a thick topping of marzipan.

'That boy's no thief.' He then explained to Robyn that she could ask him a few questions, as long as she was careful. Children were much easier to get information from without arousing suspicion.

They had to walk a fair way before the muddy bank gave way to grass and Will, who'd quite happily volunteered his name once he knew cake was involved, sat with them.

'You look a little young to be out without a parent, Will?'

'I'm seven Mistress, but I shouldn't really be down by the river on mine own.' He looked at Shay. 'I heard the crowd sayeth thee were newly-weds, art thee travelling, sir?'

'Yes lad, we've been to Scotland and we're heading home to Exeter.' Shay had learnt from experience that sticking to the truth, or at least what you knew best, was usually safest.

'Scotland?' His eyes widened.

'Near Scone Palace, actually,' Robyn added. 'Have you heard of it?' She watched him shake his head. His cake was long finished, but he didn't seem in a rush to leave. 'Some famous kings were crowned there, Robert the Bruce and Macbeth.'

'Robert the Bruce, I knoweth about that gent, mine teacher hath instructed us. I don't the other one, Mac...'

'Macbeth, he was a General of King Duncan, but killed him to take the throne himself.'

Will's mouth opened in a large 'O'. 'That wasn't nice, that gent deserved a bad end, didst he get one?'

Robyn saw Shay's warning look. It was history so she wasn't giving anything away, but she should take into account a young boy running home to his parents spouting off about a Scottish king they may not have heard of.

'Well, he was defeated in battle eventually and the son of King Duncan was put on the throne. That's it really, nothing exciting.'

'I has't to taketh my leave,' said Will, jumping up and turning to run. Then, remembering his manners, he gave a quick bow.

'No more pickpocketing, promise?'

'I promise, my thanks for the cake and the story of Macbeth. Methinks many more horrible things should hath befallen that gent.' He gave them a grin and ran off.

'You were meant to ask him questions, not tell him about the Scottish play.'

'The Scottish Play? What are you on about?'

'Err, that young boy, who just *happens* to be called Will, now thinks that terrible things should have befallen Macbeth!'

'What? No, *surely* not. Wow, oh my God. I mean, do you *really* think it's possible?'

'Who knows? Time to go, my love, before you influence any more potential young writers, or teach the town of Stratford-upon-Avon a whole new vocabulary of peculiar words and phrases.'

Chapter Eight

*'You could have this night a thousand times,
but for me, it will only be the once.'*

'You really did come back straight away, well twenty-eight seconds to be exact,' Simone looked at the clock on her phone. 'I knew you were coming, my fingers went all weird.'

'And now, I must go,' Shay smiled. 'Thanks again for your help, Simone.'

'You're welcome, are you still meeting us for lunch. I haven't mentioned anything, I know my parents are very curious about Robz's new boyfriend, though.'

He had to think for a second who '*Robz*' was. 'Err yes I'd like that. I can only eat a very light salad type of meal, or vegetable soup would be okay.'

'What? No *cake*?'

'Well yes, cake's okay.' He gave Simone a smile. 'But not too much and not too rich.'

'It seems they pop protein pills and such-like in the forty-fifth century. It's a wonder they have teeth, they seem so unnecessary.' Robyn gave Shay an exasperated look, this was something she found difficult to accept as progress. 'I doubt we'd have quite the same relationship if you were dentally challenged.'

'I'll bear that in mind,' he replied, unconsciously running his tongue over his front teeth. 'Don't believe everything this one tells you,' he said to Simone. 'Solid food is fine, we just have trouble digesting a lot of the proteins you consume on a daily basis, and we don't 'pop pills' either.'

'A weak and lily-livered race, that's what our descendants will become,' teased Robyn, changing quickly and handing the clothes back to Shay. 'Thank God they still produce gorgeous hunks of manliness.' She gave him a kiss and he felt her giggles erupt against his tongue.

'See you soon,' he whispered into her mouth.'

'The park, near the river, don't forget,'

'I don't need to know that, I'll find you anywhere, silly girl.'

* * *

Babs and Clive assisted their daughter into the MPV, then loaded the wheelchair in the back. They'd got it off to a fine art. It was a little easier now that Simone could grip slightly, whilst shuffling her body independently. Robyn watched with a feeling of pride in the advances her friend had made. During the six weeks since she'd first arrived, the changes were noticeable. Babs had remarked, only that morning, how Robyn being with them had made all the difference.

She felt a little ashamed not having spent more time with Simone. That was, after all why she'd moved to Stonehaven. Her friend had been unusually quiet after Shay left, and it had taken a while to get to the bottom of it. 'Did you see the way he looked at my chair?' she'd finally said.

Shay had previously explained to Robyn, people in his century didn't suffer from injuries or sickness of that kind, as most things were treatable. He'd let slip that damaged spinal cords would be replaced in the not too distant future. But not meaning to give that information away, he'd clammed up. Robyn had to be content with the knowledge that it would happen one day, whether or not in her time he wouldn't confirm or deny.

'Oh, *that's* nice,' Babs exclaimed, noticing her daughter's bracelet. 'Is it new?'

'I bought them at Warwick Castle,' Robyn quickly said. 'I forgot all about them until this morning when I was looking for some bangles.' Simone breathed a sigh of relief, stupidly she hadn't even thought about what to say if she was asked.

'Oh yes, you have the same, how very lovely. Proper copies of the Plantagenet jewellery, I should think. I remember seeing things like that in the gift shop when we visited.' Babs turned to her son. 'Joey, is your friend actually *coming*? Because we're ready to go.'

Simone threw Robyn an amused look, her mother wouldn't know the difference between Tudor Plantagenet or Victorian jewellery, and she'd probably assume a leather thong of Stone Age animal teeth was a contemporary fashion statement.

A car pulled up and Joey's friend Sam dashed out. His mother gave a wave and shouted she'd be back to pick him up later when he texted.

'Hi, Joe. Hello, Mr and Mrs Harman. Hello, Simone.' He looked a bit lost when he came to Robyn.

'This is my sister's friend,' Joey said casually by way of introduction. Sam looked none the wiser.

'Hi, I'm Robyn,' she held out her hand, not sure if you did that with twelve-year-old boys.

Sam gave it a shake and looked as if he'd just remembered something. 'Oh yeah, the one in the barn,' he said without thinking. The ensuing silence told him he'd put his foot in it. Pulling a face, he looked around for an escape.

'Get in the car, quick,' Joey said, clambering onto the back seat before Robyn could make eye contact.

Clive coloured a little and hurriedly took his seat behind the wheel. Babs gave Robyn a sympathetic look, as she got in next to him. She had her own theories about what was going on there, and although she didn't condone it, Robyn was twenty now, not a teenager anymore. Interference from her best friend's mother, even if they were close, would not be appreciated.

Simone waggled her eyebrows and patted the seat next to her. 'Come on Robz, you're last as usual.'

Leaping in, she cast a disparaging look at the two reprobates, who were discussing the latest Pokémon they'd found. Joey looked a bit sheepish but was quickly distracted by something that Sam was excitedly pointing to on his phone.

'Are we keeping you up?' Simone commented. They'd been travelling for less than 20 minutes and Robyn had just yawned for the third time.

'Didn't you sleep well?' Clive smiled into the rear-view mirror.

'I guess I was excited. Birthdays, you know.' She answered lamely, scowling at Simone for drawing attention to it.

'Dreaming of snogging your boyfriend?' The question was accompanied by kissing noises from the seat behind.

'Did you really want me and Shay to take you somewhere, Joey?' Robyn had a moment's satisfaction when he fell quiet, nudging Sam to do likewise.

The journey wasn't long. They were soon parked near the Winter Gardens, deciding what to do with the large picnic that Babs had packed. In the end, they chanced leaving it in the car for the morning, as it was all in cold bags. Robyn wondered if there would be anything suitable for Shay to eat. She'd seen plastic containers of cold chicken pieces and scotch eggs going into the bottomless hamper; so much for a flask of vegetable soup.

Joe, as he was trying desperately to get his family to call him now, ran on ahead with Sam. Babs and Clive sorted Simone and then grudgingly left Robyn to do the pushing, knowing the girls wanted to talk.

'I feel quite redundant.' Babs said, her brow wrinkling with concern.

'Enjoy it, Mum, I'm sure I'll need you for something later,' Simone grinned. Babs nodded, and after checking once more that the girls were okay, walked ahead with Clive to keep an eye on the boys.

'Bloody hell, what a fusspot she is at times.' Simone shook her head. 'Right, finally I want to hear all about it.' The girls walked through the tropical and desert gardens, enjoying the colourful displays of plants, moaning about the humidity and watching the fish and turtles in the stream that ran down the middle of one of the huge greenhouses. Robyn tried to remember every single detail of her trip to Stratford-upon-Avon, adding her own twist to make it more dramatic or comical. By the time they headed outside and into Duthie Park, Simone was up to date and completely and utterly spellbound.

'And there he is, Robz, by the bandstand; your very own, much better-looking Dr Who.'

'Oh, I don't know. I have quite a thing for David Tennant,' Robyn said, waving madly at Shay. 'I'll just go and bring him over, hang on.'

'Don't rush,' Simone mumbled. 'I'm not going anywhere.'

'I'm so glad you came,' Robyn said, patting his behind and murmuring appreciatively. 'Tight jeans, so much better than those massive pantaloons.'

'You're going to have to get used to period wear. This isn't exactly normal for me you know,' he gestured towards his clothes.

'No, I suppose not, I never thought about it. What *do* you wear?'

'Similar in appearance actually, but our fabrics are very different, lightweight and suitable for all climates.' He fished a small box from his pocket. 'Happy birthday, love.'

They walked slowly back to where Simone was waiting impatiently with the rest of her family. Pretending it was a first-time meeting for her friend, as well as the others, Robyn made the introductions. While they exchanged pleasantries, she opened her gift and gave a gasp at the sight of a pair of sapphire earrings sat on a plump white cushion.

'To match your eyes,' he said softly. Hoots of laughter started from the two boys and he shrugged good-naturedly.

Clive went to fetch the food, whilst Babs pointed them in the direction of the picnic benches. Luckily, the grass was short and dry, and with a bit of extra brute force and the odd swear word, the wheelchair was soon parked alongside the shadiest table.

'Would you rather sit on the bench, Simone?' Shay asked. She nodded and he swept her up into his arms as if weighing nothing and deposited her between himself and Robyn. 'We'll wedge you in and keep you upright,' he grinned.

Clive, who'd returned just in time to see this, felt slightly superfluous and was for once lost for words. That didn't last long when he discovered that Shay was vegetarian. 'You don't eat meat? What, none at *all*?' he asked incredulously.

'Dad, he's hardly the first veggie to walk the Earth,' Simone said despairingly. 'Sorry about my father, he's a bit of a caveman at times.'

Shay listened politely to all the arguments that Clive offered on nutrition and protein. He had nothing to add to the conversation, as it wasn't a question of choice or some health-conscious decision he'd come to. Animal flesh just wasn't available in his time; it hadn't been for over eighteen hundred years. Not missing something he'd never had, he didn't care one way or the other. Adam and Tarro had been known to indulge a few times and were always extremely ill the next day. At certain times if it couldn't be avoided, they were given emetics to swallow as soon as possible. Vomiting, until their stomachs had expelled all the contents was not pleasant, but it was far better than the side-effects of a digestive system that had long ago lost its adaptive ability to cope with a carnivorous diet.

'For goodness sake, Clive, stop going on,' Babs frowned. 'It's to be admired and you have to admit Robyn's chap seems very fit.' Simone and Robyn started to laugh.

Babs' face flushed red. 'You know *exactly* what I meant girls.' She turned to address Shay 'You're a healthy and fine looking young man, that's all I wanted to say.'

'Thank you, Mrs Harmon.' Shay grinned, helping himself to the tomato and avocado salad.

'Well, I don't get it,' Clive grumbled, as he tore into his chicken drumstick. 'But I'll concede the point, come to our BBQ next week. I'm sure Babs will rustle you up something tasty with a tin of baked beans.'

'I certainly will *not*, Shay, don't listen to him. I bought a wonderful vegetarian recipe book in the charity shop, I'm dying to try it out.'

'Ha, unlucky!' Joey shouted.

'I'm *so* sorry about my family,' Simone muttered through clenched teeth.'

'Don't be,' he smiled. 'It's lovely to meet them and apparently, I'm taking Joe out somewhere soon.'

Joey beamed that he'd got his name right. Even Clive smiled. 'I'd be very grateful, I don't get anywhere near the free time I thought I would,' he said with a sigh, and looked at Simone and Joey. 'I did promise my boy a few more trips out, doing some father and son bonding.'

'This won't be *just* man stuff, I'll be there too, keeping an eye on things,' Robyn added. 'We thought maybe camping for one night at one of the smaller lochs?'

'P*lease,* mum, can I?'

'Camping... overnight, I'm not sure.'

'Let him go, Babs,' Clive interrupted. 'Shay seems like a decent sort.'

'And you'll get an evening alone with Richard,' Robyn gave Simone a conspiratorial wink.

'Of course, how could I *forget*. I was just about to feel sorry for myself again, with all the talk of camping, but you're right, I'll have Rich,' Simone gave a warm smile. 'Thank you for thinking of Joey, I know you'd rather be under the stars alone with your man. I do appreciate it.'

While Babs and Clive tidied everything away, the others walked to the boating lake. Shay pushed Simone, who was quite aware that he was more interested in the chair than her. 'I'd let you have a try if I could get out and walk you know!'

'I'm sorry, it's just fascinating. Not the chair, the whole concept of it being necessary.'

'Yeah, I'm sure Sim thinks so too. *Honestly* Shay, just push the bloody thing properly or give it to me,' Robyn snapped, after watching him zigzag, stop and start and then use the back wheels only, like some child on a BMX bike.

Joey and Sam thought the whole thing was hilarious; Robyn's boyfriend was great fun.

'Why don't you jump in a pedalo, Shay,' Simone suggested. 'If you enjoy antiquated means of transport, you'll love it.'

'Come on,' urged Robyn, grabbing him by the arm and steering him to the water's edge. 'After you.' Once they were in the middle of the lake and managed to avoid the boys, Robyn gave him a piece of her mind.

'I didn't mean anything; it just seems so...' He knew he'd put his foot it.

'So... what?' she interrupted. 'Archaic? One step on from the leeches? Tell me, how would a hemiparesis caused by a head injury be treated in the year 4433?'

'I'm not medically trained, so I don't know the ins and outs of it, but it involves not much more than an overnight stay in a hospital.'

She blew out a long breath. 'Even for something like that?'

He nodded. 'Those sorts of things, we can repair. It's the things we can't that are the problem. The answers to our survival lie in the past. Or at least we hope they do.' He put his arm around Robyn and pulled her tightly against him.

'Take some more of my blood back,' she said, her voice muffled against his shoulder. 'Unless you already have?'

'No, it didn't feel right without consent. Maybe your sample mixed with a few others will be the one, who knows.'

'I'd quite like to think I was a saviour,' she smirked. 'You'd owe me big time.' They both laughed. 'Actually,' she said, reclining back, 'you'd better do the pedalling if I'm going to donate blood.'

'A few *drops*, on a disc, that's all. But by all means, *you* take it easy.'

She made him pedal the circumference of the lake before joining in and leaning over to nuzzle his neck thanking him once more for the earrings.

'Spend the day with Simone tomorrow or just rest, you're going to be tired after our long day. Time travel can be exhausting if you don't sleep properly. I'll look in at bedtime tomorrow night if you're alone.'

'Damn right I'll be alone; my bedroom is up in the attic, and until Rich arrives next week the other room up there is empty *and* the door has a lock, which I've never needed so far.'

'First time for everything then.'

Shay left them on the lakeshore with a promise to attend the BBQ and meet Robyn's future stepbrother at the weekend. They would finalise the details of Joey's trip then.

Robyn didn't make too much of kissing him in front of an audience, but couldn't let him go without a small peck on the lips. 'Where's Adam waiting for you? Or are you going back to the portal?'

'Back to the portal, Adam's already at home.' He didn't go into details about Tarro. Hopefully, after some lab experience and spending a few days with his family, he'd be ready to rejoin them.

'What a pleasant young man.' Babs commented, watching him walk away. 'What does he do again?'

'Errm, research,' Robyn mumbled.

'And he likes history, just like Robyn,' Simone added, and then asked for the loo before her mother could think of any more questions.

Sam's mother picked her son up from the house and Clive took Joey to the beach for an early evening swim. Robyn was too exhausted to accept the offer of joining them. Instead, she enjoyed the last of the day's sunshine with Simone. The two loungers were on the patio, just outside of the conservatory doors, which was a real suntrap. Babs sat with them and chatted for a while before disappearing to make a start on tea.

'She really shouldn't be back in the kitchen, we're all stuffed. I feel so lazy being here and doing nothing,' Robyn said. 'I've offered to do some voluntary work in a few of the museums to hopefully, get my foot in the door, but they haven't got back to me yet.'

'Don't worry about Mum, she's sorting the remains of the picnic, we'll be eating that again for tea. Something's bound to come up in September when all the students go back to college. Are you absolutely sure you don't want to do another course?'

'Maybe next year, but not now; not after the last twelve months.'

'A tall dark and handsome time traveller isn't the reason, is he? You do seem very... involved. You are *happy* aren't you, Robz? Everything's happened rather quickly.'

Robyn chewed her lip. What she felt for Shay was completely overwhelming, all-consuming at times, he was never far from her thoughts. She'd hadn't experienced anything like the strong emotional attachment she felt for this man, nothing had come close. Previous casual boyfriends had come and gone and been easily forgotten. 'I'm so afraid it's not going to last Sim, one day I'll wake up and know he's not coming back.' She turned her face to wipe a tear away. 'In Shay's time, I'm long dead, so this relationship can't continue, it isn't possible.'

'Think of it as a holiday romance then,' Simone offered. 'Make the bloody most of him while you can.'

'Yeah, you're right, that's how I need to look at it.' Who was she kidding? Robyn was desperately in love and given a choice, would never let him go. When the time came and she was the one left behind, she'd deal with the fallout then. 'Anyway, let's talk about your love life and a certain Mr Saunders, arriving Friday night.' She was amused to see Simone flush slightly. 'You like him, don't you?'

'Christ Robz, he was meant for *you*, at least that was my original plan. Now your mum and his dad have spoiled it all.'

'What crap, you can't wait to see him. You talk to Rich almost as often as you talk to me. It's crystal clear he fancies you back.'

'Yeah right, *wheelchair* girl!' Simone gave a short laugh.

Robyn detected the bitter undertone and gave her friend a hug. 'Not for much longer Sim, I'm sure it's hard, but some people don't ever get out of them. You're nearly there, I saw you standing with Peter and Maggie's help the other day.'

'You saw that?' Simone looked pleased. 'Why didn't you say something?'

'It was just so awesome, I didn't want to put you off. Sim, you're one of the strongest people I know, you *can* do this. If Rich is keen on you while you're still... this way, it says a lot. Give him a chance at least.'

'Yes, I will. Thanks, Robz.' She lay back and started a few exercises with a renewed vigour. With her knees bent and feet flat on the sun lounger, she lifted her hips and lowered them again. After counting half a dozen, she stopped feeling her weak leg about to give way. 'What do you think of that then?' She asked, panting for breath.

Robyn pulled a face. 'Sex with the invisible man! And he's knackered you so quickly? You need to improve your technique, my luvver.'

Babs heard the girls' laughter float through the house. Her daughter was recovering and happy, it had seemed like an impossible hill to climb just six months ago. Since Robyn had arrived, Simone was always smiling and she had a feeling that Richard would put an even bigger smile on her face.

* * *

The following day, Maggie had obtained permission for Robyn to accompany them to the hydrotherapy pool. It was wonderful to float in the warm water while Simone did her exercises.

The fact she was being watched gave an added incentive to impress, and Simone came away from the morning session exhausted, but very pleased with herself.

After lunch, they went for a stroll along the cliff walk, Joey seeing them leave invited himself along. Robyn made him take turns pushing his sister. If she'd thought it would put him off coming again, she was wrong. He ran with the chair along the footpath, making Simone shriek with laughter and fear that he'd tip her over each time they hit a rut.

Shay's bedtime visit had been on Robyn's mind all day and she was thankful her room was so far away from the others. When she felt the familiar tingle, her eyes darted around, wondering where he'd materialise.

She gave a snort when he tapped her shoulder. 'I should get used to your advances from the rear,' she laughed.

'I like the sound of that,' he replied, his dark brown eye's sparkling when she turned to kiss him. Robyn's thoughts from yesterday were still rumbling away in her subconscious, and Shay could tell immediately something was wrong. Perhaps the brain had developed over the course of two and a half thousand years so that it could pick up on empathic feelings more easily, or perhaps it was just the fact she was chewing her lip again. 'What's wrong?'

'*Nothing*, I'm really glad to see you.' Robyn was surprised that he'd asked and the insecurities started pushing through. 'You won't be able to do this forever, will you?' The moment she'd spoken the words she wished she could take them back. The last thing she wanted to do was spoil the mood. 'I mean you could have this night a thousand times, but for me, it will only be the once. Are you already visiting my future self, now that I'm an anchor for the next however many years?'

'Robyn, don't think like that, this will be just a one-off for me as well, I promise.'

She looked thoughtful. 'If you went back in time to see me, I wouldn't know you, it would be before you met me, but then I wouldn't be an anchor anyway, so I guess that couldn't happen. If you go too late, I'll be dead.' She couldn't meet his eyes. 'Christ, I'm sorry, I'm such an ass sometimes.'

He pulled her closer. 'Don't torment yourself, I've been travelling through time for ten years and I still don't understand it.'

'You must know when I'm going to die? Is that something you can look up?'

'I don't *know* and I don't *want* to.' It was a sensitive subject and the words came out more sharply than he'd meant. 'I certainly wouldn't tell you anything that would have such a resounding impact, it would almost definitely alter your future in some way.'

'It's already altered. Was I meant to meet you? Maybe I should have carried on down that country lane, ignored your car and not stopped to help. Just suppose a man had been walking his dog in that narrow lane, I may have been destined to crash and kill him. Instead, he's going to father a child, who grows up to be a mass murderer. The possibilities are endless.' Robyn's mood changed again and she realised she mustn't pursue this, it wasn't Shay's fault.

'You're overthinking things. It's difficult. I *would* say live for every minute but that sounds patronising coming from me. We're getting out of here love, right now. Put something warm on.'

'Where are we going?' She pulled a thick jumper over her t-shirt, but it seemed out of place on a warm summer night.

The next thing she knew they were in the portal and then on the side of a road. A house loomed in the darkness nearby. 'Is your anchor in there?' she asked.

He nodded, pulling her gently in the other direction. 'We've got a short walk now; I have a torch but be careful.' Eventually, after following the well-worn trail they came to the bank of a river that looked out over a beautiful, almost magical waterfall.

It was night and the area was bathed in the glow of the full moon. Robyn looked around in delight. 'How wonderful, are we definitely alone?'

'This is the Fairy Glen Falls, we're in 1916 and I can guarantee, no one will intrude.'

'One hundred years ago. Just think, we can come again in real-time, err, my current time, I mean,' she clarified. 'We'll know that we were right here, in this very spot, how cool is that?'

They lay together on the bank watching the stars, not caring that the grass was damp. Shay did his best to keep them both warm and it was only when they got up to leave that he saw Robyn start to shiver. 'If you can put up with the cold for a little while longer there's something else I want you to see. I *was* saving it.' He nodded as if affirming something to himself. 'This seems like the right time.'

'The right time? I'm intrigued.'

'We'll have a short walk at the other end, I don't have an anchor. It's imperative that you *don't* draw attention to yourself.'

She was vaguely aware of passing through two different portals and ending up behind a church which looked achingly familiar as they walked around it. 'We're heading for Church Street, I'm home! When is this? I could have been our anchor.'

'No, you can only be that from the moment of the connection, until the moment of death. Not before.' *Christ, is it even possible to be an anchor for yourself?* 'Come on, all will be revealed. Whatever we see, you *have* to keep quiet or I'll take us back immediately.'

Robyn could see there was no teasing or messing around, this was clearly something serious. She nodded her head and noted that he kept a tight hold on her hand.

Hidden in the bushes, Shay gave her a nudge and another warning to remain silent. She made a small squeak when she spotted Simone walking alone. The night was dark and a sliver of new moon in a cloudy sky couldn't help her. 'There's a car coming, you're showing me the bastard that hit her.'

Shay frowned and tapped his finger on her lips.

Robyn nodded. *Pull your hood down Sim, can't you hear it? Pay attention, it's right behind you.* She was willing her friend to change what was going to happen next. At that moment, a fox ran out, so close that Robyn felt it brush her leg. The car swerved, there was a sickening thud and it braked sharply.

A young woman got out and moaned softly when she saw the fox's body. The window wound down on the driver's side and she walked around. 'You were right Dad, it was a hard knock. There's nothing we can do, poor old thing. I hope she didn't have cubs.' The woman grabbed a carrier bag from the backseat and proceeded to drag the fox by the tail until it was under a bush, near to where Robyn and Shay stood.

She got back in the car, said something to the driver and they moved off, having no idea they'd hit a girl when they'd swerved, who'd been walking home alone, and was now lying unconscious on the other side of the road.

'I've got to help her. *Please*, Shay.'

'How can you? At this exact time, you're at home with your mother. Just watch Robyn. I know this is hard, but I'm showing you for a reason.'

She looked at him, with a mixture of confusion and anger. 'This is too weird.'

'Should we go then?' he asked softly.

'No, I'm sorry.' She leant against him, gaining strength from his supporting arms. It wasn't long before a middle-aged couple came along. They were walking a dog, which, stopping to sniff everything possible, thought all its birthdays had come at once when it discovered Simone's unconscious body. Robyn watched the scene play out like an episode of *Casualty*.

'Phone an ambulance.'

'Make sure she's in the recovery position.'

'There's so much blood.'

'I heard somewhere if the neck's broken, they shouldn't be moved.'

'Check her *airway*, the *airway* for fuck sake!'

All eyes turned to the bushes.

'Robyn, *shut up*,' Shay snapped. 'You know the rest, it's time we left.'

Flashing blue lights and a siren could already be seen and heard, everything had happened quickly. She reluctantly followed him to the path and found herself once again in the portal.

'Did I do the right thing?' Shay asked anxiously.

'It was *so* difficult to watch, but knowing it really was accidental makes all the difference. Okay, they should have paid a bit more attention, looked around more, but they really thought it was just a fox. I guess even when they heard it on the news, it didn't click either. Thank you, so much. It's been haunting me for months.'

He nodded. Occasionally, when she'd fallen asleep, he'd heard her muttering and stray tears had escaped onto the pillow. 'Now you know and it's where it belongs, in the past.'

'I love you so much.' She felt him flinch. *I shouldn't have said that.*

'Oh Robyn, I love you too... I think.'

I'll take that. If anyone else had answered her declaration of love in such a manner, she'd have been most insulted. But because Shay had no understanding of his present emotions her earlier fears and misgivings were well and truly buried, for now.

Chapter Nine

*'Can you really see Shay entertaining
ladies of the night?'*

'You're not going to be satisfied until we all have our travelling rights revoked,' Adam grumbled. 'I turned a blind eye the first time, don't expect me to keep doing it.'

'I don't expect anything from you. Just mind your own business and if I'm caught, I'll tell them you were completely unaware.'

Adam scowled. They often sailed a little close to the wind, especially during leisure visits, but this was different. Shay had taken Robyn to the past and not just once. If his friend thought he'd covered his tracks, he was sadly mistaken. 'I can see you like these new feelings; is it her or the emotions that you don't want to lose?'

Shay silently pleaded with Adam to let the conversation drop but it wasn't going to happen. 'They sort of go together,' he sighed. 'I had no idea what it could be like. If you must know it scares the hell out of me. How do you cope with falling in love?'

Adam chuckled and got his temper back in check. He was concerned about his friend, but also found the whole 'Shay in love' thing rather amusing. 'I haven't actually been in love, just 'cos my emotions are heightened, it doesn't happen at the drop of a hat.'

'Oh, I thought...'

'Because we rave about the women we want or get churlish and melancholy when we can't have them? That's normal behaviour my friend, or at least I assume it is. I'm expecting love to be something completely different to passing fancies and attractions.'

'It leaves me breathless. Robyn's shown me how things should be. I can't describe it, I just wish the situation could be different.' He thought of all the things about her that made him happy. Her Harry Potter pyjamas, her sometimes maniacal driving, her lovely smile, and those blue, blue eyes. They had to be the best of all.

'You've got it bad, snap out of it and try to put things into perspective. Right here, right now, she's been dead for two thousand, four hundred and something years.' He tried to steer away from the subject for a while. 'Tarro's been fixed, poor bugger, let's go visit and see if he's ready to come back to work.'

The two men walked across the paved concourse, where various slabs triggered small visual images. These were usually in the form of short messages called holonotes, whose meanings were personal to whoever happened to be walking there.

'Shayden Lomax — Dental check due in ten days.'
'Shayden Lomax — Deliver latest samples to lab 89.'
'Adam Beaumont — Health-Screen overdue.'

'No way,' Adam groaned. 'It can't have come around *that* quickly.'

'What's that?' asked Shay, as they couldn't see each other's messages. The holonotes stimulated something in the brain so that only the person they were directed at could read them.

'My health check's overdue, it wasn't that long ago I had one.' He started counting back the months in his head.

'Damn it, that means mine will be scheduled soon, they're usually one after the other,' said Shay, knowing that he'd have to be very careful not to draw attention to his new emotional state.

Adam started waving madly at someone, which provided a much-appreciated distraction for both of them. 'It's Mara, I'd recognise that black-haired beauty anywhere. It's quite unnerving how the two of you look so much alike and yet I fancy the pants off her.'

'Well, thank Christ my sister's not into men, at least she's safe from *you*!'

Mara waved back and hurried over. Her dark eyes shone and she gave both of them a brief hug, allowing Shay a small peck on the cheek. He immediately noticed the difference in the greetings of his reserved sister and the exuberant Robyn. How had he ever thought a show of affection could appear brash?

'One minute,' Mara put her hand up as she received her own holonote. She smiled with pleasure and a look of relief flitted across her pretty face. 'I was waiting for that,' she said. 'My foetus has reached fifteen weeks; I need to have it removed. Thank goodness. I can't wait to watch his progress in the lab. I think I'll go straight there and see if they can do the procedure this morning.'

What on earth would Robyn make of that? Definitely one conversation, I don't want to have. 'Are you and Rebecca excited?'

'Excited? That's a strange way of putting it, Shay. I'd expect a comment like that from our impulsive and over-enthusiastic friend here.' Inclining her head towards Adam, who narrowed his eyes slightly. His delight at seeing her was quickly melting away. 'We're certainly looking forward to the time we can bring our son home.'

'I shall look in on him when you tell me it's okay. Have you kept Mother up to date? Speaking of which, how are our parents?'

'*Really* Shayden, isn't it time you went to see for yourself. All your travelling and you can't be bothered to take a short trip to the South Sector.'

'I hate London, what possessed them to move there of all places?'

'You know very well; our beloved sister has produced three grandchildren, all in good health still and Mother can't get enough of them.' She silently prayed they would all get through puberty. The eldest was eleven and none of the family could ever completely relax.

The United Kingdom had been split into four Sectors. Wales and Scotland had remained roughly the same. There was a boundary line running from Bristol, to the East coast which divided the South from the Midlands. Each Sector was run independently with its own capital and counsel. For the most part, it seemed to work well. Shay tended to think that London still saw itself as some kind of supreme authority, which it wasn't. In his opinion, the people there were too full of their own self-importance. If he never had to visit the city again, it would be too soon.

'**Shayden Lomax — Deliver latest samples to lab 89.**'

'Yeah, yeah,' he muttered, 'I heard you the first time, can't even take a bloody walk these days.' He said a quick goodbye to Mara, arranged to meet Adam at Tarro's home and hurried towards the lab, unaware of the strange looks his sister was giving him.

'**Shayden Lomax — You have travelled for over 400 hours, please identify yourself at the nearest air booth and check your oxygen levels and blood purity.**'

Gritting his teeth, he veered off to one of the blue-topped booths dotted around the area. Pressing his palm to the screen and following the instructions, he left thirty seconds later knowing that his heart, amongst other things, was working just fine. He'd usually feel a smug satisfaction leaving one of the many booths that measured and reported everything from bone density to the flow of blood in his coronary arteries. Today, it just added to his irritation. He had to avoid a health check at all costs because once his emotional patterns were evaluated, there'd be no hiding the truth.

Adam brought his freshly adjusted friend up to date with recent activities. It was disconcerting to admit that Tarro was in the unusual position of being the most stable of the three of them. If he'd been looking for an extra voice to add pressure against Shay's risky behaviour, he was in for a disappointment.

'Look Adam, I feel great. I can laugh, cry, have some great sex, or not as the case may be, and feel elated or really hacked off. You're due a check soon, so you'll probably get a few tweaks and all being well, neither of us will go into meltdown again for at least a year. That poor sod Shay is finally getting a chance to experience what we take for granted. It's not fair that they can strip it all away.'

'I've given this talk to myself, believe me, Tarro. I mean, Robyn's as cute as hell, but it's not real. He's having an affair with an echo from the past, and that's all she can ever be.'

'He can pick a good day and relive it as often as he needs,' Tarro shrugged. 'I don't really see the problem.'

'That's what you or I would do, but not *him*. The latest, wait for this... he's not only agreed to *never* do that, but Robyn's also told him that she wants to see him in real-time.'

'Real-time? What the hell's that?'

'So, for instance, if he's here, like *now* for three days, then three days will have to pass in her time as well.'

'Shit, why did she suggest that?' Tarro looked completely baffled. 'It's surely better for Robyn if a week or more goes by for him and for her, it's still the same afternoon.'

'Yeah well, there's no telling them. On top of that, he won't use her for an anchor unless he's actually going to *see* her. He's got a couple of others in the area now at least.'

'Is he still in control?'

Adam nodded. 'Yeah, that's the only reason I haven't taken it further. It's this travelling together nonsense that's pissing me off, we can't let them do it again.'

Tarro grinned. 'We've got his back still, he's covered for us enough times. This... romance, it'll come to a natural end.'

Adam looked sceptical. 'And if it doesn't?'

'We'll make sure it does, maybe this real-time shit will work in our favour. By the time he's been kept away for several long periods, she'll get fed up and meet some twenty-first-century guy. Shay will eventually get fixed and that'll be that. He'll look back on it all as an interesting experience.'

'Okay,' Adam conceded. 'We'll do it your way, but I'm not playing the good cop bad cop routine again, 'cos I'm always the bad guy. When we call a halt on it, we work together.'

Tarro chuckled, 'You're thinking of our brothel, where you have to pretend to be a Bow Street runner.'

Adam snorted with laughter. 'I'll never get tired of seeing so many bare arses running out of one building. That's exactly what I mean, you're *always* the good guy. Why don't we swap sometimes?' He frowned slightly. 'The benevolent Earl of Cyberhill, who directs half a dozen of the pretty ones into his *conveniently* waiting carriage. So much for not changing the past. They're probably still looking for the randy sod who entertained them on the longest ride around London, in more ways than one! God, it's fun though, and long overdue.'

They both had a few scenarios they liked to use for relaxation. The ideas suggested by the council members were along the lines of theme parks, theatres, lake fishing or watching old battles, which the Harvesters got quite enough of anyway, or extreme sports in different centuries.

His own idea of leisure pursuits was totally different and always involved a willing female or a good fight. Fortunately, Tarro, his partner in crime, enjoyed similar predilections. In this particular favourite 'recreational visit', Tarro would stand in front of the carriage, holding his top hat and silver-headed cane, and the same rough street urchin would always approach, asking: 'Does his lordship require anything.'

'A place where a gentleman might meet a few nice ladies,' Tarro replied.

'That's easy guv, Minuit's up the lane,' he pointed. 'The black and white building with the sign 'Gentleman's Club'.' He guffawed and wiped his nose with the back of his hand. 'If you've got any particular leanings to the exotic, if you catch my drift, that's the place yer after.' Forgetting himself, he nudged Tarro's arm and then apologised profusely, wiping off some imaginary dirt.

Tarro had nearly sent him away with a flea in his ear, protesting that he didn't indulge in kinky sport of any kind, but on each subsequent visit, the banter seemed to notch up a risqué peg or two. After sharing a few fantasies, the boy had laughed even harder.

'The girls will be right up yer street guv and they're clean. Don't you be going near the docks; the whorehouses down there are full of disease. You only have to walk in and yer cock will drop off.'

At this point, they'd learnt that the nudging of the arm was not accidental. When Tarro delved into his pocket to flip the boy a coin, he discovered his purse had gone. The boy did a runner and Adam stepped out from behind the concealing curtain of the carriage, shaking his head in despair. All of their money gone in the first ten minutes.

Now when they visited, the only thing they changed was the lightness of the purse, which only held two coins. According to Tarro, this was all part of the game. 'Let him have it,' he'd grinned. 'It's early Victorian London after all.'

Money for each era was easily replicated and given out quite freely. It might have to be justified if a large amount was used, and that was a conversation, in this case, better avoided.

Realising that Tarro, was still talking Adam was brought back to the present.

'Let Shay have this,' Tarro said. 'Maybe before he's fixed we'll sweeten the medicine and take him with us for a revisit to Madame Minuit's Maison for gentlemen. I'll even be the runner this time. You seem to do quite well with the ones that are left behind and want to persuade the '*ever* so strong and handsome policeman', to let them go.'

'Can you really see Shay entertaining ladies of the night?' Adam shrugged and gave a laugh. 'Hell, why not. I never thought he'd do what he's doing with Robyn. We may need a bigger carriage if we're talking orgies.'

Tarro roared with laughter. 'That really is one step too far for our emotionally suppressed friend.'

And that was how Shay found the two of them, wearing the daftest expressions, and Tarro continually sending him knowing winks. Just what had Adam had told him?

They had a three-day trip to sometime in 1983, Adam apparently had the details. Tarro announced that he couldn't wait to get there and was ready for a plate of greasy fried food and would happily throw up all night if necessary.

Shay saw the funny side, appreciating the camaraderie of having his two friends around. His thoughts turned to Robyn, as they seemed to do easily these days. This would be the first time she'd go nearly five days without seeing him since she'd requested to move forward in real-time. Having already promised not to relive the same experiences, he'd once again agreed with her wishes.

But what if he couldn't get back for any reason, if he was grounded or sent to work abroad? The portals didn't work across water. Robyn would waste her time waiting for him, clinging on to something that Adam insisted could never be. There was little point voicing these concerns. He was learning that once Robyn had made her mind up about something, she didn't change it.

He was used to the times between visits, staying away when he had to and then, returning close to the point they'd last parted. Strangely, the anticipation, which should have been hers alone, was having quite an effect and he was desperate to see her. Even the thought of beans at the family BBQ was almost appealing.

* * *

Robyn picked her way carefully across the slippery, seaweed covered rocks. The tide had been going out for over an hour, and to her delight, there were new rock pools containing secret and colourful treasures ripe for discovery. The beach was growing quieter, with families leaving after their day out to be replaced by a smaller early evening crowd of locals who liked to come after work.

She missed Shay, why had she decided that real-time visiting would be better? During their last day out together, he'd casually mentioned over lunch that he was going to be busy for the next three or four days and would come to her room that evening, and she wouldn't even know the difference. For a moment, she'd looked forward to seeing him again a few hours later. But as it sank in, Robyn realised she didn't want to be visited like any other person, place or thing that lived in his history books, not since their declaration of love. It must also be tiring for him to fit her in amongst his full days of research, specimen collecting or whatever it was he actually did.

Picking up her towel and flip-flops, she walked back across the sand to the steep cliff path. A few lads waved, inviting her to stay and join them. She was beginning to get friendly with some of them from her constant walks to the harbour with Simone and late afternoon visits here. Two were brothers who owned a niche gift shop near the harbour, selling the most wonderful sculptures and pieces of furniture made from reclaimed wood. She shook her head and couldn't help a small glow of pleasure when one of them looked genuinely disappointed. It was only a momentary ego boost though, what she really craved was her black-haired, dark-eyed man, who was only, what? A few thousand years away.

One more day, the BBQ tomorrow and then he'd be staying. They'd have to be quiet or travel somewhere else, as Richard would be in the next room. *Rich, oh shit*. She was meant to be meeting him at the airport in less than an hour and it was a forty-minute drive. With a loud groan, she ran up the path puffing and panting, before sprinting across the field to the house.

'Robyn, you look... err, pretty shocking, actually.' Richard laughed, hugging her in the airport foyer.

'Nice to see you too,' she answered sarcastically, returning the hug. 'An hour ago, I was drying off on the beach.'

'Sounds great. How's Sim doing?'

'Good, mostly. You know what she's like, puts a brave face on everything. I've definitely noticed a big improvement in the time I've been here. She's really looking forward to seeing *you*.' A warm smile spread across Richard's face. 'Right, let's see if I can remember where the car is parked.'

'You can tell me all about this mystery man of yours during the drive back.' Richard relaxed in the passenger seat, amused to see all his maps and charts bundled into the side pocket. 'How old is he?'

'He's twenty-four, what's that got to do with anything?'

'And what did you say he did?'

'I didn't, Rich, what *is* this? You're not my brother yet, so no need to play protector, okay.'

'About the brother thing.'

Robyn swerved into the side of the road, slamming on the brakes. Richard jerked forward before the seatbelt jammed him back. '*Sorry*. What's she done now? Don't tell me it's all over. Bloody hell, I knew she'd go off on a bender or something.'

'No, not at all, just the opposite. Things are moving on *really* quickly, they've talked about getting married. I didn't mean to give you the wrong idea Josie's doing well. They're good for each other Robz. I think the wedding might be sooner rather than later, now the divorce is settled. I've got a letter here for you.'

'Oh, well okay, that's good then I guess. Why doesn't she just email?'

'Thought it was a bit impersonal I think; she did try to phone you *several* times,' Richard said rather pointedly.

Robyn looked uncomfortable. Shay didn't use a phone and because of this, her own spent much of the time on silent. She'd noticed the missed calls, but just hadn't got around to doing anything about them. 'I'll phone her later after I've read the letter. As for my man, you'll meet him tomorrow at one of Clive's famous BBQ's. He's threatened to do a hog roast. I think it's because Shay's vegetarian.'

He was curious to meet Robyn's new boyfriend. Simone seemed pretty impressed and her instincts were usually right. Richard had liked her for ages and had planned to ask her out just before the accident. Afterwards, it had been impossible. Clive announced they were moving and unsurprisingly, she became detached from everyone other than her family and Robyn.

When she'd first contacted him via messenger, asking if he'd keep an eye on her best friend, he was thrilled. It was just the opening he needed. Living opposite the Harleys was suddenly the best thing ever. He constantly tried to engineer conversations or any small convenient meetings that he could use as an excuse to report back via Skype to Simone. After a few weeks, he hadn't needed a particular reason to talk. She always seemed pleased to hear from him, even if there was an ulterior motive.

Her attempts to speak clearly and hold her phone when they were FaceTiming made him want to charge up to Scotland and tell her how proud of her he was. So, it had come as a bit of a disappointment when he first realised her motives. 'Come up and stay,' she'd suggested. 'I'm sure Robyn likes you, perhaps you can persuade her to return home and finish her course.'

Everything had happened really fast after Robyn had announced she was going to Stonehaven. His father had told him what he already suspected, that he was seeing Josie Harley and things were getting serious. And finally, he'd known he had to take Simone up on her offer of a visit and make it clear that she was the person he was interested in.

Fortune had smiled on him when Robyn found some mystery man and Simone seemed to think her friend was better off staying put. The fact that he was no longer meant to be enticing Robyn home, and Simone still wanted to see him, was good news indeed. Recently, something in Simone's manner had changed, the way she spoke, the way she looked at him. Those big hazel brown eyes gazing through his laptop screen gave him hope that the next fortnight was going to be a new beginning for the both of them. All he needed to decide, was whether or not to confide in Robyn? He glanced over and saw she was looking at him oddly.

'You were bloody miles away. I've just told you nearly everyone who's coming, did you hear any of it?'

'Coming where?'

'The BBQ, you moron. Me and Shay are taking Joey camping next week, so you and Sim will have some time on your own,' she looked at him slyly. 'She likes you Rich.'

He let out a long breath. 'Are you sure, she was trying to get the two of us together you know.' He heard a loud snort and had to laugh. 'Yeah, it was never going to happen. I am looking forward to having you as a sister though.'

'This is a really big step for Sim. I'm sure she thinks we all see her as a cripple. The thing is she's now actually starting to weight bear. If she has a fall or something small goes wrong, she blows it all out of proportion. It's not sympathy she needs anymore Rich, she gets that in bucketloads from Babs. It's a bloody good kick up the backside.' She stopped talking whilst waiting for a gap in the traffic.

Richard screwed his eyes shut as the car screeched around the bend. He was about to comment but Robyn, completely unaware that she'd scared her passenger half to death, carried on. 'She's so nearly there, but rather than chance defeat, she won't always try. I've watched her for hours and heard her physios, Maggie and Peter, tell her what to do. I'm kind of hoping you'll be the carrot.'

'The *carrot,* a very flattering analogy. Thanks, Robyn.'

'Richard Saunders, the metaphoric carrot,' she laughed when he scowled. 'You can do it, Rich. In this case, you'll be better than me. I think I've helped motivate her with little comments like, when Rich gets here, we can do this... or wait till Rich sees you walking with a frame, he'll be really impressed. Stuff like that. Look, you can tell me to mind my own business if you want, not that I will, but you haven't come all the way up here to see *me*.' She threw him a grin. 'If there's anything I can do to help the course of true love, let me know, okay.'

'I appreciate the offer, I just think this whole thing is delicate. I need to make Simone realise I'm serious. It's not going to be easy if our past conversations are anything to go by, she's very prickly about her condition.'

'The biggest thing to overcome is making her believe she's worthy, I guess we'd all feel the same if we had to rely on help.'

Richard spent the remainder of the journey staring out of the window and commenting on the scenery. He had a lot to think about it was hard to imagine how things would play out until he was face to face with Simone, alone.

Chapter Ten

'Get down and dirty, you might enjoy it.'

All things considered, it was, sort of, going well. Robyn grimaced slightly as she watched Richard hoist Simone into his arms, not quite so effortlessly as Shay had done a few days earlier, she couldn't help noticing.

They had arrived home from the airport a few minutes before, and Babs had signalled to bring Richard through the back of the house. Looking flustered, she waylaid them and shuffled her new guest into the conservatory. Whispering to Robyn, she explained that Simone had had a fall, she was fine, but embarrassed and it didn't help she was still on the floor.

Subterfuge was pointless, as Joey announced that his sister, was this minute, sprawled across the hall carpet. It was done in the same casual manner that he'd inform them she was just having a cup of tea. Hearing the frustrated argument further inside the house, they followed the racket and quickly summed up the situation.

Allowing no protests, Richard carried Simone to the living room and deposited her into the nearest comfortable armchair. Clive, who was a little red in the face from his own attempts at lifting his struggling daughter, disappeared to get some cold beers from the fridge.

'Well then,' said Babs, beaming at everyone. 'Now we're back to normal again, I'll leave you three to catch up while I prepare supper.' She took the drinks from Clive, offered them around, and then ushered Joey to the kitchen, with the pretext of needing help.

Simone looked at Richard a little shyly. It wasn't like her, but the fall had knocked her confidence. Robyn was about to fill the silence when she saw Richard take Simone's hands and give them a squeeze.

'I can't believe how well you look in the flesh. Robz says you're walking quite a bit now.'

'Err, well, yeah, sort of. You just saw the end result of that,' she cringed.

'Don't let little things like that bother you. It's amazing, I had no idea. Christ Sim, you'll be walking in no time.'

Simone looked pleased with the praise. Even if she did know he was just trying to make her feel better, it was working. 'I'm really happy to see you Rich; you do know Robyn's a lost cause, don't you? She's staying here for the foreseeable.'

'So, I understand,' he grinned. 'Any luck job hunting?'

Robyn grimaced slightly. 'Not really, although the shop manager has sent my references at last, so that's something.' She was well aware that she hadn't put in as much effort as she should. Her time with Shay had become precious and was something she was jealously guarding. The thought of any outside influences, like job hunting, encroaching on it were becoming hard to juggle.

'She's sent her CV to loads of places,' Simone said, quickly jumping to her friend's defence.

Babs came in carrying a large tray with cutlery and drinks. 'Casserole, if that's alright with you, Richard? I thought you may be needing a hot meal.'

'Casserole in the front room?' Simone asked dubiously.

'They don't want you falling on your ass again,' Joey sniggered, carrying a plate of bread and butter and avoiding a slap across the head from Clive, who carefully juggled with a large steaming crockpot, before gingerly putting it down on the coffee table. 'Did you *want* to go camping next week?' he asked his son, sternly.

'Don't tease him, Dad, I'm fine. It was just a stumble, a bit of lumpy carpet or something.' Simone sighed as her mother rushed to the hall, obviously to inspect every inch of the floor. 'Mum,' she groaned, 'come back and eat with us.'

Robyn tried not to find the whole thing funny, but it wasn't long before both girls started to giggle. Joey and Richard grinned, and when they heard the sound of heavy stamping by the front door, even Clive began to chuckle.

'Dad, go and get her. I don't really think it was the carpet.'

Babs came back, tutting and muttering, took one look at everyone's face and broke into a huge smile. 'I knew things would be even better with you here as well.' She looked at Richard fondly. 'Simone never stops talking about you.'

'Thanks for *that*, mother,' she looked down at her bowl, pretending to fidget with the thick handled spoon. Hopefully, if everyone concentrated on their own food, she'd be okay. After a comment like that *and* being watched eating, she may as well give up now. A gentle hand on her arm, just for a moment, and a soft voice telling her to enjoy her meal made her take a deep breath and feel a rush of pleasure. Could it really be remotely possible that Richard liked her? First thing tomorrow, she was going to step up her physio. After all, Maggie and Peter had been pressing her to be more confident. Robyn had certainly helped with her motivation, but now she had a very important reason to try and when Simone Harmon set her mind on something, she never failed.

* * *

Robyn had spent all morning helping to prepare food, just leaving enough time to get ready. She wanted to make an effort and show Shay what he'd missed. He knew everything was starting around mid-afternoon and decided it would be best if he arrived by car, as appearing out of nowhere could lead to awkward questions. She wondered what Adam and Tarro would have to say about bringing the Merc to Stonehaven. Would they be pissed off if they needed it further north, or had their work finished there now? She also wondered what comments Clive would make. Simone's dad was great but he did have a habit of judging everyone by their annual salary. Once he clocked a brand-new Mercedes S-Class parked in his drive, the questions about Shay's job would start again.

Chewing her lip nervously, she sat in front of the dressing table mirror and applied the finishing touches to her makeup. The straighteners were cooling on the side and her blonde hair looked longer without the usual thick waves. Robyn examined herself critically and shunning the customary jeans and shorts, she took out her new purchase, a short, sleeveless, royal blue cocktail dress. Her eyes sparkled and reflected the sapphires earrings. *Too much blue?* she wondered. *What the hell. Shay likes blue, it's his favourite colour.*

Friends and work colleagues of Clive, starting to gather in the large field. Joey his friend Sam, plus a few other children, took over the three barns, happy to be away from their parent's watchful eyes. Clive had taken all the ladders away, not chancing any accidents. The last thing he wanted was his boss' eight-year-old climbing into the hayloft and falling through the first storey loading doors. A bit paranoid at times, he only had to take a look at his beautiful daughter to bring it home that some things were out of his control. Granted he wasn't responsible for the half dozen children that were here this afternoon, but he still couldn't totally relax.

The constant feeling of helplessness over Simone had many other negative effects on him, looking for weaknesses in others was just one of them. He'd never been like that before and whilst he was aware of this, he didn't know how to overcome it. Watching Richard Saunders bring a certain type of smile to Simone's face – the first one from her he'd seen for a long time – tore him in two. Jealousy warred with genuine pleasure at her obvious happiness. He gave out a loud sigh. Hopefully, it was just a 'dad' thing and not a sign that he was turning into some kind of evil tyrant.

He also felt bad about his needling comments towards Robyn's boyfriend. He was important to her, and Clive had very nearly let himself forget that crucial fact.

Here she was now, as pretty as a picture. His heart surged with a paternal feeling for his daughter's best friend. She was almost as dear to him as his own children.

The hog roast gave off tempting smells and he felt a small measure of satisfaction as he watched his boss inspect it, and give him a thumbs-up after breaking off a small piece of crackling.

'Anything you want me to do, Clive?' Robyn asked, handing him a cold drink.

'No thanks, dear girl. You just have a lovely day. Don't get any hot fat on your dress,' he warned, as she neared the spitting sizzling meat.

'God, no.' She backed away from the hot metal grills crammed with sausages and burgers. 'I bought this last week in Aberdeen, in the sales, I could never have afforded it otherwise.'

'You are *okay* for money, aren't you Robyn? You would tell me?'

She put her hand on his arm and smiled. 'Thanks, I'm still okay for a while, Mum transferred some more of my money from Dad. I wish you'd start taking some rent now.'

'I know you want to pay your way, but we wouldn't dream of it, not until you're working. I'll give you some money towards the camping next week.' He saw she was about to protest. 'I'm adamant and also very grateful, please don't refuse. Look a car's coming,' he gestured towards the narrow road that ran next to the field. 'Shay perhaps?'

'Hmm, not in a red car, I'll make sure they know where to park.' She walked around to the front of the house and watched as the Mini Cooper convertible pulled in next to her Audi.

Shay leapt out and grinned at her surprised expression, then held his arms open. She ran over and let him swing her off her feet as she planted a huge kiss on his eager lips.

'I thought something a little more understated might be wise.'

'I wouldn't say it's understated, exactly, but it certainly won't open a debate about your finances. Not that they're anyone's business, of course. I love it.' She walked around and had a quick look inside. 'It won't be big enough for our trip next week, which is a shame.'

'Big enough for me to take you out tomorrow, though,' he gave her another kiss and kept holding her hand as they took the long way around the house.

'Really, you have the whole day free tomorrow as well?'

'Today, tonight and tomorrow,' he smiled. 'And I happen to know that next Thursday and Friday are going to be nice, so maybe we can camp overnight then. There're a few good places, not too far from here, plenty of water, woods and hill walks.' He stopped when she looked a little unsure. 'That's what you want isn't it, camping, a hike through the great outdoors?'

'Y-yes, I guess.' She'd imagined sitting comfortably reading a magazine outside the tent, or maybe swimming in one of the lochs. Marching up and down hills hadn't really come into it. She was about to ask how he knew the weather would be good and realised that he'd probably already done a recce. 'Quite handy having my own futuristic weatherman,' she said, squeezing his hand. 'Come on, I want you to meet my soon-to-be stepbrother.' On the way past the kitchen door she stopped and sifted through a large box of fresh vegetables that had been delivered earlier in the day. 'The stuff from the organic farm shop,' she explained. 'Babs has a twice weekly order. It's good cooking what's in season, instead of just opening the freezer and grabbing the first packet of peas.'

'That's filthy, Robyn.' He watched mesmerised as she gave a large carrot a quick rinse under the outside tap and bit into it. 'I do mean in the brown muddy sense,' he added quickly, realising what he'd just said could have two meanings.

She tried not to laugh at his obvious discomfort. 'Don't you ever eat earth?' she teased.

'Are you *serious*, do you have any idea what's in it?'

'No idea at all, and I don't care. My granddad grew all his fruit and veg. He'd dunk something off quickly in the rain butt, then we'd eat it, just like that. Lighten up and stop looking so appalled, this is why you're all so bloody precious in the forty-fifth century.'

'So, let me get this right, you're suggesting I tell my people to eat mud?'

'Why not,' she winked. 'Get down and dirty, you might enjoy it.' Throwing the remainder of the carrot on the compost heap, Robyn told Shay he wasn't the only one who could offer advice with a second, more suggestive meaning.

Simone waved madly to get their attention. Before the poor man could have apoplexy, she dragged him forward.

'Shay, meet Rich. I told you my mum's shagging his dad, didn't I?'

Richard raised his eyes. 'Always a nice turn of phrase, Robz.' He gave Shay a friendly grin and held his hand out. 'Actually, they've set a date for the wedding, which Robyn well knows, now she's finally bothered to phone her mum.'

Robyn pulled a face, she had taken her mother's letter to her room after supper yesterday evening. Reading it, she immediately began to feel guilty. After what seemed like years of constantly having to worry about her mother, Robyn wasn't sure how she felt about it being the other way around. It appeared that Josie Harley had well and truly turned her life about. The months of anxiety, watching her generous cheerful mother turn into a sad pathetic mess, finally started to fall away.

The letter was full of heartfelt recriminations. Robyn was genuinely relieved for both their sakes, pleased that her mother had eventually found the strength to do something about it, but sad and a little angry that she – her own daughter – hadn't been enough to make this happen earlier. The date of the wedding was set for Boxing Day. Obviously, the thinking was she'd be home for Christmas.

Richard could assume that she'd already made the call all he liked. She'd do it when she was ready. Scowling slightly, she was aware of Shay's hand stroking her back. She'd become tense and he could obviously tell. 'Let's go and grab some beers and make ourselves comfy here. If we start wandering around, you'll get bombarded with questions.'

Overhearing, Simone grinned at them. 'Rich has already had to suffer the Spanish Inquisition from Dad's boss. People think their position gives them a right to be nosy. Robyn's right, tuck yourself away with us Shay, we can take it in turns later to run the gauntlet for food.'

They spent a pleasant afternoon eating, drinking and laughing. As the four of them became increasingly louder, they got their wish to be ignored. Richard took to Shay's easy manner and although he would have liked to find out a little more about him, he remembered Simone's earlier warning not to ask too many questions. He wasn't quite sure why, but a few beers later, it didn't seem to matter much anymore.

Babs approached them, and after noticing how much they were drinking, she invited Shay to stay the night. A blow-up bed on the floor in Robyn's room was the exact offer. At least that way she could ignore whatever went on with a clear conscience. If Clive had any misgivings he didn't voice them.

Shay sent Robyn a secret smile. They both knew that he'd end up there tonight, anyway. At least now there'd be no pretence of driving away first. 'I may regret this,' he said, studying the bottle of ale in his hand.

'You've had a couple cans of larger, they seemed to go down okay. You do have alcohol in your time, right?' Robyn whispered.

'Yes, we do, but that doesn't mean this stronger ale will agree with me, the fermentation process is a little different, I believe, I'm not going to chance it.' He swapped it for a fruit juice. The last thing he wanted was their first full night together to be ruined because he was in the bathroom with his head down the toilet. 'I wanted to take you somewhere later, but the thought of having all that time alone together in your room is too tempting. Do you mind if we put it off?'

'No, of course not, where were you thinking... just out of interest?'

'Well, sometime not *too* far back, so we wouldn't have needed special clothes.' He chuckled as she was trying so hard not to care. 'You listen to a lot of music, don't you?'

'Yes, you know I do, especially when I'm driving.' She gave his arm a hard nudge. '*Tell* me.'

'1976, London.' He shuddered slightly when he said it. 'The King's Road to be exact. I thought you might like to witness the rise of Punk Rock.'

'Oh, my God,' she squealed, lowering her voice when Richard and Simone both looked in their direction. 'That was such an iconic time, I can't believe you've even heard of it.'

'Actually, Tarro has a huge interest in ancient music, especially around this time. He was telling me it influenced songwriting for the next hundred years.'

'You've just broken a rule, bad man.'

He looked puzzled, her eyes were dancing with mischief. 'Ah, damn it, I told you about the future, didn't I? Oh well, considering you know a lot more about my time, I suppose I'm just going to have to trust you not to report me.'

'*Report* you, as if and who to? No doubt you'd get your brains sucked out for such a terrible infraction of the rules.'

He didn't tell her she wasn't far off the mark. They became distracted by Clive bringing in a large tray of bits and pieces that were cooked to perfection. A plate of succulent pork, Chicken drumsticks, some burgers in bread rolls and dishes of savoury rice and avocado salad were laid on the table next to where Simone was sitting.

'This one is a veggie burger,' Clive grinned, as he put what looked to Shay like a small brown disc of carpet tile to one side. 'Enjoy.'

'Am I imagining things or has that guy improved since our last meeting,' he whispered very quietly into Robyn's ear, not wanting to offend Simone.

'He's a sweetheart really,' she whispered back. 'I think Babs may have had a go at him after the picnic.' She leant forward and added a dollop of corn and onion relish to Shay's designated burger, then heaped a few spoons of salad on the side. Her own plate consisted of two fat slices of pork, a piece of chicken and a large piece of crackling.

He watched for a moment, wondering how people never broke their teeth on the hard-cooked pigskin. Still, she seemed to enjoy it. The grease shone against her lips and he had the strongest urge to lick it off. Instead, he concentrated on his own meal, and taking a bite, was pleasantly surprised.

'Good?' Robyn asked. Looking at the remains of her chicken drumstick and wondering if it had been cooked through properly.

'Very. I can detect tofu, nuts, mushrooms and wheat I think, maybe flax as well.'

Richard stopped his conversation with Simone to stare at Shay.

'You sound like some sort of food analyst,' Robyn giggled. 'Stop being all forty-fifth century.'

'Sorry,' he mumbled between mouthfuls.

Simone caught Robyn's eye and winked. They were going to have to come up with a feasible explanation for Shay's sometimes bizarre comments. Either that or she'd have to try and give Richard plenty of other things to think about and distract him over the next fortnight.

By mid-evening, most families with children had drifted away. Only Sam and his mother remained and that was because Joey was having his friend stay over. Once his boss had left, Clive totally relaxed and joined his family, who were huddled together on blankets around a small fire. Robyn and Simone were toasting marshmallows for everyone. At the first sign of looking like she needed propping up, Richard was at Simone's side, offering his body as support.

Robyn crawled onto Shay's lap, not caring one bit about the teasing comments. Noticing that he'd gone a bit quiet, she asked him, 'Are you okay?'

'I was just reminded of actions and repercussion a moment ago.'

'Why, what happened?'

'Joe nearly burnt his hand, it could have been quite bad.' He pointed to a large charred lump of wood on the ground. 'It rolled out of the fire and... well, I pulled his arm away.'

'What's wrong with *that*? Of course, you would.'

'Yes, but *I* did it. In theory, *I* shouldn't be here,' he said, struggling to explain. 'Just suppose he'd had to undergo a few weeks of burns treatment. It could have put him on the path to becoming a plastic surgeon or some such thing, now that may not be the case.'

'Bloody hell, that's *exactly* the point I was making, about driving down the lane and killing the potential father of a murdering deviant. You told me to stop over thinking things, you hypocrite.' She laughed at his stricken expression. 'I'm joking, but I thought you said history couldn't be changed, it had already happened.'

'It's what people chose to believe when they first travelled to the past, perhaps we've come to that conclusion to placate our own consciences.'

'You've changed *my* life completely, I shouldn't worry about every minor decision you make. I hope you'd save me if a runaway tractor was bearing down on us?'

'I certainly would,' he grinned. 'But you could argue you wouldn't be in its path, had I not been with you at that particular time, so it cancels out your imminent death.'

'I give up,' she said, forcing a very hot sticky marshmallow in his mouth. 'Chew on that and count your lucky stars you have such an understanding, old-fashioned girlfriend, who incidentally *would* like that trip to London after all.' She watched his face fall. 'Not tonight, though, we'll go early in the morning before the others are awake. No need to worry about real-time if we're together, is there? We can leave and be back before breakfast.'

'That'll work,' he perked up. 'I have a few old English pound notes, so we can buy a drink at least. The best time to arrive would be a summer evening, it was an extremely hot summer that year, so at least you'll see all the weird outfits, without coats and things covering them.'

Robyn remained silent. Shay wouldn't understand that the weather had little to do with what people wore if they went out clubbing. She and Simone had both frozen many times, wearing revealing tops or short skirts, rather than bother with a coat or jacket. You just hoped in the early hours of the morning, a taxi wouldn't take too long. Living in a small village, usually meant a trip to Exeter or Plymouth, which involved crashing with a friend overnight. Clive and Babs had been frantic at times if Simone didn't text. Her own mother had probably been totally unaware. Angry with herself for letting her thoughts drift back there, she speared another marshmallow and cuddled tighter into Shay's lap. She could feel his breath and small kisses at the back of her neck. The sooner the evening drew to a close the better.

* * *

As the sun shone through the curtains, Robyn could feel her stomach cramping. She moved her legs from the tangle they'd gotten into with Shay's and padded quietly into the bathroom. The bed creaked and she could hear Shay getting ready. The airbed was a mess; they had decided to christen it, so at least he wouldn't have to lie if Babs asked him if it was comfortable. He could just say, 'It had done the job nicely, thank you', and Robyn would ensure she didn't catch his eye when he said it.

'Ready?' he asked, catching hold of her hand tightly. He couldn't risk them coming adrift in the portal, that would be one disaster he never wanted to face. Just the thought of it made him feel sick. Without the means or knowledge to enter or leave the vortex, Robyn's body would be torn apart. 'Hold on tight,' he reminded her.

'Don't let me go, Shay,' she smiled happily, having no idea what would happen if he did.

'Never,' he smiled back.

'London, in one of the hottest summers ever recorded, reached temperatures well into the mid-thirties,' Shay reeled off, sounding like a travel guide. 'At least it's evening. Still too warm for me, though.'

'I'm glad I just slipped the same dress back on, we won't exactly mix with the locals though.' Robyn eyed a couple walking past, both with a shock of green spiked hair. The man was wearing a blue tartan suit held together with heavy buckles, and his girlfriend a pink tutu with a black vest, sporting a Sex Pistols logo. 'Wow, I feel slightly underdressed.'

'It's safer that way, you'd stand out far more if we made a token effort. Better we just embrace being the tourists we are, who've come to gawp at the punks. They don't seem to mind.'

'If you say so.' Robyn caught a hostile glare from a bleached blonde guy, wearing a studded collar around his neck. 'I think we should at least walk up and down a bit, or we'll draw attention just standing here. Is your anchor in sight?'

Shay inclined his head to a small newsagent with a flat above. 'Keep hold of my hand, if there are any problems, we'll disappear and hope whoever sees us is high on drugs.'

'They didn't *all* take drugs you know, no more than any other group of young people. Look, most of them here are teenagers, they just earned such a bad press 'cos people felt intimidated.'

'I wonder why,' he frowned, getting his shoulder knocked by the next three spiky haired individuals that barged past. 'Maybe this wasn't one of my best ideas.'

'It was... it is. Look over there. The Great Gear Trading Company, let's go in.'

Shay earned a few more disgruntled looks, mainly because he insisted on walking in tandem through the tightly packed aisles. They battled their way around a few more shops until he'd had enough and hailed a black cab asking the driver to take them to the Ritz. Robyn couldn't say she was disappointed.

'That was amazing,' she said, sipping a second cocktail that had all but depleted their stash of one pound notes. 'How's your sparkling water?'

'Irritatingly fizzy and hugely expensive. Still, it's worth it to bring you here. You look stunning by the way. I love you in blue,' he added. 'Are you feeling better now?'

'Better? I'm perfectly fine, thanks.' *Damn it he must have heard me in the night.* 'Thank you for this, it's quite something. Completely different from seeing the documentary stuff on the telly.'

He didn't mention that she was looking pale, hopefully, it was just tiredness. Whatever it was she'd deny it anyway. He'd planned the day so they would be doing a lot of driving, maybe she'd catch up on some sleep that way. 'Think of somewhere you want to go next, we'll try and do a proper overnight visit, so choose carefully.'

'Ooh, how far back can we go? I'd like to see the building of the pyramids or Stonehenge.'

'We can't travel across water, I explained that before, and although it is possible to go a long way back, it would flag up on the system. Most of my activity, although recorded, is never examined. Something like that would definitely be questioned.'

'Oh, okay. Somewhere we can spend the night in a comfortable coaching inn then, an earlier time period than the Tudors.'

'The further back we go, the transport and inns aren't going to be so grand, remember. How about a fayre and jousting tournament, followed by a stay in a local tavern?'

'Ooh, medieval times, I could wear a pointy hat.'

'And a chastity belt, with a great big lock.'

'I'll treat that comment with the contempt it deserves! You better bring me some nice clothes.'

'They didn't go for much in the underwear department,' his eyes flashed teasingly.

'Nor for the men either, authenticity is everything,' she wagged her finger at him. 'Can you get the currency for that time?'

'Those sorts of details are no problem. Don't worry, we just can't splash it around too much, we have to blend in, like always.'

'I know. Will this be after our camping trip next week?'

He nodded. 'If we're keeping to this real-time thing, then yes, it will take me a little while to get it organised. And now, as wonderful as it is, sitting in the Ritz and knowing the sun is setting, we should be getting back for breakfast. We have the whole day to enjoy.'

Chapter Eleven

'Are we in Lapland?'

She didn't need the tingling she'd felt earlier to confirm her friend had been away. If Robyn was looking a bit pale, the fact that her eyes were shining with excitement was a dead giveaway and Simone was pleasantly aware that she didn't feel the burn of envy that she'd experienced the last time. Perhaps it was due to the fact that Richard was busy spreading jam on her croissant.

'Where are you off to, or rather, where have you already been?' she asked as Robyn wheeled her into the conservatory after breakfast was finished.

'You don't mind Sim, do you? I couldn't really come in at five-thirty this morning to ask if it was okay.'

'Don't be daft, it'll always be okay. Tell me quickly, before the others come in.'

After relaying her visit to London, Robyn produced a folded scrap of cloth from under her top. 'This is for you, stash it quickly.' She handed Simone a black t-shirt, one shoulder was ripped and the other had a zip attached at an odd angle. The price ticket was ripped off.

'Wow retro, what did you pay for this?'

'Um, I didn't,' she replied, looking guilty. 'Hide it quick.'

'You *nicked* it! That's not like you.' She tutted and shook her head in mock disgust. 'I'll lean forward, stuff it down behind my back.' She shuffled forward a bit until it fell far enough down to be properly concealed. 'Christ Robz, you feel a bit clammy, are you okay?'

'I was up three times last night, I think it was the last piece of chicken I took. I thought it looked a bit pink but I'd eaten it by then.' Quickly adding some blusher to her pale face, she wondered if her stomach would settle now. 'Thank God for the posh toilets in the Ritz,' she grinned. 'How do I look?'

'Not great my luvver, if you spend half the night shagging, the other half sat on the loo *and* fit in a trip to London what can you expect?' She used her good hand to blend the blusher into Robyn's cheekbones. 'That's better, are you going to be okay? I really think...'

Shay took that moment to enter the room and didn't miss the look Robyn gave to Simone, which implied: *'Drop it'*. 'You've told Simone about our trip?' he asked.

Robyn nodded, fluffing up Simone's cushion. She felt extremely guilty, first for pinching the t-shirt from one of the shops in Carnaby Street, something she'd never ever contemplated doing before, and secondly for bringing it back through the portal when Shay had told her emphatically he needed to know about anything they moved from one time period to another. She wasn't sure why, but she shouldn't really ignore something that may have a consequence. How on earth he hadn't noticed her small shoulder bag bulging at the seams she'd never know. It was a heat of the moment thing, a gift that Simone would appreciate. 'Are we off?' She turned and gave him a bright smile.

'Yes, it's a long drive, we should get going.'

'A magical mystery tour, lucky girl.' Simone grinned, the smile lighting up her eyes as Richard joined them. 'Laters.'

'Laters,' Robyn replied. 'I'll just nip to the bathroom first, meet you by the car, Shay.' She ignored her friend's look of concern.

The cool breeze was glorious and Robyn seriously considered trading the Audi for something small with a folding roof. 'Where exactly are you taking me?' she asked after they'd been travelling for a while.

'Drum Castle for our first stop, we're nearly there now,' he grinned. 'It's got a thirteenth-century square tower I thought you might be interested in seeing.'

'Oh, yes I am. Where else, why the thick coats on the back seat in the middle of summer?'

Ignoring the question, he carried on. 'We'll either find a nice lunch stop or drive on and eat in Inverness.'

'Wonderful, but it's still *summer*, even in Inverness,' she stated quizzically.

'That's for a surprise before we go back this evening, you'll find out later.'

'It's a long way for you to drive, all the way back to Stonehaven.'

'We won't be driving. Tarro's in Inverness, I'll leave the car with him. We can use Simone to get you home.'

Robyn gave a sigh of pleasure before starting to wonder how Tarro would act today. Adam, she'd become used to, but Tarro scared her a little and she gave a small shiver. Shay, assuming she was chilly, immediately put the roof of the car up. She didn't have the heart to ask him to put it back down.

'What beautiful roses.' The perfume had hit them before the large blooms had even come into view. 'These gardens are beautiful; I don't know much about this castle. I suppose I need to read up on local history a bit more.'

'Robert the Bruce gifted the forest and tower to Sir William de Irwyn,' Shay told her. 'He married the King's granddaughter, I believe.'

'That must have been the early 1300s,' Robyn pondered. 'I'm up to date on most the Scots Kings and Queens because I've been applying for jobs in the museums. You never know what they're going to ask. If I ever get an *interview* that is.'

Shay took her hand, wishing he dared pick a rose to give her. Maybe there would be something suitable in the gift department.

They spent three hours exploring every corner, as they had done at Scone, and before leaving, Robyn made a beeline for the shop. Shay browsed, not seeing anything he wanted. It would be so easy to whisk himself away to find some wonderful English country garden full of roses. He could be back before she even knew it, but having promised her real-time visits only, she may not appreciate his vanishing act. The rose would frustratingly have to wait.

'A few bags of sweets and a scarf for Babs.' Robyn showed him the muted bronze and brown flowered material.

'Looks nice,' he answered non-committedly, arching a brow when Robyn rolled her eyes. 'On to Inverness, all being well about two and a half hours. If you want to stop, just say. Or perhaps close your eyes and have a nap?'

'Why do you say that? I'd rather stay awake and keep you company.'

'Because, my love, I think you're looking a little unwell, should we turn back?'

'Don't you dare, I'm fine,' she insisted. They travelled on listening to the radio, chatting and admiring the passing countryside. When Robyn did fall asleep, Shay did everything he could to make sure their continuing journey was as smooth and quiet as possible.

Inverness, like all the larger towns, was busier than usual during the holiday season. Shay parked a fair way out, grabbed Robyn and the bag of clothes from the back seat, and arrived in the small bedroom of a city hotel, using Tarro as an anchor.

'He must know we're coming. Is he nearby?'

'Probably in the bar right below.' Shay smiled and threw the coats and other bits onto the bed. 'If you want to freshen up I'll wait.'

'Err, no you go on, I'll find you.'

'Are you okay, Robyn, you still look very tired, do you want to lie down for an hour.'

She saw him look dubiously at the coats. 'I'm fine, really, it was just a piece of dodgy chicken yesterday, we're not cutting our day short. Whatever surprise you have in store for later on, I *want* it.'

He laughed at her stricken look. 'Okay, promise me that you'll catch up on sleep tonight then.'

'I will, honest, lights out at 9 pm. Go and find your friend, I'll be right behind you.'

Shay left her in peace, but rather than go downstairs, he waited in the hall. He was aware she was a little wary of Tarro and preferred to arrive holding hands as if presenting a united front.

When they reached the bar and she saw the friendly, smiling face, she could hardly believe it was the same person.

'At last,' he said with a loud laugh and threw the broadsheet newspaper down in a heap of creases and folds. 'Bloody great thing,' he grumbled. 'Hello Robyn, looking lovely.' Her expression of astonishment caused him to laugh again. 'What's up? You usually have plenty to say, or so I've been told.'

'What's *that* supposed to mean?' she couldn't help but smile, his whole cheery demeanour was quite infectious. 'You've been fixed,' she whispered quietly, looking around to make sure no one could hear.

'That obvious, eh?' he winked. 'Don't tell anyone.'

Shay shook his head in despair. 'Will you be here later, as we arranged?'

'Would I let you down, my friend? Hurry back after the lights... err, the other trip.' He looked guiltily at Robyn, worried that he'd spoiled the surprise. She didn't look like she'd noticed. Lowering his voice, he turned and made sure that only Shay could hear him. 'When you've finished for the day we need to join Adam. There's a lucrative incident, sixty years from now, it's just been discovered by the researchers. He'll need our help.' He checked to make sure that Robyn still wasn't listening. 'It's really big, there's a second team there as well. Now you're doing this 'real-time' shit with 'Blondie', you'll be missed and you can't afford to come under the spotlight.'

'I know, I'll make this afternoon a bit shorter. It may be for the best, I don't think Robyn's very well and I want to take her to Strathy Point, even if it's just for a quick look.'

'Yeah, she'll enjoy it, is your anchor in place there?'

'For the time we're going, yeah, I've checked him out. I check everything before I take her anywhere. I don't know what I'd do if something happened.'

'Bloody hell man, pull yourself together.' Tarro gave Robyn a stunning smile. 'Sorry sweetheart, he's all yours. Take him shopping, or whatever it is you're going to do in Inverness.'

'My God is that what fixing someone does?' she asked the minute they were out of earshot.

'For the likes of Adam and Tarro, yes, they need it. You saw what he was like before.'

'Well, yeah I know, but...' she stopped, not wanting to admit that fiddling with his brain had actually improved him. 'Anyway, what's on the itinerary for us?'

'Lunch for a start, something light to settle your stomach.' His anxious look was enough to keep her from arguing.

They walked into one of the main shopping areas, food chains loomed in every direction. Shay, obviously having somewhere particular in mind, ignored them all and took them to a side street.

'We're still going to do whatever it was later, aren't we?' *It has to be travelling, with those winter clothes.*

'If you're okay after lunch, we will. Ah, here we are.' He opened the door and gestured for Robyn to go in first. From the outside, it looked like a small tearoom, which actually gave a completely inaccurate impression. Inside it was way more and wonderful cooking aromas wafted out from the kitchen. 'I don't want to tell you what to do, it's your choice, but I suggest soup.'

'Okay,' she normally wouldn't have capitulated so easily. The meaty smells were out of this world, but she was still a bit queasy and nothing was going to put their next visit on hold.

He was right, damn him, she brooded while spooning the last of the delicious butternut squash soup into her mouth. And they'd both managed to order the same thing and eat it together, which was kind of nice.

'Next time you don't feel well, tell me, all that driving wasn't a good idea.'

'Don't be mad. I was so looking forward to a proper day out on our own.'

'I'm not mad, Robyn, I just don't like to think of you suffering.'

'We had such a fabulous night and then London, I didn't want our time together to end. One day you'll only have these memories of me.' *Noooo, stupid bitch why did I say that?*

'Don't think that way.' He was saddened to see her upset and not sure how to deal with it.

She gave a small sigh, aware that he struggled with any emotional topics of conversation. 'I'm just being sentimental. I don't mean to say these things.'

'We'll work something out.' An air of doom had taken hold and he fought hard, trying not to let it show. 'Let's go, there's a lot to do and we only have a few hours. Unfortunately, I'm depending on Tarro to be here at a certain time so I can get back.'

'Righto,' she kept her voice light and grabbed his hand, cursing herself for nearly spoiling things.

'We'll head for the old town, there's a 19th-century cathedral, an 18th-century church, umm, and a Victorian market selling all the usual sort of stuff, food, clothes and craft stuff. We won't have time for the museum or art gallery today. Maybe another time,' he suggested, sounding more cheerful.

'I'd definitely like to do the market. After Drum, I don't feel the need to see the cathedral. Well, maybe a walk around the outside would be good.' She tried not to giggle. Shay sounded like a travel guide again. It was the no-nonsense way he spoke. His friends weren't like it, so it wasn't necessarily a 'futuristic' thing.

The indoor market was busy and the unique range of shops kept Robyn occupied for the next hour and a half. Shay was happy to follow behind. When he'd seen the real thing before, in its real time, this replica didn't hold a lot of interest, he was just pleased she was enjoying it. Something did catch his eye in a small jewellery shop, however, a tiny silver rose on a chain. He bought it immediately, and on the way back to the hotel, stopped in the shelter of an arched doorway.

'I've had roses on my mind since the gardens this morning.' He said, patiently waiting while she examined it. Robyn kissed him and held her hair out of the way so that he could fix the clasp. It reached just to the base of her throat. 'Beautiful,' he smiled.

'You're so generous, I want to spoil you too.'

'How about you be the camp cook when we take Joe on Thursday, just no partly cooked chicken, okay?'

'I'll have a look at the vegetarian cookbook and see what I can adapt to cooking over a campfire. I know we don't have to be completely 'back to nature self-sufficient' but I think Joey would enjoy it. I may have to do a few fish fingers for him, just in case.'

Fish fingers? He didn't ask.

There was no sign of Tarro when they walked back to the hotel. Robyn was feeling much better, the soup really had settled her stomach, and the emotional wobble, well and truly forgotten. Shay had a duplicate key to the room and they began to put the warm clothing on immediately. The coat, hat and gloves were fine, the thermal socks which he insisted she wore, posed more of a problem.

'This could be the deal breaker,' she grumbled, having difficulty refastening the strappy sandals over the thick wool.

'I thought I'd covered everything, I forgot about your summer footwear.' He picked up two scarves and put one around his own neck and the other around her eyes, like a blindfold. 'Trust me,' he said softly, chuckling at her outrage.

'What the hell? This better not be some kind of snow bondage. I have no wish to freeze my ass off thank you.'

'Robyn *really*, do you think I would do that to you?'

'Stop *laughing*, it's creepy when I can't see your face.'

'We're going to the wheatfield portal, and then to a place, not that far from here. I found one of the optimum times, thirty-two years ago to be precise. It's quite sparsely populated and the anchor I'm using died shortly after. Remember to...'

'Hold tight at all times,' she chanted in a sing-song voice. It was disconcerting not being able to see, but his arms were locked around her and she felt totally safe. 'We're in the portal, I can feel it,' she said, paying attention to the shifting swirls of air. 'Now it's different, I'm guessing we're moving towards your anchor. Strange, when one of the main senses is taken away how the others kick in. People always say that.'

'Okay, we're here. Don't take the scarf off for a minute. I just want to get away from the buildings and find the best possible place. He led her carefully over the stony uneven ground. When she stumbled for the second time, he picked her up and carried her. 'I've brought a blanket, let me just put it over this rock and we can sit down and watch the show.'

'The show?' For a split second as Shay removed the scarf, she was terrified. The night sky was lit up with swathes of dancing green light. Totally unaware he was wrapping the scarf around her neck, her lips curved up in a delighted smile. 'The Northern Lights,' she said in wonder, giving a gasp, as pinks purples and whites broke through the green that was fanning out right over their heads. 'This is spectacular.'

They watched together for over an hour. Sometimes the lights would dip away and peek above the horizon, like some kind of enchanted purple sunset. Other times they appeared so close that Robyn stretched her hand out thinking she might touch them. 'Are we in Lapland?'

'No, I keep telling you the portals can't cross water. Actually, John o' Groats isn't too far to the east, we're right up on the North coast. It's not unusual to see the Polar Lights from here, but this one night, in particular, is pretty spectacular.'

She nodded and turned to kiss him. 'Do you know what I'd really like to do?'

He shook his head, just as enraptured by the phenomenon as she was, even though he'd seen them many times before. Watching her pull the blanket to the ground and gesturing towards it, he smiled. 'There's nothing I'd like more, but you've been shivering for the last thirty minutes.'

She dismissed his concerns by kissing him again and moved her hand downwards until she felt the telltale bulge in his trousers. 'The cold doesn't seem to be affecting you too much. Come on *please*, under the Northern lights, can you imagine?'

He could and didn't need any more coaxing.

Afterwards, they wrapped themselves in the blanket and huddled together watching the ever-changing lights for a little while longer, neither of them feeling the cold now. All too soon Shay begrudgingly took her hand and said they must go. Bringing this magical time to an end was the last thing he wanted to do but, regrettably, Tarro would be waiting.

Later that evening, she tried to describe the best thing that had ever happened in her life to Simone. She left out the most amazing part, making love on a blanket under a million stars, with the Aurora Borealis casting heavenly patterns all around them, preferring for once to keep it to herself. Shay had told her they could do it again, any time they wanted. It was a nice thought, but somehow, she knew it could never beat what they'd shared there today.

* * *

Robyn and Richard had spent most of the morning swimming and sunbathing. Seeing Simone's transport return, they raced each other up the cliff path to meet her.

'Hi, guys,' she grinned. 'Not having too much fun without me I hope.'

Maggie got back in the car and told her to tell her friends what she'd achieved that morning. Both Richard and Robyn were amused to see her blush a little.

'Tell us then,' Richard said, grabbing the handles of her wheelchair and pushing her up the drive.

'I walked a few steps unaided, I mean, like *completely,* no frame, no stick, nothing. Maggie's told me to try and use the frame or crutches in the house from now on. The chair's only for when I'm out of doors.'

'Wow Sim, well done.' Richard stopped pushing to give her a hug.

Robyn noticed how her friend was basking in Richard's approval. He'd already said he was staying a few days longer and would come back at the end of October during reading week. Simone's improvement was bound to continue with a goal like that to aim for.

Everything was good, why then did she keep thinking back to the comment she'd made in the tearoom yesterday? Perhaps because she knew this wonderful thing she had with Shay couldn't last forever and felt a tinge of envy that Simone and Richard might well have the relationship she couldn't.

She mustn't think that way, No one deserved happiness as much as Simone. As for herself, she'd enjoy her time with Shay as long as possible.

'There's post on the kitchen table,' Babs said, while handing them all mugs of tea.

Robyn went to have a look and tentatively picked up one of the letters, another job rejection no doubt. But it was just the opposite, in fact. She had an interview for the position of Education Officer's Assistant. Waving the letter in her hand, she ran whooping to join the others, back in the conservatory.

'So, what exactly will you be doing?' Richard asked while trying to peer over her shoulder.

'Umm, it says developing educational resources for families and schools, things like guided tours, helping with activities and workshops, putting together teaching packs. Also, developing reading material for general visitors, guidebooks and audio tours.' Her face fell, 'I won't get this, who am I kidding. I don't stand a chance in hell.'

'Don't you *dare* say anything so bloody stupid.' Simone cried angrily. 'Unless they have someone earmarked, and there's not a damn thing you can do if that's the case, you'll walk it. That job has got your bloody name written all over it.'

Babs had come rushing in to see what all the noise was about, and Robyn mutely handed her the letter. 'Oh, Robyn dear, this is just the thing. Go into Aberdeen tomorrow and have a look at the place, tell them in person you'll be coming for the interview.'

'Rich will go with you,' Simone said, brooking no argument from either of them. She turned to smile beguilingly at him. 'You said you wanted to see the city.'

'Yes, I did say that, didn't I?' He'd really wanted to stay and watch Simone's therapy, but realised this was far more important to her. 'Okay then Robz, looks like it's you and me tomorrow morning again.'

'Lovely,' she muttered. *And now, I have to make that phone call to Mum.* Excusing herself, she went out in the garden as far from the house as possible.

Josie answered almost immediately and burst into tears on hearing Robyn's voice. The conversation was a bit strained, to begin with, but the bridges had started to be built before Robyn set off on her road trip to Stonehaven, so hopefully, things could only get better now.

Both mother and daughter were smiling twenty minutes later when the call ended. Josie had been hoping that Robyn would have mentioned her new boyfriend. The news had filtered down some weeks back, via Simone to Richard, then to his father, who had relayed it to her. When it wasn't forthcoming first hand, she felt disappointed to think they couldn't share that sort of conversation. Small steps, Steven had advised her, don't smother. Steven always gave good advice, as he'd done with her drinking. Filled with new feelings of self-worth, she hadn't had a drink for over a month. Robyn had sounded happy and that was all that mattered, so whoever this boy was, she was grateful to him.

Chapter Twelve

*'Think yourself lucky they're not a pair of
budgie smugglers.'*

Why on earth had they decided to travel in the rush hour? The train had been full and because they hadn't booked, they had to stand the whole way.

From the station, Robyn had taken them to where she thought the museum was, but now studied the building in front of her with uncertainty.

'Are you *sure* this is the right place?' Richard asked doubtfully. 'They don't even open till half ten. 'Let's get a coffee somewhere and you can tell me all the secrets about Shay.'

Robyn glared at his back, as he led the way. How dare he act in such a high-handed manner, this brother stuff was going to his head. 'It's strictly on a need to know basis,' she muttered, following him along the crowded pavement until they came to a cafe. 'And *you* certainly don't need to know.'

'Over there,' he ushered her to a seat in a quiet corner. 'Latte?'

She nodded and began to think furiously of plausible reasons and answers while he was in the queue. Damn Richard, he'd just completely and utterly spoil her morning.

'I don't think it's unreasonable,' he started, staring into Robyn's mutinous face. Changing tactics slightly, he began again. 'Look Robz, when Sim asked me to keep an eye on her '*besty*', I knew exactly what her game was. At first, I thought, yeah okay. I didn't exactly fancy you, but that was only 'cos we didn't really have anything in common.' He was teasing her and stopped when he saw her lips twitch.

'Nothing in common is a *polite* way of putting it, I suppose,' she grinned. 'You were like the boffin geek across the road.'

'And you were the strange little goth kid, who got a tattoo at fourteen.' He watched as her eyes narrowed. 'My mum obviously heard from your mum. It was quite the talk of the cul-de-sac.'

'Bloody hell.'

'Anyway, you grew up and improved somewhat, so, when Sim asked, I...'

'Thought you'd spy and try and get into my pants at the same time?'

'No, of *course* not. Christ, I can't even think of you in that way now, and anyway it was always for Simone.'

She choked on a mouthful of coffee, trying not to laugh at his incensed expression. 'I'm joking, Rich. Look it's fine, even if you weren't my potential brother, I wouldn't have been interested.'

'Thanks, I think. May I ask why not?'

'For every reason in the world. You're too safe for a start. I bet you have the future all mapped out. Simone's the same, do you know she had a ten and twenty-year plan for fuck's sake? That's not me. I have no idea what I'm doing tomorrow, let alone in a year's time.' *A year's time... will Shay still be here?*

Richard nodded. 'The more I spoke to Simone, the more I liked her. You know the rest, and yes, I have got a ten-year plan *actually*.' He laughed. 'Which could change if necessary.'

'Are you that serious Rich? I can see how you two look at each other, it hasn't been that long though, not really.'

'Says you, who's only known this guy for what, two months' tops? What do you really know about him, where does he work? Where does all his money come from? Simone mentioned a Mercedes. He rolled up in a different car on Saturday.'

Robyn sighed, she'd unintentionally brought the conversation full circle. 'The Merc belongs to a friend, I never said it was his. I don't appreciate the Spanish Inquisition, he's nice, what's the problem?'

'Why the *secrecy*? Every time I tried to make conversation on Saturday, Sim kept shushing me and telling me not to ask questions.'

'He does historical research for a small agency that sells the information to museums, authors, um, playwrights, anyone that has to have correct facts for… err, whatever,' she finished a bit lamely. Shay had suggested she stick to this story if Richard or Simone's parents pressed her. He'd made it sound much more impressive when she'd been playing with the few dark hairs on his chest. It really would have helped if she'd paid proper attention. 'Don't ask me the name of the firm, or his annual salary. I have no idea and it's none of your business.' Richard sat back and for the first time that morning looked more at ease. *He's bought it*, she thought, relieved.

'Okay, that's obviously all I'm getting. It's a start at least.' He checked his watch. 'They should be opening now; I'll wait for you here.' Grabbing a newspaper from the rack, he went to order a second coffee. 'Good luck Robz, make an impression, preferably a *good* one.'

The front of the building was tall and narrow, giving a deceptive expectation of what awaited inside. The old-fashioned dark mahogany pay desk was charming, but not so the clerk, who did nothing to hide his irritation at being bothered by someone, first thing in the morning.

'The lights are nae on yet,' he grumbled, doing his best to ignore her. 'Ye ken?'

'Sorry, I thought you were open.' Robyn wasn't impressed so far, and when she heard him tut, nearly turned and walked out. It was only because she so desperately needed a job that she bit back a sarcastic comment. 'Is Mr Fraser available, would you know?' she asked in an exaggerated honeyed tone. He'd had the decency to turn and face her, so at least she wasn't speaking to the back of his head. She waved her letter briefly under his nose.

'Fraser, ye say?' he peered over half-moon glasses.

'Yes, I did say that. Is he, um, available at all?'

Tutting loudly, he picked up the phone, punched in three numbers, mumbled something into the receiver and slammed it back down. 'Upstairs foremaist on the left, canny the lights...'

'Aren't on yet,' she finished, and let a small smile escape at his slightly perturbed look.

Almost every step she stood on creaked loudly. Did schools really come here on visits? Twenty or more youngsters running up and down this ancient staircase would give her a headache in no time.

The first door on the left opened on the landing above and a middle-aged, rather dapper gentleman smiled warmly. 'Please, Miss err...Hadley, is it? Come this way.'

Robyn waited for him to offer a chair, which was quite a feat in itself, as every surface was covered with memorabilia or stacks of paper. 'Mr Fraser, I'm Robyn Harley. I received an invite to come for an interview, and as I was in town I thought perhaps I could introduce myself.' His look was blank, it was obvious he didn't have the slightest clue who she was. Once again, she produced the letter and slid it across the desk.

'Aah, I understand,' he muttered as he read the first line. 'I'm Frazer with a 'Z' you see, Miss...? Sorry, I didn't catch the name.' He spoke with a soft Scottish burr, which in any other situation would have had Robyn feeling at ease immediately.

'Harley, Robyn *Harley*.' This wasn't right, she was in some kind of time warp. If it had been possible, she'd have thought Shay was playing a trick. He wouldn't do that though, not her straight-laced lovely man. Adam or Tarro on the other hand...

Mr Frazer with a 'Z' looked up. 'You're in completely the wrong place lass, we are part of the same foundation, but in the remotest sense. This is purely storage and archiving.' He carried on reading her letter. 'We certainly don't open to members of the public.'

'Oh, right. You have a pay desk downstairs, though?'

Mr Frazer smiled. 'Just for show, it's old and came with the building. This used to be a theatre in the late nineteenth century. We do let historians, representatives from various magazines, researchers and such like in, by appointment. If Clem doesn't scare them away first,' he chuckled.

'Clem, as in the receptionist?'

'That's a rather posh word for him, the resident caretaker would be more appropriate.'

'I'm sorry to have bothered you, I better Google the museum again. I obviously didn't take enough notice of the two different addresses under the letter heading.'

'Google? Are you competent with computers Miss Harley?'

'Well, I can do the basics, word, spreadsheets, that sort of thing.'

'I have no idea what you're talking about. I can just about answer an email,' he shook his head. 'We have the most expensive equipment gifted to us, but unfortunately, we really don't use it.'

Robyn looked over in the corner where he was indicating and saw the latest all singing all dancing Mac.

'Could you... do things on that?' he asked. 'We need everything catalogued. Apparently, the software's all set up.' He shrugged helplessly.

'Yes, I could, would they send me over here? If I got the job?'

'Let me make a phone call to Charles Fraser, that's Fraser with an 'S',' he smiled. 'He would have conducted your interview next week. I'm assuming you have references?' He saw her delve into her bag and produce a large brown envelope. 'If I can be honest with you, there are eight candidates for the other job, including yourself, four of which are their permanent staff. I know that because my niece applied, she didn't even get shortlisted. Would you be interested in working here instead?'

Robyn thought of the dismal foyer and Clem who was in need of a personality transplant; could she work with people like that? 'May I ask why your niece isn't working *here*?'

'The lassie's far too large and clumsy. I wouldn't have her anywhere near the objects we keep downstairs. Some of them date back hundreds of years.'

Robyn's interest was caught. 'How many staff do you employ?'

'Clem, who you've met, Mrs Rhodes, the cleaner and general tea maker, and the odd student who comes for a work placement. Actually, they never stay long, not when they discover the fast pace of our sister building. Oh, and the accountant, he comes in once a fortnight, sorts out the salaries and stuff. My son Jack, he's around your age, often pops in to help downstairs. Not on the payroll, you understand, just voluntary. I give him a little cash incentive from my own wallet. Can't get him anywhere near the office though.' He glanced again at the large computer sitting idly in the corner and sighed. 'Look, Miss Harley, have a think about it. By all means, go for the other interview if you want to. I can only offer you four days a week, thirty hours, that may not be enough?'

Eight candidates and four of them already employed. Robyn didn't have any experience, she'd only worked in a castle gift shop. Regardless of what Simone had said, she was pretty sure she was only making up numbers. Thirty hours was better than nothing, it would give her more time to spend with Sim and Shay. 'Yes,' Robyn said quickly before she could change her mind. 'I can't start for a fortnight though, would that be okay?' She thought of her medieval assignation with Shay; nothing was going to come between her and a jousting tournament. It would also give her time to ask Rich a bit more about Macs; she had used them occasionally, but wasn't as confident as she would be with Windows.

'That's ideal, I'll let Charles Fraser know,' he grinned.

'Are you sure it's okay to take me on like this, without advertising the job?' She didn't want to be out on her ear within a week due to some employment law technicality.

'We'll combine it with the job you applied for, don't worry Miss Harley.'

'Please, call me Robyn,' she offered quickly. 'I do have one more question. The salary, will it be the same?'

'Well, fewer hours, of course, but I can match the rate. To be honest Miss... Robyn, the other job, in the education section, if you were to get it, would be far more dynamic, *and* you'd receive the occasional tip. I can't match that. You have to really love the work to spend hours amongst all the boxes and crates here. At the moment, apart from Jack and Stella – that's Mrs Rhodes – I'm working mostly alone.'

'Could I have a quick look around before I go, Mr Frazer?'

He got up and led her out onto the landing. 'The other rooms here are filled with files, they all need to be scanned and put on um, discs? Is that the right word?'

Robyn grinned. 'Sort of, it may be more work than I can manage alone. I don't really want to be sat at a computer *every* day.' She looked with dismay at the floor to ceiling piles of brown A4 files.

'Perhaps with you here, Jack might be tempted to work upstairs sometimes,' he chuckled. 'We have a lift, which is rather noisy, but as it's only one flight, we only use it when necessary.'

At the bottom of the stairs, she was taken into what had previously looked like a dark cavern when she'd arrived earlier. Clem had put the lights on and she gave a gasp. 'Wow, it goes back forever. Like that scene from Indiana Jones, when they hide the crate away at the end of the film.' She heard laughter and turned around. Clem had joined them and actually looked *amused*. 'I wish I could start work right now, but I have commitments, Mr Frazer.'

'Call me Stuart, we all use first names here, except Mac, the accountant. He'll introduce himself as Mr MacDonald, and I doubt he'll invite you to call him anything other than that. You'll see when you meet him.'

Robyn saw his eyes twinkle and suspected that Mr MacDonald may be a bit of a character. Her hands were itching to start exploring the hidden depths of this vast room. If she was cataloguing everything, presumably she'd get to see it all in time.

'In answer to your earlier question, you wouldn't be at the computer all day. There's a lot of sorting needs doing here, that's the main job really. I'll be in touch, Robyn.' Stuart Frazer still had her letter in his hand. 'I have your details, let me check your references and sort the formalities.' He saw her face fall. 'Don't worry lass, you're perfect for this job. I shan't be letting you slip through our fingers. We'll see you here two weeks today, I'll confirm everything in writing.'

Bouncing back into the café, she grabbed Richard's arm. 'Come on, I want to get home and tell everyone my news. Guess what Rich, I've got a job, a weird, wonderful job. Awesome, or what?'

* * *

Robyn woke up smiling, life was perfect. Stuart Frazer had phoned her the next day to confirm the job was definitely hers. On Wednesday, Simone walked the length of the hall alone, with just a frame. And today would be best of all, as she was seeing Shay and going camping. Even the fact that this trip was all about Joey was absolutely fine.

Clive had looked out the two brand new fishing rods he'd bought when the family first moved to Stonehaven and handed them over after breakfast. 'Um, the price and wrapping are still on,' he said a bit sheepishly.

Joey frowned and spoke to Robyn, ignoring his father. 'That's 'cos he promised we'd go every weekend and we haven't even been once yet.'

'I'm sorry son, I'll make it up to you, now your sister's getting better.' His shoulders slumped as he said goodbye and left for work.

'Give him a chance Joey... Joe,' she corrected herself quickly. 'I know you feel a bit left out, but I'm sure he'll have more time soon.'

He let out a kind of harrumph wanting to believe it, but not building up his hopes. Babs kept out of it for once and made herself busy clearing the table.

Robyn had forgotten how much Babs had loved her part-time job, working as a teaching assistant in the local primary school. She'd given it up without a second thought or murmur, even before Clive mentioned moving to Scotland. All any of them wanted was for Simone to walk again and the family to get back to normal. At least now, thanks to Shay, her own anger had gone. It was just the unfairness of something so random affecting her dearest friend and indirectly, all the others members of the Harmon family, that still rankled.

'Okay then, we have the rods. Did you buy all the worms and stuff, and if so are they in a tight plastic box?' The thought of mealworms escaping onto the back seat of the Audi would be her worst nightmare.

Joey started to laugh. 'It's fly fishing, stupid, and before you ask, they're not alive.'

'I know *that*,' Robyn said a bit too quickly, she hadn't known at all, she knew absolutely nothing about fishing. The fact that the rods were brand new and looked like they needed assembling had already dissolved her wonderful euphoric mood. 'Um Joe, do you have any idea how these rods work?'

Rolling his eyes, he laughed even harder. 'They're only in two pieces Robz. Jeez, *what* a girl. I hope Shay likes fishing.'

'I don't think he's done it before. I'm sure you can show him, eh Joe?' *While I lie on a blanket and read my book.*

'Cool, and you can gut the fish and cook them for our supper.'

Robyn pretended she hadn't heard, with any luck they wouldn't catch any. The instant noodles, tin of tuna and small packet of fish fingers she'd packed would suffice. Or ratatouille, in Shay's case, the enthusiasm over the vegetarian recipe book, long forgotten.

'A loaf, biscuits and tea bread. I've wrapped the butter and bacon for the morning in foil and put a cold gel pack around it. Be careful with the eggs.' Babs handed her the picnic bag. 'Clive's put everything else in the boot of your car. Oh, and he's fitted the bike rack on as well, we only have the two bikes though.'

They heard a car pull up in the front and Simone smiled. 'I quite miss going all tingly when he arrives the normal way,' she whispered. 'Have fun, Robz. If you wear Joey out, I'm sure you'll get an hour alone tonight.'

'That's okay, hopefully, we'll be staying at an eleventh-century coaching inn of some kind next week.'

'Hmm, rather you than me, those bedbugs crawl in all sorts of moist dark places.'

'Erugh, *thanks*, Sim,' She pulled a face. 'He'll never let me take a clean sheet through the portal.'

'Don't look like that,' Simone started to feel bad. 'I was *joking*, Robz.'

'The awful thing is, you're probably right. I can't think about it now; I'll worry next week when the time comes.' She pictured the night ahead instead, Joey tucked into his sleeping bag with the tent fastened, and herself and Shay sitting by the dying remains of their campfire. Another night, albeit chaste this time, under the stars, with the memory of the last one still blissfully fresh.

Shay kissed her cheek. 'You were miles away.'

'I was wondering how clear the sky will be tonight, we can look at the stars.' She saw her own emotion reflected in his eyes. They were both thinking of the Northern Lights.

'Yeah,' Joey piped up, 'I'm going to stay up *really* late. Do you know all the star names, Shay? Maybe we'll see a satellite, or a meteorite, or a comet or something?'

Shay laughed. 'A UFO perhaps?' He waggled his eyebrows over Joey's head and gave a wolfish grin. 'A cosmic explosion would be very pleasurable.'

Simone giggled as Robyn gave a small gasp and began to busy herself taking the picnic bag to the car. Had she really thought of him as straight-laced only the other day? Shay had certainly come a long way from the man who tentatively admitted he'd wanted to see her again after their journey to Stonehaven.

* * *

A two-hour drive brought them to a large parking area. From there, it was a short walk to the shore of the most beautiful loch Robyn had ever seen, not that she'd actually seen one before, except on the television. The surrounding hills were mostly covered with thick pine and the thought of hiking had suddenly become appealing. She couldn't wait to walk through the hidden trails within the green forests.

'We can either camp here,' Shay pointed out some nearby sites, which quite a few families had already claimed. 'Or find somewhere more remote?'

Robyn knew what her choice would be, as far from civilisation as possible. But this was Joey's treat, he may like to have some other children close by. 'What do you reckon, Joe?' she asked.

He was helping Shay remove the bikes and instructing him on how they could load them up with their gear. 'We could go a *bit* further along the shore, don't you think, Robz?' he said excitedly. 'Shay's just suggested a place about half a mile away.'

'It'll still be popular,' Shay smiled. I happen to know that the water shelves nicely if you want to swim.'

'What about fishing?' That seemed to be uppermost in Joey's mind.

'Well, I don't know much about it, but we can't fish where people are splashing around. We'll have to walk along the bank and find a quieter spot I think.'

'Right then,' Robyn gave both of them a large backpack each and pulled her own into place, before throwing a few things over the handlebars of the larger bike. 'Give me your bike Joe, you won't be able to ride it with all this stuff. You lead the way, Shay can push your dad's.'

That was how they proceeded, Joey running on and coming back to report on everything ahead, while Robyn and Shay took in the beautiful scenery, feeling utter contentment and serenity in each other's company.

Shay listened to her news about the job offer, en route, pleased it was so obviously what she wanted, and needed. It had been tempting to look ahead a few months and find out what she and Simone were doing. Adhering to his promise of experiencing all the ups and downs together, he refrained.

The tranquil mood lasted as long as it took to bang in the first tent peg. Like the fishing rods, the tent was new and had not even been put together in the garden. Worse still, it appeared to be minus any instructions, or perhaps they'd been printed on the small sheet of paper that had blown out of Robyn's hand and fluttered away into the water. She swore, threw the mallet on the ground and raised her arms in the air in utter hopelessness. Shay finally led her to the water's edge with an order to sit and stay put. Or if she couldn't manage that, go and collect some wood for the fire.

She watched as he marched away, feeling convinced they wouldn't manage without her input. Joey looked a little alarmed, but it wasn't long before the two of them seemed to be winning, and their canvas home for the night was most definitely taking shape.

Armed with enough firewood to last till breakfast, she returned to the smug faces nodding towards the fully erected tent. They stowed all the non-valuables in the front, behind the zipped opening, and the car keys and mobiles further in, buried under the groundsheet.

'That's probably the most obvious place ever,' Shay said, taking a few long looks at Robyn as she changed into a bright yellow bikini, while he made a token effort of holding the tent flap closed. 'Wow, makes me wish I could go swimming with you.'

'Why can't you?' she demanded, 'I know you can swim, you've mentioned it before.'

'I didn't bring anything to wear.'

'Christ,' she muttered. 'Who comes to a bloody loch with no swimming shorts? It's a good thing I have a present for you then.' She fished out a pair of black trunks from amongst her clothes, pulling the price tag off before handing them over. 'I had a feeling you wouldn't be fully prepared, think yourself lucky they're not a pair of budgie smugglers.'

'Budgie smugglers?'

Joey, overhearing, put his hand up to Shay's ear. 'They're so tight they show your nob off,' he whispered.'

'Right, I get it, hence the budgie. In that case,' he said, quickly examining the trunks, 'Thank you, my love, much appreciated. You and Joe carry on, I'll be right behind.'

'So, I don't get to watch you change then?' Raising her eyebrows, she turned and looked at the inviting water. 'Race you, Joey.'

'It's *Joe*,' he shouted, quickly overtaking her and standing waist deep, ready to splash freezing cold water the moment she came anywhere near.

Stopping for a few minutes to get the fire going, Shay joined them, by which time the other two were acclimatised and had joined forces to welcome him to the loch with much splashing and an eventual dunking. At one point, they were afraid their play had gone a bit far when he failed to break the surface. Panicking, Robyn dived down, fearing what she may find. Frantically coming back up for air, she saw him calmly wave from a good distance away. He was smirking, she could tell.

'Cool,' Joey shouted, swimming out in his direction. Robyn smiled, as much with relief as admiration. Shay was obviously a much more competent swimmer than he'd let on.

Later, once they were dry, they enjoyed a cup of tea with water that had been boiled over the fire. Joey, still desperate to catch a fish, puzzled over the plastic boxes of fluffy and feathery dragonfly looking objects. Robyn picked up a container that was full of something very colourful. As she peeled back the lid, her lap was covered in a shower of yellow blue green and red 'maggots'. She gave an ear-piercing scream and proceeding to re-enact some kind of Native American rain dance, or that was what Shay most likened it to.

When her foot nearly stamped in the fire for the second time, he stood up and swept a hysterical Robyn into his arms. 'Calm down, love,' he said quietly. 'I don't think they're real.'

She groaned, hearing Joey's laughter rise up from where he was sitting on the ground. A few other campers nearby had turned around when they'd heard the scream, and she was just in time to see them all look away.

'Robyn Harley, is that you, dancing around the fire?'

A vaguely familiar voice called from behind Shay's back. She burrowed her head in his shoulder, trying to remember who it was that owned the warm Scottish burr. When she connected the voice to a face, she groaned.

'This really is a coincidence and I must say a *most* pleasant one. May I introduce my father?' Stuart turned to the much older man at his side, 'Angus Frazer.'

'Nice tae make yer acquaintance, lassie?'

Robyn wriggled herself free from Shay's arms. 'Mr Fraz... Stuart, and Mr Frazer senior, a pleasure. Won't you join us for a cup of tea and some cake? Or a cold drink, if you'd rather.'

'A cuppa will be just braw.' Angus Frazer sat on the blanket next to Joey, giving him a wink. 'Your lummies are escaping laddie.'

Joey picked up one of the small coloured worms. 'Do you mean these, Mr Frazer?'

'Aye, they're nae braw, but ye can catch a trout if you ken where to fish.'

'Err, this is Joe, my best friend's younger brother. I told you I was staying with her family.' Stuart nodded. 'And this is Shay, my boyfriend.'

Shay grabbed the older man's hand in a strong grasp. 'Nice to meet you, Mr Frazer.'

'Please, call me Stuart. Are you taking a boat out?' He inclined his head at the fishing rods.

Shay shrugged helplessly. 'I have to confess that I've never fished, but Joe is keen and Robyn has promised to cook anything we bring back.'

Stuart heard a tortured moan and laughed. 'In that case young Joe, we must definitely help you. Firstly, the coast along here is pretty shallow, so you'd need to wade out a long way. Do you see all the small boats out in the middle of the loch?'

'We thought they were just pleasure boats,' Robyn said, pouring two cups of tea. She noticed Angus take a small hip flask from his pocket and add his own 'extra'.

'A few belong to the locals. My father's boat is moored around the corner, about a ten-minute walk.' Biting into a slice of Babs' tea bread, Stuart licked the thick butter from his lip and eyed a second slice, which Robyn quickly offered. 'Delicious,' he nodded his thanks. 'That's why we're here actually. I usually bring Dad on a

Saturday morning, but as I'm being hassled to take some leave, I decided to take today and tomorrow off.'

'Can Clem hold the fort?' Robyn asked sceptically.

'We've got no appointments booked, he'll manage.'

While the conversation continued, Angus quickly and adeptly fixed the rods together and showed Joey how to attach a lure. 'Ye can show yer mukker afterwards.' Joey giggled at this and Angus' eyes twinkled. 'Would ye care tae come oot in the boat wi' us? There's ainlie room fur four, though.'

'Would you mind if I don't go?' Robyn asked Shay quietly. 'I don't want to push you into spending time doing something that you don't want to do, though.'

'I'd really like to actually,' he grinned. 'Not that I want to be apart from you, sweetheart.'

'Listen tae they big wet haddock.' Angus guffawed. 'Feart his love will hae bolted afore he gets back.'

Robyn put a hand over her mouth and laughter spluttered out around her fingers. 'I'll never bolt from ye, don't be afeart.' She giggled at the bemused look on Shay's face and turned to the Frazer men. 'This is very good of you, but Joe... I'm not sure,' she said hesitantly. 'He can't swim that well.'

'*ROBYN!*' he shouted angrily.

'Sorry,' she gave him a quick hug. 'You're my responsibility for two days.'

'We've enough life jackets to go around. I always wear one. Dad won't I'm afraid, he's a stubborn old bugger at times.'

'When mah times up, tis up. A jaiket will make nae difference.' He put his cup down, gathered up the equipment and then signalled to Stuart to give him a hand. 'We'll motor this way lassie, gies a wave 'n' a bonny smile as we go by.'

Robyn waited about twenty minutes before she heard the quiet engine and saw them all wave enthusiastically. The boat looked a little larger than the others with a covered area, where she assumed their fishing tackle was stored. Bored with the whole fishing thing, she lovingly unfolded a magazine and made herself comfortable on the blanket. Maybe a walk after supper would be nice, after *supper*! Oh, no, in the company of two experienced anglers, they were bound to bring some humungous, fat-bellied fish for her to gut.

Chapter Thirteen

'Holy shit, what have you done? You're a madman.'

Silver and pink trout fillets were skewered onto thick twigs and hung over the fire. 'We have to watch them all the time,' Joey told her, keeping his own eyes fixed on the fish that was gently cooking above the tempered flames. 'If you don't, the sticks will burn through. Stuart says they only take a few minutes.'

'I can't thank Angus enough for preparing them,' said Robyn, who had smiled with glee when she woke up and saw their supper already cooking. 'I wouldn't have wimped out, though.'

Shay gave Joey a knowing look. 'Th' bonny Sassenach lassie won't dae it, were the exact words Angus used. And anyway, I didn't fancy you smelling of fish later,' he grinned.

Robyn kissed his cheek, handing the plates around with thick slices of buttered bread. 'Are you going to eat one?' she asked. 'The veg and noodles are almost ready.'

He peered longingly at the white flaking flesh. 'Maybe a taste, there's not much point being a hunter gatherer if I can't eat my prey.'

The fish was taken from the wooden skewers and transferred to the waiting plates. Shay was given a generous portion of the noodle concoction, while Robyn and Joey shared what was left.

Not particularly want to see its dead staring eye, Robyn cut it off below the gill, before pushing it under a paper serviette. Joey, on the other hand, took great delight in forcing the prong of his fork into the withered socket.

'This is tasty,' Shay announced, eating his small portion as he eyed Robyn's plate. She offered more but he declined. 'If I can keep this down, I'll be happy.'

'Why wouldn't you?' Joey asked, puzzled by his statement. 'Cos you're supposed to be a vegetarian?'

He sucked in a breath, it was hard to remember to be careful about what was said when he was so used to talking freely to Robyn. 'Yeah, sort of, my stomach isn't used to it. I got a bit carried away with the fishing today.'

Joey nodded, seemingly happy with the explanation. 'Sam's sister says she's a veggie, but we saw her stuffing a sausage roll the other day.'

'Ah well, I won't be doing *that*. As I said, this was more down to curiosity. Um, how about a walk or a bike ride?' he asked, changing the subject.

'We can take turns,' Robyn suggested, as they only had the two bikes. 'It's 7 o'clock now, so there're a couple of hours of daylight left.' *Not only that but I want you worn out, my little friend*. She looked affectionately at Joey. He really was very good company and seemed quite in awe of Shay.

They walked and cycled through the trails until the light finally forced them to return to the tent. Shay had proved himself surprisingly adept on a bicycle, so much so that Robyn was able to sit on the handlebars in the places where the terrain was kind to them.

When they did get back, she was mightily pleased to see Joey fall asleep minutes after cleaning his teeth and changing into pyjamas. What she hadn't planned, was that she'd soon be joining him, as she also fell asleep almost immediately.

Shay looked at his two camping companions, snuggled up in sleeping bags. Smiling he brewed a cup of tea, took a sip and felt the electrodes in his wrist start to pulse. Whichever of his friends had chosen to interrupt his interlude, they would no doubt have a good reason.

Adam looked unusually nervous. Excited, anxious, deliriously happy, in a fervent rage, or anything in-between, Shay was used to dealing with, but not nervousness. 'What's happened?' He motioned his friend towards the shadows.

'Channing knows something's up, he's pulling your records.'

'What, *how*?' It was Shay's turn to look nervous.

'Something must have flagged up, perhaps the number of visits you've had in this exact time portal, some foreign object that hasn't cleared, who knows? You have to come home with me now.'

'I can't, I'm not leaving Robyn stuck here on her own, how would she explain that to Joe and her friends?'

'Stop this ridiculous visiting in real-time. Stay away for a few months, do some work four hundred years from now, anything mundane that will stop him looking for discrepancies. Robyn will still be here in the same tent, hell, having the same dream for that matter in a month, or a year. Come back then if you feel the need.'

Shay shook his head. 'I'm staying tonight and I've promised one more trip. I have to at least do that for her. Damn Christopher Channing, I hate him with a passion.'

'Hate and passion, curious concepts for you Shay. Think carefully about what you're doing, he's far too important to ignore. The council re-elections are due in a few months, if he gets in, everything will change. He wants complete policing of all portals, the man's power crazy.' He saw the determination on his friend's face. Shay had promised something and he wasn't about to back down. The fact that they could all be in trouble didn't matter. 'Right, wherever you're going on this next trip, *I'll* bring Robyn and meet you there. We'll think of some excuse to tell her. You have to avoid this particular portal in this time.' He put a hand on his friend's shoulder. 'There was never going to be a future for the two of you, not one that you could share at any rate.'

Shay tore himself away, but recognised Adam's concern. When he spoke again, he gave nothing of his feelings away. 'You'll need some blood, I should have given you or Tarro some weeks ago when I first took Robyn travelling.'

'Or at least told one of us exactly where you were all the time. What if something had happened to you? What if Channing knows?' Adam said with a horrified realism.

'I know, I wasn't thinking. Wait here.' He went back inside the tent and took a small black disc from the pocket of his jeans. An item none of them ever travelled without. Pressing it to Robyn's arm, the sample was taken, swiftly and painlessly. She would know because he would explain it in the morning, how much he'd say at this point he wasn't sure. They had a two-day trip to look forward to. If that was to be the last memory they'd share, it was going to be good, for both of them.

'There's enough there for Tarro as well.' Giving the disc to Adam, and making a tentative arrangement to speak again the next day, he made his way back to the tent and crawled into the empty sleeping bag. Sneering slightly at the ludicrously primitive design, he rolled over, pulling Robyn, bag and all, into his arms. How would he ever be able to let her go? And with that thought in his head, how would he get any sleep tonight?

* * *

Exhaustion had eventually won out and the next thing Shay was aware of, was the smell of bacon wafting in through the opening of the tent. Not a smell he was usually tempted by, this morning it seemed to taunt him. Voices from outside filtered through the canvas, then soft laughter as Robyn tried to keep things quiet. The flap opened and Joey grinned, shouting back that Shay was wide awake, no need to whisper.

Perhaps if he tried to believe it hard enough, things would be okay, at least for another week or so. *Just let us have our trip together and then she can get caught up in her new job. That'll make it easier*, he tried to justify. *As soon as she's been there a few days, I'll come back and say goodbye.*

'Something smells good,' he said putting on a smile.

'Not for you,' Robyn announced. 'There are a couple of tofu strips frying. I did share the pan,' she confessed. 'Perhaps a minuscule amount of bacon fat won't upset you and may make the err... pretend stuff a little more palatable.' She waited until Joey had grabbed a bacon butty and a few fish fingers and disappeared to the water's edge, before asking questions. 'Were you okay, after the fish? Your stomach, I mean. Why didn't you wake me when you came to bed last night? I know we could only have a cuddle, but I was looking forward to it.'

'I'm feeling okay so far, it was only a few mouthfuls, maybe a small amount of protein in such a pure form isn't so bad after all, and I did have a cuddle, even though *you* snored all the way through it.'

Robyn pulled a face at his reference to snoring. 'Here, try this.' Slapping two slices of the plastic-looking bacon substitute onto a slice of bread, she squirted some ketchup on top. 'Enjoy, there's a mug of tea poured out for you as well.'

With breakfast finished and everything packed away, Joey was given the choice of what to do next. He wanted to swim again, so they took a ball into the water and played around for a while. If Robyn thought Shay was even more quiet than usual, she didn't mention it, still assuming it was the fish and not wanting to make him feel awkward.

'When we drove by one of the towns on the way here, I think I saw a fair,' Joey hinted strongly. 'There were definitely stripy tents.'

'Are you up for a ride on the dodgems Shay?' Robyn asked.

'Of course,' he answered, not too sure what he was agreeing to. This was really hard, but luckily Robyn suspected he wasn't feeling great. She certainly wasn't a million miles from the truth, but for a completely different reason. He did feel sick, but it was a sickness in his heart, if such a thing existed. This was most definitely the negative side of experiencing unsuppressed emotions.

The walk back to the car was much slower as they took a longer route through the forest, stopping to pick a few wild mushrooms.

'Wow are these really safe to eat?' Joey wanted to know.

'Absolutely,' Shay said, examining them carefully. 'When you get home, look them up online. There are some very similar to this that would make you extremely ill.'

'You can do it with me before you go.' Joey grinned when Shay nodded in agreement.

'He's really taken to you, do you have younger brothers or sisters?' asked Robyn, who didn't recall him speaking much about his family.

'Two *older* sisters actually and I'm an uncle a few times over now. Don't look too much into Joe's adoration, you should have seen him hanging on Angus' every word on the boat yesterday when I knew next to nothing.'

'Yeah, I suppose their allegiance changes easily at that age.' She wanted to slip her hand in Shay's, but there was too much to carry and he was pushing one of the bikes. Joey was pushing the other. 'We didn't really make much use of these, did we?'

'Maybe we can fit something in after the fair, let's see how the time's going.' He didn't want to admit that he'd been looking forward to a proper bike ride. There was something vaguely similar in his own time, but it was more efficient and business-like. This mechanical machine was pure fun for him.

'I could always drop you two off, a few miles before we reach Stonehaven, then you could cycle to the house?' Robyn suggested, aware that it would be another hour or so she'd be apart from him. In that moment, with his eyes shining in anticipation, he looked more like Joey than a grown man. She had to smile.

'This was a brilliant idea, Joe, I had no idea fairs were like this...' Shay just stopped himself from adding, 'in the twenty-first century'.

'What do you mean you had *no* idea?' Joey looked at him curiously.

'He means,' Robyn stepped in quickly. 'We thought it was going to be all waltzers and loud music. This is like, really old fashioned. Look over there, a coconut shy.'

'Yeah, boring or what?' Joey whined. 'They glue them in you know!' he shouted in a loud voice. A girl who was about to throw her ball and the stall owner both looked over. One now seemed indecisive, the other angry.

It certainly hadn't been the fair Joey had in mind, despite there being a few rides, but he made the best of it. They all had their fortunes told, Robyn would meet a tall, dark stranger and travel, well that was true. Joey was to become a premier footballer one day. He'd rolled his eyes and laughed, having no interest in football, apart from the odd kick around. Had the pretend gypsy said he was going to become a top Engineering Geologist, he'd have been won over instantly.

Shay settled with the knowledge he was going to move house shortly and have a change in career. 'Well, that was fifteen pounds wasted,' he grumbled and licked a sugary mountain of fluff from Robyn's finger. 'Christ, that's sweet. I've seen it before, can't say it ever appealed. Although, actually,' he pulled off another piece and stuffed it in his mouth, 'it is rather addictive.'

'Hold that,' she handed him the stick, with a warning not to eat it all, and proceeded to buy wrapped toffee apples and a few sealed bags of candyfloss. 'To take back for the family,' she grinned.

Joey disappeared with an arrangement to find them later and with Shay's arm around her and just the two of them sharing the candyfloss, Robyn felt a wave of contentment. They passed a few booths, trying their luck at rifle shooting and darts, but neither of them won a prize. Shay was about to suggest they find a seat in the sun, where they could wait for Joe, he followed Robyn's gaze towards a small tent. Lots of inked designs on stands adorned the outside.

'Most of these are temporary, stickers or henna,' she explained, pointing to various patterns. 'He does real tattooing as well.'

'Who on earth would do that to themselves?' Shay asked, forgetting Robyn's little circlet of flowers around her navel.

'Well not you *obviously*, far too rugged and manly a thing for such a futuristic, forward-thinking guy,' she teased. 'Why express yourself when you can blend into the background?'

Whether it was the thought of Christopher Channing still in his head, or the inner rage and heartbreak at knowing his time with Robyn was coming to an end, he wasn't sure. But a deep desire was forcing him to rebel, and if this was the only way he could do it...*Blend into the background*, he'd show her. 'I'm going to have one,' he said, gratified to see the look of incomprehension on her face.

'T-think carefully Shay, you should never rush into...' Why was she bothering? In his time, he could probably remove it with a lotion. 'What will you have?' her curiosity got the better of her. 'And more importantly where?'

'Wait and see, stay there while I find out if he can do what I want.'

The man had come out and spotted what he hoped was his first real customer of the day. As a bona fide ink artist, this is what got his blood excited, not blobbing a few henna patterns on children's pale spotty arms. 'Hi there, I'm Ben, anything you like the look of mate?' he asked. 'I could do something freehand if you have an idea of your own.'

Robyn couldn't hear what was being said or see exactly what he was looking at. They were pointing to a design; a lot of nodding was going on. She wondered if Shay had the slightest idea of the pain he was about to endure. He'd probably thought it was nothing because she had one. Betting he'd chosen a small Celtic cross, or maybe a Scottish thistle, she then tried to guess where he'd have it. Obviously, somewhere it could be well hidden, perhaps his chest? She managed to hold out for fifteen minutes before following inside the tent.

'It's okay love, you can come over and watch,' he said when he noticed her hovering.

The outline was already taking shape and Robyn could see a tortured look on Shay's face. She couldn't stop a gasp of surprise, it looked like a small bird. The tattooist was working on the inside of Shay's right wrist and as time went on, he started adding brown and then red. She knew exactly what it was. 'A *Robin*' she exclaimed.

'It hurts like *hell*, why didn't you warn me?'

Ben gave a muffled laugh. 'Not much longer, about twenty more minutes,' he estimated.

Shay nodded resolutely and watched as the robin seemed to come to life. Small feathers and even tiny claws were defined, the whole thing looked extremely life-like. The completed image was about two inches long, its beak pointing towards his hand.

'What do you think?' Ben directed the question to both of them, pleased with his work and hoping they would be as well. He took great pride in what he did, free hand designs being his absolute favourites.

'I think it's wonderful.' She gently clasped the small silver rose between her thumb and forefinger. 'Ever since you gave me this I've been racking my brains to think of something significant that I could give you in return. What could be better? Let me pay for it, please?'

When she put it like that, Shay had to agree.

Robyn tipped Ben extra, over the agreed price. She was so touched by the whole thing, and the man had done such an excellent job. He gave Shay a few instructions and covered the tattoo with cling film.

'I feel a bit light headed is that normal?'

'Come and sit in the shade for a while. We can wait for Joey and you can tell me a little about the future.'

Perhaps because he was feeling woozy, a little vulnerable and still cross with Christopher Channing, it didn't occur to him to refuse. Did it really matter now? He'd started telling her things that he shouldn't have, weeks ago. 'This isn't for Simone's ears.' He saw her nod and started to pick out relevant bullet points, that she'd find interesting.

'I'll start at the year 3000 — numbers had grown so rapidly that euthanasia, both legal and illegal, was enforced. People would have been living long healthy lives if the planet, which was unable to support them, hadn't virtually shut down.

It was also a time of cosmetic selection, eye colours from the brightest pinks, through to the greenest emerald, purples, golds and even silver were favourites. There was hair every colour of the rainbow, not just dyed, permanently transformed and noses were robotically sculpted and grafted. Everybody wanted to look beautiful and if advanced chemicals could change body shape, why not use them? Perhaps it helped them forget the reality they actually lived in?'

'I can't imagine genetic selection on such a scale. I don't think I'd want plastic surgery unless I broke my nose or something.'

'Your nose is perfect.' Shay said kissing the tip of it. Perhaps he'd better jump ahead a few centuries. They'd be here all day otherwise.

'Two momentous natural disasters over the next three hundred years reversed the population growth and were followed by the 'mutation' wars, that at least gave the planet time to recover. It didn't last, though, by the end of thirty-fifth century, the population was once again growing too quickly. People were unstable and anger issues had given rise to terrible acts of violence. It was around this time that the world power committees chose to release certain substances into fresh water supplies. These would alter emotional states, similar to the effect that lithium had on schizophrenics back in the twentieth century.'

'We don't seem to ever learn, do we?' Robyn said, morbidly fascinated by these revelations.

'The natural look was also the only option left, as no money or time was available for cosmetic selection, and it died a natural death. Maybe the grey and blue-eyed genes were weaker and hadn't survived, no one knew for sure, but everyone's eyes were now various shades of green or brown, mostly dark brown like mine. 'Now you know why I love your eyes so much.'

'Not just my eyes I hope.' She smiled. 'I always think of your eyes as black.' She peered long at hard at him. 'They're brown of course like you said, but so wonderfully dark.'

'Have you heard enough?' he asked, a little flustered from her close scrutiny.

'No, I want to know everything.' He'd never been so open, this may be the only opportunity she'd ever get to really learn about the sort of life Shay led.

'Well then, within a hundred years, irreversible damage was done. The toxins were so powerful that children were being born with either heightened or almost non-existent emotions. Completely out of their depth, the huge pharmaceutical organisations pumped more and more money into developing a cure. It would take another few hundred years before mind control of some kind was mastered technically.'

Robyn stopped him and went to buy some cold drinks. What she was learning was fascinating, but Shay did have a habit of telling it like he was reading from a history book. 'Here,' she said, handing him an orange juice. 'I'd like to know up to your time, make it quick before Joey comes back.'

'Make it *quick*!' He laughed and drank the whole drink in one go. 'I'll do my best. Constant trials and breeding programmes resulted in the second and more damning issue, the total breakdown of our immune systems. No one organisation was prepared to claim responsibility. A high percentage of foetuses stopped developing in the second trimester, and those that did survive to full term often always died within the first few months.'

'Thankfully enough must have survived.' She murmured more to herself.

He nodded absently and continued. 'The fortieth and forty-first centuries were very bleak and went down in history as The Two Hundred years of Despair.'

'I don't think I do want to hear any more after all.' Robyn was fighting back tears, torn between a thirst for knowledge and a huge feeling of regret that she'd carry this with her for the rest of her life. Shay was right, he shouldn't have said anything.

'I'm sorry Robyn but they began to see a breakthrough only after the discovery that nurturing babies in laboratory conditions increased their chances of survival, and the earlier they could be taken from the uterus, the better. With the population, low again and children facing an uncertain future after reaching puberty, people looked to the newly discovered method of time travel for answers. And that really is pretty much it, the future in a nutshell.'

'I had to ask, didn't I? Christ, what a weight you have on your shoulders. Every sample you take back you must hope it's the one.'

Strangely he didn't feel guilty for telling her, but he did feel bad knowing that she'd worry. 'There is nothing *you* can do about any of it love. Just live your life and forget about it. Treat this as one of your sci-fi stories.' He stood up before she could argue or ask even more. 'Let's find Joe, I'm feeling okay now.'

It wasn't until they were unhooking the bikes from the rack that Joey finally noticed. His eyes nearly popped out of their sockets, and he couldn't stop the envious exclamations of 'Wow and cool' and 'Can I get one?'

Shay didn't care what Adam, Tarro or Christopher bloody Channing thought. Without giving consent, there was a high probability he'd be 'fixed' sooner rather than later. He may not be able to feel the emotion behind the little bird afterwards, but he would at least remember the relevance.

* * *

'Holy shit, what have you done? You're a madman.'

'Adam, I grant you it wasn't my most sensible moment, but I kind of like it.'

Tarro chuckled. 'Could have been worse. I'm not quite sure how? Give me a while to think of something.'

'Get rid of it before someone reports…'

'No,' Shay said firmly. 'There're no laws against it. I've been through contamination, everything's good. Calm down.'

'It's not a case of whether or not it's *allowed*,' Adam spluttered. 'It's the fact that Shayden Lomax, as known to everyone here, would never contemplate such a thing. What's Mara going to say?'

'He can keep it covered, winter's not far off. Stay out of the temperature controlled domes Shay, volunteer for snow clearance duty.'

'Shut up, Tarro,' Adam growled. 'You're not funny. That's most likely all he'll have left once his travelling rights have been revoked and the electrodes dampened or worse, permanently removed.'

'My sister may not approve, but she won't say anything to anyone else.'

'Are you quite certain about that?' Adam asked. 'If Mara thinks you're going into some sort of crisis, and you refuse to go for a check, she'll call an evaluator, and it'll be for what she considers, are the best reasons.'

'As long as I can avoid a deep scan, I can fake it. And as for this,' he flicked his wrist, 'I'll tell her the truth. I just fancied it, wanted to experience something. Come on guys, even the emotionally stabilised appreciate a little fun and danger.' He watched Adam rake his hands through his thick head of hair. Tarro looked amused, but the underlying worry wasn't completely hidden. 'I know I have to let her go, I've accepted it, okay. Just let me do it my way. Look at this tattoo as a *memento* of a happy time, something I... needed, and that's an end to the discussion.'

Tarro patted him on the shoulder. 'Anything we can do to help. Speaking of which, have you ever heard of Madame Minuit's Maison for gentlemen?'

'I don't think that's the kind of help he needs right now,' said Adam, giving a small smile. 'Channing really would know something was up if he went there with us.'

'I need to get a dress for Robyn.' Shay ended the discussion about nineteenth-century brothels as quickly as he could.

'I'll take it to her,' Adam offered. 'The least amount of times you go back there before you call it a day, the better.'

'You're right, I didn't get around to telling her about the DNA though. She'll freak out if you turn up in her bedroom.' He scowled, not sure he liked the idea of that either. 'I'll stick a note in with the dress and if you leave it in her room a day or two before, it'll at least explain a few things. I'll tell her everything in more detail face to face.'

* * *

Now that Simone was able to stand and turn around, she could manage the loo, with minimum assistance. She persuaded her mother that with Richard and Robyn's help, the three of them could finally make an attempt to visit Dunnottar Castle.

Robyn explored every corner, as usual, of the thirteenth-century ruined cliff top fortress. While Richard explained to Simone that as castles went, this wasn't the best and they really weren't his thing anyway. He was quite content sitting with her and enjoying the surroundings from ground level. Simone, who was growing closer to him by the day and continuing to improve her mobility, couldn't be happier. He'd already decided to stay an extra week, using the excuse that he'd like to see how Robyn got on during her first few days in the new job. The flights for October were also booked.

Robyn wondered whether Richard might consider transferring to the University of Aberdeen for his final year. By then, the first stage of the barn conversion would be complete. If all went to plan, she and her new stepbrother might be renting the small units from Babs and Clive. Closing her eyes, she tried to imagine her bedroom; maybe it would share the same view as the first floor of the barn. She and Shay could stand at the window and watch the sunrise over the sea.

* * *

A couple of days before the next trip, Robyn was a bit put out to find a parcel on her bed. It contained some of the appropriate clothes and a note telling her exactly when to be ready and the usual boring instructions about the gown. It had happened during a film that she'd been watching with the family. Feeling a prickle in her arms, she flew up the stairs and searched every room. There was no sign of Shay and she felt a burning disappointment that he obviously hadn't been able to wait. It really must have been just a drop-off, but as she'd made the rules about real-time visiting, couldn't complain when it didn't suit.

Giving the dress a quick once over, she flounced back down the stairs. The film would be on pause, but it didn't matter anymore, she couldn't concentrate. 'Carry on,' she called to them from the hallway, 'I'll make some drinks.' Waiting for the kettle to boil, Robyn emptied a packet of digestives onto a plate. Her mind was all over the place. The bronze coloured dress, which she'd only glanced at fleetingly, appeared so much nicer than the previous Tudor gown. If she had something to wear, he must know exactly where and when in medieval England they were going. The knowledge that he'd been in her room a few minutes ago was worse than frustrating. Sometimes this whole travelling issue really sucked.

Before turning the light out, she glanced at the note again, still not reading it properly. It was a bit 'to the point', but then that was Shay all over. They were meeting the day after tomorrow, at nine in the evening. So, tomorrow night she needed to feign a headache, which would explain her going off early to bed and having a lie in the next day. This time she wanted to be better prepared and fully awake. Stratford-upon-Avon had only been one day, and she'd yawned her way around the market. This trip was going to be overnight if she had her way, and all being well, bedbugs notwithstanding, they wouldn't be getting much sleep.

Stuart Frazer phoned the next morning, firstly enquiring if they'd all enjoyed the remainder of their camping trip, and secondly to double check if Robyn was still on course to start the following Monday. There was a contract coming in the post, she should read through and then bring it in signed.

She took the opportunity to ask about a dress code, thinking about suitable outfits for the office, as well as scrabbling around in the dusty storeroom.

Stuart suggested casual for the first week, as they only had two appointed historians coming in, and there was no need to dress up for them. Maybe she'd like to keep a set of clothes hanging up, just in case? Overalls were also available if she felt the need.

The best bit of information was that there was free parking in a small yard at the back. Robyn was ecstatic, it would save her the daily train fare, and even if Aberdeen rush hour traffic was busy, so were all the other commuter routes. Ending the call, she sat back with a big smile. This job was a blessing and it sounded more and more like a match made in heaven.

Not long after she finished the phone call, a large parcel arrived from her mother, the majority being the contents of Robyn's old wardrobe. But there were quite a few new items mixed in amongst the old. It was generous and not to say extremely thoughtful. Another phone call would have to be made, this time she found herself looking forward to it.

Robyn took to her bed after supper, feeling guilty when Babs fussed around bringing Paracetamol and cups of tea to her room. 'I'm fine really, I'll sleep in tomorrow. That's all I need, a bit of catch up.'

'If you say so, although I do think you look a little pale dear. The last thing you want is to come down with something just before you start your new job.'

'Really, Babs it's just a headache.' Thank goodness Simone was in on it, she could never lie to her friend. Although her head really was beginning to hurt, maybe it served her right.

* * *

Twelve hours of solid sleep, plus a few hours dozing, took Robyn nicely to midday. Now all she had to do was sit around reading, watch daytime TV or just chat with Simone, anything to conserve her energy.

Once nine o'clock came, she'd be off and wherever they were going, the day would start somewhere new, all over again. She wondered if Shay had managed to rest. If he'd been working as normal, he'd be exhausted. That might put a dampener on their night in a medieval coaching inn.

There was no underwear with the dress, did that mean the women didn't wear any or had he forgotten to include it? They'd joked about that when he'd mentioned the 'chastity belt'. She studied the gown and browsed some pictures on her laptop. It appeared to fasten at the collar and around the waist. Stripping off, she held it up critically, examining her reflection. The rich bronze would complement her blonde hair, but surely there should be a headdress of sorts.

Her arms tingled, Shay was coming, she thought joyfully. Dropping the dress, she turned, ready to step into an embrace, only to see *Adam* leering at her. Swallowing a shriek, she got the garment over her head and yanked it down her naked body in record time. 'What the *bloody* hell do you think *you're* doing here? Where's Shay?' She should have been furious but was too shocked to think properly.

'Didn't you read his note?' He choked back a rumble of laughter.

'Yes, well… no, not properly, it said something about bringing a few other accessories. Adam, stop *staring*. Where's Shay?' she asked again.

'He's meeting you there. It did say if you'd read it.' He handed her shoes, a cloak and a hat. 'You need to plait your hair and leave a few curly bits around your face. Are you listening?'

She was too busy re-reading Shay's message. After the few sentences, which said what clothes were still to come, he'd written about her hair, and also that Adam would be collecting her, adding that it was nothing she should be concerned about, all would be explained.

'Your *hair*,' Adam emphasised. 'Christ, take those earrings out.'

She reached up to remove the sapphire earrings, placing them lovingly in the small white box. 'They were from Shay, for my birthday.'

'Yeah, yeah, very nice. Hurry up we need to go.'

'Help me with these buttons then,' she snarled, yanking her pants back on, annoyed at herself and also with the situation. It didn't help that Adam chuckled wolfishly the whole time. 'You better not be getting off on this!' It helped even less when he finally gave in and exploded with uncontrollable laughter.

After plaiting her hair quickly, a tight jacket was added, which fell to her hips, but there was *no* pointy hat. She was given a sort of a cap instead. The shoes were the only pointy items. 'Christ, clown's feet.' She moaned, slipping them on.

'One more thing,' Adam said, reaching into his pocket and pulling out a gold belt that he fastened around her middle, and a gold chain, which he placed around her neck.

'Are these the real *thing*?' Robyn looked in the mirror, fingering the heavy yellow metal links.

'No, they're very good replicas. It would take a real craftsman to tell they were fake.' He took a step back and looked at her. 'Lovely inside and out,' he chortled.

'Shut up now,' she warned, and as they flew through a series of portals, she was uncomfortably aware of Adam's arms holding her much tighter than was necessary.

Chapter Fourteen

'Sir Robert Lacey at your service.'

'May 1271,' Adam announced as they left the portal. 'We just have to home in on Shay and then… ah yes, got him. His anchor is an old nurse who used to live and work in the castle, now she has her own home, which is far more convenient for us. This is the last year, month actually, that he can use her.'

'You mean she'll die soon?'

'Yeah, a few days after this event. He's got a seven-year window here with this one. Tarro has another that follows straight on, which is fortunate.'

'Can you find out when everyone dies?'

'Not unless there are proper records to research and that's an awful lot of work, why would we bother? It's helpful to know with our anchors, though.' Adam realised he was on dangerous ground when he saw more questions coming. 'He didn't want to know about you, so don't ask.'

'He said something like that to me once before.' What she really wanted now was Shay, and Adam to bugger off and leave them alone.

'I won't be cramping your style, don't worry,' he said as if reading her mind. 'I'm not really dressed for it. These peasant clothes, tunic and hose, cover quite a few hundred years if you're just melding into a dark corner. They wouldn't stand up to close scrutiny, though.'

'Do you know, I didn't even notice.' She gave him a quick once over. 'I was too busy trying not to look at you earlier,' she frowned.

'Charming. I, on the other hand, could hardly take my eyes off you,' he said, narrowly avoiding a slap.

Pulling a hood over his hair, he grabbed her hand. 'Shay will be inside a building, a small two-roomed hovel,' he said the words dismissively. 'You mustn't make a sound, do you understand, not even a squeak. The old woman is as blind as a bat, but her hearing's bloody good for a crone.'

A blind OAP! and they were using her disability to their advantage; Robyn was too excited to worry about what was politically or morally correct in the thirteenth century.

'Right, we're off again. Remember to keep quiet. If I give your ass a squeeze, you'll have to enjoy it quietly.'

'Adam don't you bloody dare!' She gritted her teeth and had to hope he was teasing, there seemed no way to tell, recently.

Shay was waiting in the smaller of the two rooms, which was really only one, divided by a large hanging blanket. He'd found this particular anchor in 1264 when he and Tarro had been working with Rebecca, his sister's partner. A few skirmishes around the Northampton Castle area during the Second Baron's War, in the reign of Henry III, meant this was a lucrative time for the Harvesters.

Even though the old lady was beginning to lose her sight, she was still able to walk a good few miles and pick through the corpses. She would not normally have been Shay's choice of an anchor, especially as he already had one nearby, but she'd brushed past him as he was crouched and mistaken him for one of the dead. Her hands, rough and bleeding, clasped his arms as she mumbled an apology. Rebecca had been appalled, wanting to decontaminate him there and then, but Shay used his disc on some of the blood. She was old and strong, he'd argued, who was to say her DNA wouldn't be useful.

So, there he was, waiting behind a moth-eaten blanket, sharing a room with a poor excuse for a bed and a bucket half full of stinking urine, trying desperately not to make a sound. It was only because this house was so convenient for the nearby fort, which was hosting the May Day celebrations and a jousting tournament, that he put himself through it.

He could have been breathing the glorious fresh air outside, where the sun was shining, but it was teaming with villagers. So, instead, he waited in the damp, fetid smoke filled house. She must be the only peasant to burn wood so late in the season.

No doubt Adam was responsible for the delay. This whole idea of his friend fetching Robyn was playing on his mind. He should have cancelled this trip, told her the truth and called it a day. But the selfish part, the part that convinced him he was doing this for her, to give her one more wonderful thing to savour, also had to admit that it was just as much for his own sake. He drew his thumb across the small robin tattoo, which was covered by a long-sleeved cotton tunic worn beneath a leather jerkin. This would be the hardest thing he'd done in his life. To pretend that nothing was wrong when he knew that in a week's time he'd pay her one short final visit to say goodbye forever.

His electrodes pulsed and the air fractured slightly, giving a telltale shimmer to those that knew. A second later she was there, his heart sang and everything else was forgotten.

'God, I hate the smell of piss,' Adam whispered.

'Who goes?' the crone shouted from her one decent chair behind the curtained blanket. 'John, is that thee?'

Shay glared at Adam who was looking way too jovial and unconcerned that he could have alerted a 'native' to their presence. They exited by the only door and thankfully, the outraged shouts from the old lady were quickly swallowed up by the much louder shouts of the crowd.

'Idiot,' Shay hissed, spotting something in Adam's eyes, which were shining unnaturally. He sighed, they'd just got Tarro back to normal, was his other friend going emotionally off the scale as well? 'You can go, thanks for your help.'

'That's okay, I'm going to have a quick wander around while I'm here. I won't bother to come back and say goodbye. What do you want to do about seeing Robyn home tomorrow?'

Shay looked at her puzzled expression. 'I'm in a bit of trouble, too much travelling,' he said by way of explanation. 'I'll tell you about it later, it's better if one of the others take you back from here.' He turned back to Adam. 'Shall we say the forest portal, 5 pm local time?'

'I'll be there, that way my friend, you can go directly home, not via any of the other portals.' He gave Robyn an awkward hug. 'It was a pleasure, in more ways than one.'

'Do I want to know?' Shay asked, a bit perplexed by what he'd just heard.

'I was bloody starkers when he came,' Robyn said between gritted teeth. 'I was expecting you.'

Shay's mouth fell open. 'I s-said in the note,' he stuttered.

'I know that *now*. Let's just say, I'm that person who never reads the instructions past the first couple of lines. Anyway, more to the point, why? Adam shouldn't be coming to my room at all. How could he, unless...' The wheels started turning in her brain, 'You gave him my DNA, without telling me?'

'I'm so sorry, Robyn.' He pulled her to one side as they were caught in the flow of people and carts making their way through the entrance to the fort governed by Lord Anarod, a favourite of King Henry. 'It was done at the loch the other night. That was the first I knew about a problem. I meant to tell you at breakfast.'

'What exactly is going on?'

'As you know, I'm not allowed to take someone travelling. I don't know if it's ever been done before. If so it's one of the best-kept secrets.' He shrugged and gave her hand a squeeze. 'I've certainly ignored the rules where you're concerned. The situation has become a bit more serious, in a political sense. It's complicated. Look, I don't want to spoil this time here for us.' He pointed ahead to a giant maypole, where red yellow and blue ribbons hung down. 'The dancing will start soon. I really did mean to tell you about the DNA.'

Robyn believed him. 'It makes sense I suppose. I guess we'll just have to be careful until whatever trouble you're in, dies down. At least if Adam can fetch me I still get to see you, that's all that matters.' She felt Shay kiss the top of her head, aware that he didn't confirm what she'd said. 'I don't want to talk about it anymore, we're missing things.' She grabbed his hand and forced a smile. 'Come on, let's explore.'

'First,' he slipped the wedding ring on her finger again. 'It's safer,' he smiled.

The fortified castle looked down over large flat fields. Wooden benches, set high on podiums, were covered with brightly striped canopies, all in the blue, red and yellow of Lord Anarod's colours. His standard flew above the battlements and the coat of arms, two black wolves on a yellow background, seemed to be displayed indiscriminately around the grounds. Robyn had never heard the name Anarod before and for once, didn't want a history lesson. The atmosphere and sharing it with Shay was more than enough.

Young girls in pastel gowns ran giggling to the maypole and started to dance as three castle musicians played a merry tune. Further along the path, a group of troubadours were reciting French poetry. Robyn's knowledge of the language was passable, but she only recognised a few words. Stalls selling sweetmeats and pies cropped up every hundred yards or so.

'Where's the loo, do you think?' she asked, beginning to feel a little desperate.

'I'm not sure. Just don't ask for the bathroom, you'll most likely be directed to the nearest river, they'll assume you want to bathe. '*Prithee* and *Grammarcy*', please and thank you, don't say anything more than that. I'm sure it'll be a tent with a few buckets, follow your nose.' He conveyed a look which said she wasn't going to like it.

Great, she did as he said and soon found what was needed.

'Just hover over the top,' he suggested. 'I'll wait downwind if you don't mind.' It was less than two minutes before Robyn returned, her face frozen in a tight grimace.

'I need a bottle of disinfectant,' she moaned. 'I was feeling peckish, but that experience has just killed my appetite stone dead.' She scowled at two men who were giving her an odd look.

'Watch what you say,' Shay reminded her quietly. 'It's even more important than our last trip. 'Keep a low profile, remember.'

'Yeah sorry,' she whispered back. 'We better not upset the serfs.' The crowd was becoming denser, and a wave of excitement seemed to be flowing. In the distance, people began to move to the sides, creating an opening through the middle.

Shay stood protectively in front of Robyn. 'Everyone's picking up a stick, I have feeling this is a punishment. Shall we go?' It was too late. Shrieks turning into bloodcurdling screams could be heard and running footsteps were getting closer.

'What are they doing to those poor men?' She watched open mouthed as a baying crowd beat two youths with what looked like birch twigs. 'Shay,' Damn, he couldn't hear her. 'SHAY.' They'd become separated by the mass of bodies cramming to see what was happening. He was uncommonly tall for this time, at least she could still see him, even if the hustle and bustle had swept them further apart.

A hand snaked around her upper arm and pulled her deftly to one side. She looked up into a pair of laughing blue eyes. *Oh, my God, Sir Lancelot.* Or it might have been if he hadn't opened his mouth. Not only was he missing a tooth right in the front, while his remaining tombstones were black, but the reek of wild garlic and onions nearly knocked her senseless.

'Sir Robert Lacey at your service.' He gave a small bow. 'Sodomites,' he said with relish. 'Caught in a flagrant act of depravity.' He mistook her look of incredulity for innocence. 'Mine humble apologies to speak such words. I heard thee pondering over their punishment. Mayhap a maiden, such as yourself, has no knowledge of these matters.'

How young did he think she was? This day and age, most girls would be wedded, bedded and on their way to producing a third child by the age of twenty, if they hadn't died during the birthing of numbers one or two. She probably did look a lot younger than them. The sound of the men's screams forced her back to the awful events unfolding on the raised stage. 'What wilt become-eth of them?' she asked. Not really wanting to participate in any conversation, but a morbid fascination made it impossible to turn her back on what was happening.

Luckily, he was fascinated with her gold necklace, if her speech was odd he didn't take much notice. 'It's punishable by death,' he shrugged. 'Lord Anarod is usually merciful, they may receive gelding only. For now, they will be pilloried, the final decision anon. Shall we desire, for all our sakes, the Castle Knights win the jousting tourney? It will put his Lordship in a goodly humour if they fetch him a hefty purse.'

Robyn felt herself grow faint and looked frantically in Shay's direction. Thankfully, he was making his way towards her. 'Ah my husband comes,' she said and noticed how Sir Robert's face fell. 'Grammarcy so much for saving me from the crowd.' When he grabbed her hand and took it to his lips, she fought hard to disguise the look of disgust.

'My love,' Shay said loudly and firmly, propelling her to his side. 'Who is your new friend?'

The Knight gave a quick bow and answered, 'Sir Robert Lacey. Thy good lady wife was rather swamped in her eagerness to see the sodomites punished.'

'No, I certainly was... OW!' She glared at Shay, who had given her a hard dig in the ribs.

'Of course,' he smiled. 'Prithee excuse us, we're in need of refreshments.' He quickly steered her away before the knight could make any offers to show them to the large food tents. It would be rude to decline if that was the case.

'We have to help those men; they're going to have their willies cut off.'

'*Willies*?' he looked puzzled until he glanced down and saw where Robyn was looking. 'Ah, of course. You know we can't do anything, I'm sorry. You have a romantic notion of the past, but this is the harsh reality, it was brutally unfair. Don't cry Robyn,' he said, looking back at the platform where the men were standing in front of the jeering mob. 'It didn't always end so badly; they may well get way with a flogging.'

'Christ, I never thought I'd actually hope that two men would be whipped. I suppose they'll count themselves lucky. Is there really nothing we can do?'

'No, they'll have a guard standing by all day. I'm sure families and friends will petition on their behalf.'

'Lord Anarod is generally fair, according to Sir Onion-breath.'

'Good, because if we did somehow manage to free them, what do you think they'd do?' He saw her shrug. 'They wouldn't run away, they'd throw themselves on the mercy of the Lord here, who would be furious they'd escaped in the first place. He'd be cutting off a lot more than their — willies. I know you see this as a grave injustice, but look a bit closer to your own time period, or all time periods in fact, and you'll find the mistreatment of minority groups.'

'You're right, it just seems so sad that two young men have to suffer so badly, and still can't be together, or not officially. Still, I suppose you come back to my time and think we're all ignorant?'

'Not all, certainly, not *you*.' He gave her a brief hug, desperately wanting to show more affection, but it wasn't wise here in front of everyone. If they weren't careful it would be them in the stocks, Shay for unseemly behaviour and Robyn for displaying herself like a strumpet.

They found a quiet spot to sit and eat lunch. Shay had what appeared to be a heavy brown lump of bread with lentil broth in a wooden tankard. Robyn was tucking into a meat pie, trying not to guess what the lumps of sinew and gristle might be. It was actually delicious and she mopped up the last of it with the pastry crust.

'There are so many places I'd like to go with you,' she said wistfully. 'They don't all have to be so far back as this. Queen Victoria's coronation, the war years, the summer of 67 or London, New Year's Eve 1999, I was too young to enjoy it the first time around.' She stopped abruptly. 'I guess we can't if you're in trouble. What's exactly happened?'

'I'm sure it'll be okay; I've just got to stick to where I should be. Things will die down, they always do.'

She dug her pointy shoe into the dry earth, kicking up a load of dust. He didn't sound convinced, nor particularly reassuring. 'Is it going to affect us?' There was no answer, so she looked up. Shay was distracted with something happening further along, near the podiums.

'The jousting is about to start,' he said, standing up and offering his hand. 'Come on, this is what you wanted to see. We'll put the dishes back and make our way over.' He'd heard the question but was unable to answer it without lying.

'Dear Lady,' Sir Robert rushed across as soon as he saw her. 'And thy husband as well, how fortuitous.' He addressed Shay, 'May I ask for a small favour from your good wife, just for luck.'

Shay smirked and gave a nod.

'I don't think I have anything to give you,' said Robyn. The Knight looked so downcast she felt awful. 'Just one moment.' Running behind a tent she reached under her skirt. After Adam had got an eyeful, she'd pulled her pants back on, not caring that they were totally contradictory with this time period. She tugged at a piece of lace. Really, it was so small, he'd probably be insulted?

'Black lace,' he was in awe. 'I can only imagine from whence it has come.' He looked her up and down avariciously, 'from your...?'

'From a kerchief, Sir Robert,' Robyn finished quickly. Trying to avoid Shay's eyes, which she knew without

217

looking would be narrowed and possibly glaring. He would recognise the lace, as he'd once commented on that particular set of underwear.

'How the hell did you manage to hover over the bucket?' he asked as soon as they were alone.

'With great difficulty and subterfuge. I had to share that tent with two other women who were also using the conveniences. Anyway, don't start being a grouch, it wasn't done on purpose. I just couldn't think properly with *Adam* in the bedroom!' She grabbed his hand, pulled him over to the tiered seating and they headed for the middle block. They were dressed more finely than serfs, but not as richly as the nobles sitting in the front rows. Middle ground, Shay always said, was least likely to attract unwanted attention.

There was no fear of Sir Robert Lacey winning a tournament and bringing Robyn into the spotlight, as he was unseated in the first round, his lance broken and also his nose. She'd gasped as he went flying through the air, and winced when he hit the ground with a sickening thud.

'There goes another tooth,' Shay announced cheerfully.

The rest of the afternoon was far more exciting and colourful. They found themselves standing, clapping, cheering and booing along with everyone else. Training for the tournaments kept the Knights in excellent physical condition, and their weaponry skill, supreme strength and fitness did not go unnoticed. The jousting, it turned out was only one of many events for them to display their prowess in combat and the codes of chivalry over the next three days. 'Will we have time to come back tomorrow?' She leant over and asked Shay, unable to tear her eyes away from a particularly tall armour-clad fellow receiving a purple scarf from one of the daughters of the house.

'Don't tell me,' he laughed, 'you want to watch the Club Tourney?'

'I do, yes. I'm not sure what it is exactly, but the women next to me have been talking about it for the last twenty minutes.'

'Basically, they have two teams.' Shay explained. 'Using blunt swords or clubs, they have to knock the crests off their opponent's helmets. I never realised you were such a bloodthirsty little thing.'

'Neither did I, it's so exciting. I love everything, from the size of the horses to the complete reckless abandon of the competition. Look at the women, they absolutely adore it, they're the original groupies. I have no doubt up close, they all stink and have rotting teeth, but from here, everything is shiny and wonderful. God, I'm looking forward to tonight.' She saw his face and laughed out loud. 'Doesn't it affect you, just a little?'

'Watching *your* reaction affects me,' he grinned. It hit him hard, this would be their last night together. Closing his eyes for a moment he got himself in check. He'd make sure this was good for the both of them, but especially for Robyn.

As the afternoon gave way to evening and more barrels of strong ale were rolled out, Shay suggested it may be best to find their lodgings. Inns with nicer rooms were found near the larger towns. At the risk of heading into the unknown, Robyn chose to stay locally and they paid a farmworker, who promised to take them in his covered wagon to a fine inn nearby.

The wattle and daub straw-roofed Alehouse was, unsurprisingly, owned by the farmer's sister and of the three rooms, only one was still vacant. There was no courtyard or stables and it had only a small lean-to, which could just about accommodate two horses.

Shay looked around dubiously. 'I haven't had a chance to check this place out, we could all perish in a fire tonight for all I know.'

Robyn was delighted; somewhere he'd never been, another first for both of them. 'Let's take it,' she urged. 'The place looks free from dirt, that's good enough.'

The bedroom was sparse but, most importantly, clean, like the downstairs area. The bedding was aired and Shay pulled back the sheets to make sure the ticking that covered the mattress was intact. When he was finally satisfied, they paid the landlord and ordered an evening meal.

'Don't expect meat,' he told her. 'The pie you had earlier was baked specially for the celebrations, they mostly eat vegetables and grains.' They were amused to be told there was a choice of main dishes. One seemed to be stewed vegetables, the other boiled, both amounting to the same thing – a heap of sludge in a wooden bowl with a mound of barley mixed in. Rye bread was served with thinly spread butter.

'Salt and pepper?' Shay offered, delving into his pocket when no one was looking.

'Breaking the rules!' Robyn pointed out with glee.

'It's the only time I do,' he grinned. 'The food is so bland around this time.'

They were assured the jug of ale that appeared was good quality. 'First rate,' the kitchen boy said. He came back to take their empty bowls, replacing them with pudding, a sweet almond custard, which was by far the best part of the meal.

When they'd finished, it was still early. Disregarding the time, an unspoken need to be alone together – something they hadn't been able to take advantage of for quite a while – had them both heading towards the stairs.

'Privy's in the yard, sir.' The landlady called after them. 'Pots will be emptied anon.'

'Oh hell, much as I don't fancy it, I think I'd better,' Robyn said, looking miserably at the door.

'I'll come as well,' Shay offered. They headed to the lean-to, which now housed a sorry looking pony. Next to it stood the privy, consisting of a smooth plank of wood over a stone base, with two holes cut side by side.

'Two? Are they for different... um, things do you think?'

Shay chuckled. 'No, my love, you can use either. I'll stay here and make sure you don't get an unwanted toilet companion. Here you go, I've broken the rules again.' He discreetly handed her an ultra-thin pack of wet wipes. He could have been giving her the crown jewels by the grateful look she gave him in return.

Shay made use of the facilities as well and told Robyn she was not to come down here alone during the night. If she could share a bucket in a tent with strangers, she could use a pot behind a screen whilst he was asleep. She agreed, wishing it was possible to hold herself until returning home tomorrow afternoon. But after two large tankards of ale and a large helping of vegetable, lentil and barley stew, that wasn't going to happen.

Finally, they were alone behind a bolted door. Robyn stripped off quickly and stood in her black lacy undies. 'There's no possibility of Adam suddenly appearing is there?'

'Absolutely not, and by the way, those pants are completely contraband. I think I should confiscate them.'

Robyn desperately tried to keep her eyes open. Lying awake, in the aftermath of their lovemaking, was better than any dream she may have when asleep. 'I want this moment to last forever,' she murmured.

'Me too, you don't know how much.' He pulled her into the crook of his arm.

'You've given me so much Shay. I left home hoping to start a new life in Scotland with Sim. I never in a million years expected to pick up a stranger and fall in love.' She wriggled until she could look at his face. 'The things you've shown me, places I could only imagine, time travel I mean, and to do it all with you, that's what's made it so wonderful.' She went quiet and when he remained silent, pulled herself across him and stared into his dark eyes. 'Even if you were Mr Fred Ordinary, the local window cleaner, I'd still have fallen in love with you. Don't think it's all about this,' she said, gesturing around the room with a sweep of her arm.

'I never really questioned things before. All my life I've accepted what we were taught, how the mistakes of the past must never be repeated. There's nothing wrong with normal emotions, mine shouldn't have been tampered with. Over the years, it's caused enormous problems for the likes of Adam and Tarro. Their kind will always need help but I don't, not anymore, I'm perfectly okay this way.'

'Damn right you are, it's not a sin to love deeply or have your heart broken. Those are human traits, it's okay to hate someone as well. It's just how you *act* on the impulses that matter.'

'This is getting too deep, let's get some sleep, there's more to see at the castle tomorrow.' He kissed her into silence and listened until her steady breathing gave way to soft snores.

Once he finally said goodbye, he'd no intention of treating their time together as if it had never happened. Someone needed to go up against Christopher Channing.

Robyn really had shown him how much better it could be to feel real passion. No wonder everyone was content to maintain the status quo. The reason issues weren't debated or argued over properly was because the council members consisted predominantly of emotionally stable citizens. In his opinion, they needed a much fairer mix. Discussions would be a lot more enthusiastic, dramatic and vehement. People would be stirred up enough to look past a sensible or comfortable conclusion. Channing had ruined everything for him and he had to pay a price for that.

* * *

The next morning a light misty rain fell. It wasn't unpleasant at first, although after a while it did begin to seep through their clothes. There was no sign of the two young men punished due to their sexual preference the day before. Shay assured Robyn that had they been hanged; their bodies would be on display. Much more likely that, having overwhelmingly won the jousting competition with his own Knights the Baron, Lord Anarod, had pardoned all criminals, and it was a pretty good bet the cells beneath the castle would be empty. From rapists and murderers to the thieves of a bread roll, the perpetrators would have all been treated to the same clemency. Neither of them wanted to think what might have happened if the visiting Knights had won instead.

Without the sun shining, the musicians or dancing displays, the atmosphere out of doors was very different. Until the rain stopped, everyone was directed to the main hall of the castle, where entertainment had been temporarily set up. Robyn started walking ahead, and just as Shay was about to catch her up, he spotted a familiar face. If anything convinced him that his time with Robyn was over, this was it.

One of Channing's lackeys, obviously sent to spy. Shay could see him searching the crowds. Slouching, so as not to be given away by his height, he moved as far away as he was able, while still keeping Robyn in sight. He didn't want her to turn and start calling his name. If he left it too long, she was bound to look for him.

Sir Robert Lacey, thank God for small mercies. Shay clapped him on the back. 'Heigh-ho Sir Knight, could thee possibly go ahead and tell my lady wife that I'll join her anon?' He tried not to stare at the man's swollen and bruised nose. Lacey nodded enthusiastically, hurrying to Robyn.

It gave Shay the time he needed to skirt around the castle and enter from a back entrance. By the time he located her, she was far from happy, but something in his face must have cautioned her outrage.

'There's a problem isn't there?' She hissed, throwing a simpering smile back at Sir Robert.

'We need to leave here *now,* but not together.' He turned once again to the Knight, who seemed hell bent on impressing Robyn, regardless that her husband was standing right next to them. 'Could I beg of thee one last favour, Sir Robert, I'm afraid it's a rather big one.' He saw him incline his head. 'My wife left a valuable item behind in the inn we stayed at last night, and I have some business with err... Lord Anarod, I very much must speaketh with him.'

'Of course, It will be mine honour,' Sir Robert leered, not believing his luck. 'My dear lady,' he started to grab her hand.

'One moment if you... prithee, I must have a quick *wordeth* with my Lord.' She turned to Shay whispering, 'What the bloody hell are you playing at?'

'It won't be for long, as soon as you're far enough away, just say you need to relieve yourself, find some bushes, anything. I'll come to you and we'll be at the portal within seconds.'

'Christ, this better work. If garlic features puts his hands on me, I'll punch his lights out, and then yours!' she fumed.

'If he lays a finger on you, I'll be doing the punching,' Shay soothed. 'Please Robyn, I can't risk you being seen here with me.'

'Someone's here, from your time?' she started to look around, unable to stop herself.

Shay nodded. 'Try not to draw attention.'

'Sir Robert,' she smiled sweetly. 'I'm so grateful for your kind offer,' she lowered her voice and attempted to flutter her eyelashes. *Such a handsome man, such a pity about his lesser attributions.* 'My husband sees fit to neglect me this morn, it seems.' Robyn had no idea if her speech was acceptable, she'd never expected to have to engage verbally with one of the locals so intensely. Quite frankly, she was past caring. Shay was in some kind of trouble.

If Sir Robert looked a little askance, his lust overrode any misgivings he may have. 'Oh, my lady, it's my *greatest* pleasure.'

Shay quietly seethed as he watched the oily Knight hold Robyn far too closely as he led her from the great hall. He spent the next twenty minutes giving them time to clear the castle grounds and avoid Channing's, man.

When he did find Robyn, he hung back until he was sure they were alone. Unfortunately, it looked like Sir Robert was also taking advantage of the fact that no one was around. Approaching quietly from behind, Shay gave him one blow to the back of his neck and Lacey screwed his eyes up in pain.

'Ha, how do you like them apples?' Robyn quipped sarcastically as the knight crumpled to the ground.

'Apples?' Shay asked. 'Where?'

'Never mind,' Robyn arched an eyebrow and wished she hadn't used that phrase, as she'd have to explain it later because Shay never forgot anything.

By the time Sir Robert recovered, his heart's desire had disappeared and the bemused knight was left wandering around the outside of the castle with a sore neck, trying to work out what had just happened.

'We can't wait for Adam. I'm going to take you home, but then, I'm sorry, I'll have to go.'

Robyn felt the pull of the portal and recognised immediately when they reached the wheatfield, even though it was bathed in moonlight. It was another second before they stood in her bedroom. Shay kissed her deeply and desperately, and she felt an awful foreboding.

'I'll see you soon... won't I?'

He didn't want her first few days at work ruined, even though prolonging things wasn't a good idea. For now, Robyn's need outweighed his own risk, however much Adam and Tarro would disagree. 'It won't be right away, but I want to hear about the new job,' he said honestly, feeling her body relax in his arms.

When she awoke the next morning, the feeling of doom she'd had in the portal wouldn't go away.

Chapter Fifteen

'I want to be able to tell you I had a good life.'

Regardless of everything that had happened over the past week and her constant niggling feeling that something bad was going on with Shay, Robyn managed to put it to the back of her mind on the first morning at work. A burst of excitement and anticipation flooded through her body as she parked the Audi in the small courtyard at the back of Frazer Storage. The building's name, she'd learnt from Stuart Frazer, was chosen to deter unwanted attention, theft or malicious vandalism because there was nothing in the title to alert the wrong sort as to what was inside. The building's treasures were held on a strictly need to know basis, and were certainly not advertised or open, as she'd first thought, for public viewing. While priceless items were locked in vaults beneath the main museums, Frazer's stored the more quirky and obscure pieces. On the very rare occasion something of real value came to light, it was moved immediately to a more secure setting.

Stuart opened the back door and gave a cheery wave. 'Are you ready for your first day Robyn?'

She nodded enthusiastically. 'I can't wait to get stuck in.'

'I thought you could spend the morning just familiarising yourself. Go where you want, have a poke around, we have no appointments today. After lunch, we'll go through all the necessary paperwork, staff training, health and safety, fire procedures,' he looked dubiously up at the rickety fire escape. 'You must never put yourself at risk, lass. We have procedures in place to try and save some of the antiques, I'll give you a copy to study. We'll also sort you out a key for here and a pass for the main building.'

'Will I have to go there?' she asked.

He gave a shrug. 'Sometimes two or three times in one week, then maybe not for a month or more. It's mainly if their Curator requests anything we have. That's why the cataloguing is so important. We're really behind I'm afraid and the pressure from above can't be ignored any longer. Also, you should attend if they are running a course or study day that you'd find helpful or interesting. I'm glad to have you here Robyn.' He stopped for breath and broke into a beaming smile.

'It seems I've got a large task ahead of me.' She replied. That was fine, she wanted a job where she could make a difference and lose herself entirely. If there were going to be longer periods between Shay's visits, which was sadly looking likely, something consuming to occupy herself was ideal.

At 11 am on the dot, Clem's very strong, virtually un-drinkable coffee appeared with two chocolate digestives. This prompted Robyn's offer to make the next one. She hadn't wanted to become the '*tea girl*' and when she saw his sly smile, wondered if he'd done it on purpose.

'Stella sorts us out with drinks,' Stuart grinned, knowing Clem's game. 'She works, Tuesday, Wednesday and Thursday mornings. Most of her time is spent dusting and she does do some filing as well, that seems to be an endless task.'

'What *exactly* does Clem do? Surely there isn't that much regular maintenance.'

Stuart laughed. 'He'll always find something, lass. Old buildings like this need looking after.'

Robyn spent the morning walking up and down the lines of artefacts. She was pleased to see they were in some semblance of order, but knew the actual cataloguing would include cross-referencing dates and places of origin, as well as recording where each piece was originally discovered, bought, sold, donated by whomever, et cetera. It was going to be a monumental job.

The miscellaneous section was two rows wide. Authenticity and valuations still had to be made on many of the objects, which fell into Stuart's remit. He did most of that work alone and even though the Parliamentary Treasure Act of 1996 didn't apply in Scotland, it was best to make sure that everything had been reported to the coroner, and the paperwork, in that respect, was up to date. Robyn was fascinated to learn he had a degree in archaeology and had worked in one of the top auction houses in London.

She stood with her hands on her hips and surveyed the endless rows of wooden boxes. There was a lot more to this job than she'd first thought.

'Are ye okay lassie, is it too much fur ye?'

Robyn nearly jumped out of her skin when she heard Clem cackle. 'It all depends on what the time limit is I suppose,' she frowned.

He led her to a small desk and pointed to a pile of exercise books. 'Jack's been coming here fur the last six months. He's bin scribbling notes, something there may help ye.'

Robyn started to leaf through pages of drawings and written descriptions. Small neat meticulous script leapt off the pages and it made her wonder what Jack was actually like.

'Lunch time, Robyn.' Stuart called a bit later. 'If you want to go out and stretch your legs feel free. I tend to work through. If you'd like to do that and finish earlier, you can.'

'I probably will most days, if that's okay, then I can get away before the main rush hour.'

'That's what I thought. When you're ready, come up and we'll do the paperwork. You can put it all on the PC at the same time.'

She gave an inward groan. Richard, bless him, had spent a good few hours over the last week, time he'd really have preferred to spend with Simone, showing her his MacBook. It had been an enormous help, but having no idea about the software she'd be using caused her palms to go clammy. She'd more or less stated that she could do whatever was needed at her 'interview'. Hopefully, her limited computer skills would be enough and she'd be able to decipher the programme. The fact that even the young Jack Frazer preferred to use pen and paper, didn't bode well.

Because she'd worked through, Robyn began her journey home an hour earlier, feeling quite pleased with herself. She'd managed to put all four of the staff's details onto the Mac. That was fairly easy. Feeling more confident she'd opened the main programme and played around with it for a while. Stuart Frazer looked over every so often and gave her a confident smile. Perhaps she did look like she knew what she doing and that had to be half the battle.

Tomorrow, she decided she would check Jack's notes and transfer them. Smiling into the steady flow of traffic, she felt happier. What she'd really like to do was sit in the barn and tell Shay about her day.

Instead, she told Simone and Richard, and their reactions and confidence boosting almost made up for him not being there.

'I'm going to get a flight home tomorrow,' Richard announced. 'I can get a couple weeks of full-time work before term starts.'

Robyn glanced at Simone, they had obviously discussed it earlier because her friend didn't look surprised, just a little sad. 'So, are you still planning on coming back at the end of October?'

He nodded. 'I'll have to bring some uni work, but that's okay. I can do it while Sim's at therapy.'

'Actually, I'm cutting down to two mornings a week,' she grinned. 'If Dad wasn't paying privately, I'd probably have only gone once or twice a week for the last few months.'

'You'd still be doing brilliantly,' Richard said. 'It's the way you are Sim, so focused about everything.'

'Hopefully, the frame will go soon as well. I've been practising with two short crutches and I could be down to one by Christmas. Pete and Maggie are so encouraging.'

'That's bloody marvellous,' Robyn smiled. 'Everything's going well for us.' Her voice hitched a little, which no one else noticed. Damn Shay, why hadn't he said when he'd be back?

* * *

The next three days only confirmed to Robyn that she'd made the right job choice. Meeting Stella Rhodes was a pleasant surprise. For some reason, she'd expected some friendly, mumsy type who liked baking and loved cleaning. This was not the case at all. On Tuesday morning, a young pretty dark-haired woman, wearing jeans and a David and Goliath hoodie, sought her out to say hello.

Guessing Stella to be around thirty, Robyn learned she had a one-year-old daughter and a husband, who was a Marine and currently overseas. On top of all that she was in the middle of an Open University degree. By the end of the morning, Robyn felt a new friendship had very definitely been forged.

Wednesday and Thursday morning were spent on the computer, with endless cups of tea and cakes provided by Stella. She'd been correct about the baking at least. Robyn began to think she was winning a huge victory when she read the first few pages of Jack's notes back to herself from the large monitor.

* * *

'What do you think then, hasn't he grown in the last few weeks?' Mara asked proudly, waiting for her brother's reaction.

Shay smiled at the squirming pink bundle. 'He's quite something.'

She looked at him a little oddly. 'Quite *something*, what exactly does that mean?'

Rebecca grinned. 'It means, his Uncle Shay thinks he's a gorgeous special little creature,' she leant across to give Mara a kiss. 'And his mummies can't wait to get him home.'

Mara tutted. 'You, I understand,' she said, looking fondly at her partner. 'But you my dear brother… your health check can't come quickly enough.'

'I'm going in today, but you know that, don't you?'

'Don't be cross Shayden. If you were stable, you wouldn't be frowning at me. I'm beginning to feel quite anxious about you.'

'For God's sake Mara, I'm not a machine.' He sucked in a long breath and watched as both pairs of eyes regarded him with curiosity. For the last few days, Shay had felt as if he was walking on a knife-edge. A complete health check was scheduled on the very day he was going to see Robyn. Real-time had gone out the window for this visit. He wanted to see her on the Thursday night, that way she'd have three days before going back to work. Three days to hate him, forget him, nurse a broken heart and deal with whatever else her emotions threw at her.

For him, he didn't want to forget and he certainly didn't want to revert back to how he'd been before he'd met her. He was coping, he got angry and yes, he felt like his own heart would never mend, but he wasn't about to run down the street waving an ancient meat cleaver and blaming it on his mental instability. Really, what was wrong with feeling a little more deeply than what was regarded as socially acceptable. 'I'm perfectly fine, don't concern yourselves.'

Mara looked slightly placated by this, but that was probably because she knew he was about to have a brain scan.

Becky saw right through him. Just like Adam, Tarro or any emotionally unstable person would. 'I like you better this way,' she whispered in his ear.

The 'invitation' for a mandatory health scan, stamped and initialled by Christopher Channing, was lying like confetti on the floor of the house that Shay shared with Adam and Adam's older brother, Hale. The living arrangements worked well, Hale preferring to work abroad, which suited Shay as it meant one less person close to him to make a fuss about the changes in his emotional state.

Not so the case with his sister. Meaning well, as Adam had predicted she would, Mara had responded to the health request on his behalf. The first and second date, he'd declined. It was only when he suspected Channing was going to make his life difficult, did he accept the third and final demand to present himself at the main centre.

Walking across the paved square, no less than five different holonotes sprung up in front of his eyes. He wanted to bat them away like pesky mosquitoes, but instead forced his hands into fists and kept them tightly in his pockets. It had been nearly three weeks since he'd seen Robyn. The emptiness he felt was unbearable and he still had to go and say goodbye. Adam had tried to convince him not to bother, constantly dropping reminders that she'd been dead for over two thousand years. The cowardly side of him wanted to cling on to that fact, but the side that loved her wouldn't allow it.

Both of his friends tried to be supportive in their own way. Tarro was a lot more sympathetic, he seemed to have developed a genuine soft spot for Robyn. Adam, on the other hand blatantly admitted to fancying her, Shay preferred not to listen to his suggestions or observations.

RESEARCH UNIT 18. The sign blazed in front of his eyes. Shay closed them for a second, pinched the bridge of his nose and summoned the detached demeanour that was expected. Large transparent doors seemed to melt as he walked through, only returning to their solid state the moment no human DNA was sensed. The temperature and air quality were suddenly as pleasant as a warm spring day. His usual was Lab 30, down the corridor, turn right, turn left, politely acknowledge the smiling medic and the one offering a seat. Don't let them know you'd really like to put your fist in their faces.

'Shayden Lomax, physically you're in perfect health, but as you must be aware, you're a little off the scale. Unusual for you, we can put it right in minutes.' The Medic showed him to a couch and asked him to lie down.

'What if I'm content the way I am?' He may as well have asked for the moon; the Medic's expression was so incredulous. 'If I don't give consent, you can't change anything, right?'

'Mr Lomax, I don't know what you mean.' He beckoned for help from his assistant, while all the time strategically positioning probes.

'I said *NO!*' Shay felt the instant the switch was flicked. He imagined his brain and the piece of his memory that carried his feelings for Robyn disappearing like wisps of candyfloss. Oh God, Robyn eating the fluffy mess and giggling as she pushed bits into his mouth. He pushed the equipment to one side and pulled off the probes, doing his best not to show anger. If Christopher Channing had been working today he'd be forced back onto the couch, for his 'own good' and he was certain the procedure would go ahead with or without consent.

'I really am well,' he said, trying to smooth over what was happening. 'You're right, I am a little off the scale,' he added, his acceptance appeasing them somewhat. 'But I believe it isn't a bad thing. I'll come back if it becomes a problem.'

There was a lot of head shaking and discussion. 'Mr Lomax,' one of them started to say. 'We can't just let you leave, only five percent of the balancing has been completed, it will make a difference, but not nearly enough.'

'You can't keep me either. Sorry guys.' He headed for the exit while they were in a nervous state of agitation. Really, he had to wonder at the stability of some of the actual practitioners.

Before any reports could be acted on, he made his way to Tarro's house and informed his friend he was going now, while he still could.

* * *

Robyn was in a deep sleep, so he'd have to wake her to say goodbye, neither of which felt right. The duvet was pushed down in a heap around her thighs, as the room was always too hot. For some reason, Simone's parents thought it would aid their daughter's recovery by keeping the place like a sauna. Perhaps Scotland in September felt chilly for West Country folk.

The Harry Potter pyjama top was the same one she'd worn on the first night they spent together in the B&B. It very nearly broke his reserve and fighting against reason, he was tempted to just ask her to run away into the annals of history somewhere. She might enjoy being a Victorian housewife or they could go further afield, catch a plane to America, disappear into the 1800s and become pioneers in the Wild West.

He gave a sigh, that wouldn't do. Robyn had a life to live here, there were descendants to produce, it wasn't for him to interfere. If he could get her to believe his emotions had been wiped, he may just survive this. It wasn't a total lie; the tiniest fraction had been blasted away, but thank God, the process had been stopped. He deserved to feel this, to hurt as she would be hurt.

Gently shaking her awake, he watched as her face went from confusion to joy, then back to confusion as he didn't share her welcoming smile. 'Put your dressing gown on, we need to talk somewhere away from the house.' He waited, seeing a thousand questions start to form, and dreaded everyone. 'Simone's in the house, isn't she?' He needed to know he could get her back again.

Robyn nodded, pulling on thick socks and fleece bottoms over her pyjamas. She didn't utter a sound as he whisked her away through the portal to a beach. A few remote houses nearby most likely housed the anchor. They could be anywhere at any time, but right now the only thing she cared about was what he was going to say.

'I've come to say goodbye.' He didn't, couldn't make eye contact. 'I'm very fond of you Robyn, but this is best for both of us.'

'You're *fond* of me? What's this about, why have you come in the middle of the night to tell me that?' She fell silent, forcing him to look up from the ground. 'I thought you loved me.' His deep brown eyes weren't exactly lifeless, as there was certainly regret lurking somewhere in the darkness, but the shining light was definitely switched off. A fat tear rolled down her cheek and she started to chew her bottom lip.

'Don't bite your lip,' he said softly, feeling surprised that he'd notice, let alone mention it with so much inner turmoil to control.

She felt a lighter tingle in her arms as Adam and Tarro appeared, both looking concerned. 'The cavalry's arrived,' Robyn said scornfully. She turned back to Shay, something about him was different. 'They've *fixed* you, haven't they? I didn't notice right away. How could you let them do that?' she shouted at Tarro, who'd started to move forward. 'He's your friend, doesn't he deserve to be happy?' She completely missed the puzzled expressions and Shay's warning look, telling them to keep quiet.

Moving quickly, they both took one of Shay's arms. 'I'm so sorry Robyn,' Adam said.

She watched and noticed Tarro hesitate, he looked like he wanted to say something, but obviously changed his mind. 'Then I've lost, I can't give a passionate argument to a man that doesn't care.'

'I *care*,' Shay said fiercely, composing himself quickly. 'Of course, I care,' he repeated, in a steadier voice. 'I'm looking at the bigger picture, for us both.'

Tarro was struggling, he wanted to scream the truth. 'Channing's got a lot to answer for,' he murmured quietly.

'It's fine really, everything's as it should be,' Shay replied.

'It's not fine,' Tarro growled. 'I know we told you things couldn't last with Robyn, but she was *your* choice, maybe it's possible…'

'No, it's *my* choice to walk away. It's the kindest thing to do.' His voice hitched at the end and he felt bewildered by his uncertainty.

Robyn put a hand on his cheek. 'Will I ever see you again?'

He shook his head. 'I don't think that would be a good idea.'

'Just *once* more, would you do that for me?'

'Robyn, no,' he said softly. 'What good would that do either of us?'

'I don't mean now. I want to see you before I die, as in, the day I die.' She watched him shake his head. 'Do this for me, *please*. Whatever happens in my life, I have to know that for eleven glorious weeks I loved you and the places we visited and things we did together were real. I… I'm afraid I'll forget, or, as I grow old, will think it was all a dream. I don't care how confused or frail I become and I don't care if I babble a lot of, what the nurses will call, nonsense, but I have to keep my own faith.'

'You won't know me in seventy or eighty years, I'm not sure it's a good idea.' It would mean he'd have to research the cause and date of her death, and he didn't want to go there. 'Are you talking real-time?'

'No Shay, not for this. Well, that is to say, for me, it will be. Hopefully, at least another eighty years. I intend to live till I'm one hundred.' She gave a small sad smile. 'I want to see you as you are now, so I'll know.' She touched his hand.

Shay turned his face and closed his eyes, the pain of her words burned through his whole body.

'You can do it tomorrow if you want, your tomorrow. Get it over with so to speak, then you really don't have to see me again. Please, Shay?' She hesitated. 'I want to be able to tell you I had a good life, so you don't spend the rest of yours feeling bad.' She gave a high hysterical laugh. 'Forget it then, if you don't want to do it. I'm being silly.'

'Yes,' he heard his voice somewhere in the distance. How could he not do this last thing? Even now, when he was saying goodbye, she was thinking of his well-being. 'If it's what you really want, then I'll do it.'

Adam was going to intervene but thought better of it, perhaps if Shay saw her as an old lady it would reinforce the inevitability of the situation.

The next thing Robyn knew they were all back in her bedroom. She reached up and pressed a light kiss to Shay's lips. 'Live well, think of me sometimes.' She turned and faced her dressing table, feeling the moment he left. Only then did she collapse on the bed and silently scream her heartbreak.

Shay let Adam and Tarro guide him back to the portal. *'Think of me sometimes'*, there wouldn't be a day in his life from now until he died that he wouldn't think of her.

'Why did you let her believe you'd been fixed?' Adam asked as soon as they were in the portal.

'It was the only way she'd accept what he said,' Tarro answered the question. 'And he was fixed a little, wasn't he?'

'Hardly,' Shay cut in, 'they took me down a few percent. I refused the rest. For a moment, I thought they were going to try and carry on regardless.'

'If Channing wins the next council elections, that's how things will be,' Adam growled. 'Are you alright my friend? Will you do what Robyn asked?'

'At the moment, I feel like I'll never be alright again. And yes, I'll do it I promised her. Not tomorrow, though. Not for a while. I guess... when I can face it.'

Tarro gave him an awkward hug. 'The worst part's over.'

'*Over*? It's just the beginning. Now I have to start living my life knowing she'll never be part of it.'

* * *

Waiting for Simone's therapy to finish, something occupational in the kitchen which involved boiling a kettle. Robyn took herself to the beach and walked her usual route across the rocks, as far as the incoming tide would allow. Most of the holidaymakers had long gone, schools were back to normal and the September visitors tended to stay nearer the town and harbour. The weather was turning, a continuous drizzle made the already slippery rocks even more hazardous. Giving into another bout of crying, she took to the safety of the flat sand and let the sea spray mingle with the already salty tears running down her cheeks.

With a huge sigh that even she recognised as despair, she climbed the cliff path and walked towards the comfort and wisdom of her best friend.

'Robz, I'm so sorry, what a complete bastard. How could he *do* that to you?' Simone struggled to her feet, using the armchair for support. Favouring her stronger left side, she listed slightly, giving the impression that she'd had one too many Jägerbombs, a one-time favourite drink of both the girls. 'I want to give you a hug, but I daren't let go.'

Robyn rushed across the room. 'Sit down, idiot. Shay certainly isn't worth falling flat on your face over. He's not a bastard, though,' she added quietly.

'Really? You're more forgiving than I would be.'

'He's got a point. I was fooling myself thinking we had a future together.'

With great self-control, Simone chose not to say what she really thought.

'Don't tell Rich right away. It's not a secret or anything, but give it a few days. Your mum will be hard enough.'

'I'll tell her to go easy,' Simone said, knowing exactly what Robyn meant.

'No, let her get it out the way in one fell swoop, I couldn't bear all the walking on egg shells for days in case she upsets me.'

'Dad won't understand what all the fuss is about,' Sim grimaced. 'He'll just say, 'They've only known each other five minutes' and 'plenty more fish in the sea'.'

Robyn managed a small smile. 'Clive isn't really known for his tact, is he?'

'No, wish I could say the same about his clichés.'

That managed to raise another smile. 'Think of a Disney film to watch Sim, I'll make us a cheese toasty.' Robyn walked to the kitchen unconsciously playing with the little silver rose that nestled at her throat. *I should really hide you away at the bottom of my jewellery box.*

Chapter Sixteen

*'Ne'er push a lassie tae dram if
she doesn't wantae.'*

After Shay's visit, Robyn phoned Stuart and asked if she could have the Monday off and work Friday instead. It gave her one extra day to pull herself together before having to pretend everything was normal. Maybe that was the point, things really were normal now. She didn't have a boyfriend who could materialise through portals in different time periods anymore.

Changing her days meant her path crossed with Jack when he came in for the afternoon. The first time she'd started to copy his work onto the Mac, she'd left a scrawled message on top of the open page, checking he was okay with it, and if so, would he be prepared to work with her and focus on specific items. He'd agreed, via a neatly written reply in his notebook. He'd also said he was looking forward to meeting her.

Jack was red-haired and blue-eyed like his father and grandfather and managed to make her laugh within the first ten minutes, something she hadn't done all week. Since then, they'd communicated by the odd text or written note, usually regarding a particular object in the ongoing cataloguing process.

The software programme Robyn used offered a large space for description. Uploading photos from her phone worked well, but a well-written paragraph was needed to accompany each item. That was where she hoped that Jack would help. He seemed to have the flair she lacked, even after completing one year of an English Literature degree. He could stick to the facts, yet make the most boring of clay pots come to life with his expressive and articulate prose. His hope was to become a writer and confessed to only having a passing interest in the work he did here, which was a reasonably interesting means to an end.

Robyn appreciated the honesty. He needed the money and was pleased to help his father, but as soon as uni was finished, he'd be pursuing a career with a publishing firm in America, one he was already in contact with.

Telling Simone about Jack had made her realise that she envied someone who was so driven and focussed. Never having an end goal was probably why she was floundering so badly in the aftermath of her breakup from Shay. The job helped, it just didn't replace the large void she felt so acutely.

By the middle of her fourth week at work, and nearly three weeks since Shay had said goodbye, Robyn was still wearing her necklace and still crying, albeit in private, and her affirmations that she was fine weren't working.

Simone didn't know how to make things right. She tried even harder to walk with one stick, maintaining that she'd be better company if she could be more independent.

Also, Stuart Frazer wanted to know where the bright-eyed, keen as mustard, lassie had gone. He may not have known her long, but both he and Stella were quite aware that she was desperately unhappy.

* * *

'Robyn, will you come to the office later when you have a minute?' Stuart's voice crackled over the ancient intercom system.

She put the notebook down, chuckling at the funny picture of Clem that Jack had drawn. He must have come in for a few hours the evening before. He did that sometimes, and occasionally they overlapped before she left work at the end of the day.

Should she go straight upstairs? She shrugged and moved between the aisles, dragging a cushion. He'd said later, so best to crack on here for an hour. The floor-level boxes were the worst. It was easier to sit cross-legged and join them, rather than lift and carry each individual box to the desk.

'I thought I may find you down here still.'

Robyn looked up questioningly at Stuart. 'Was I meant to be doing something else? Oh damn,' she looked at her watch. 'You wanted me in the office, didn't you? I completely lost track of time.'

'No problem,' he said, and knelt gingerly on the floor next to her, unable to ignore the dust that began to swirl and cling to his black trousers. 'I shall tell Stella to bring her duster to this area if it's where you're working. He noticed her sad smile, something was definitely wrong. 'Robyn, lass, I haven't known you very long, so forgive me if I'm speaking out of turn.' He hesitated, unsure of how to proceed. 'Did something happen after your first week here? Have you changed your mind about working with us perhaps, and you don't know how to tell me?' He was completely dismayed when she burst into tears and giving her a consoling pat on the back, resorted to waiting patiently until she was ready to speak.

'It's not the job, really, I love it here,' she sobbed.

'Shay, or your friend in the wheelchair?' he offered tentatively.

'Simone's not in the chair now, well hardly ever. She's doing really well. It's Shay, we've... split up.'

'Ah.' Stuart went quiet. A father of four boys, he felt somewhat out of his depth. 'I'm sorry to hear that, is there anything I can do?'

Not unless you can transport yourself to 4433 and bring him back to me. 'No, thank you, Stuart, it won't affect my work, don't worry.'

He clicked his tongue with exasperation. 'I'm not worried about that; your work is faultless. Look, lass, we've just moved house recently. Moira, my wife, has been going on about a house warming so we're having a small party on Saturday. Nothing special, everyone from work, except Clem who never comes to anything, will be there. You can meet Mac... Mr MacDonald. Bring Simone, if she's able. Jack will be there with a couple of his friends.' He looked at her questioningly. 'Have you been out much since Shay, um, left?'

'Not really, it's a kind offer. I just don't think I'll be up to parties for a while. I do appreciate the invite, though.'

'Party isn't really the *right* word, just a social get together. Bring Joe as well, the twins are about his age.'

'You have twins?' Robyn perked up a bit.

'Stephen and Andrew,' he grinned. 'They'll be fourteen on Christmas Eve. That was quite a year I can tell you. My father had to cook the turkey!'

Imagining the somewhat eccentric Angus Frazer getting to grips with a turkey and producing a full Christmas roast caused a small giggle.

'We had haggis stuffing,' Stuart laughed. 'He'll be coming and I'm sure he'd enjoy seeing the laddie again.' He gave her a comforting smile. 'Do think about it at least?'

Robyn nodded. She'd never thought for a moment that the photos of various aged, red-haired, cheeky faced boys in the office, must all be his offspring. Next time she went up to use the computer, she'd have a closer look at them. 'Three sons?' she asked with a smile.

'Four actually, Alec's my eldest, he's on his fourth gap year. A bit of a rogue, albeit a loveable one. Thankfully, he's in Borneo at the moment, working at an orangutan rescue centre.'

'*Thankfully*, why do you say that?'

'Because Robyn, if he saw a bonnie lass like you, he'd soon be spinning tales of magical faraway places. You'd have a backpack strapped on before you could say Timbuktu, ready to join him on his latest jaunt.' He gave a sigh. 'Each time he runs out of money and comes home, he stays a month or two and then goes off again, usually with some poor lass in tow.'

Robyn actually laughed, she was sure the stories were embellished for her amusement and they were doing the trick. Stuart had no idea that the things she'd heard and the places she'd been would make Alec's idea of excitement pale into insignificance. 'I will come, thank you. I'll do my best to persuade Sim. Joe won't need asking twice, he hasn't stopped talking about Angus since the afternoon at the loch.'

'Good, that's settled then.' He got up to leave, then turned and looked down at her. Clearing his throat, he said a little awkwardly. 'I can't imagine what Shay's reasons were, but to coin a favourite phrase of my father's, th' Sassenach jimmy doesn't hae a brain in his heid.'

Robyn looked dumbfounded for a moment. She watched Stuart walk away and once again, now she was left alone, her smile disappeared. *Shay where are you and what are doing now?*

* * *

Shay carried out his designated work like an automaton, his friends always close by. The powers that be had wanted to split the trio, feeling sure they'd all known about and then covered up what was going on. When Shay, even in his logical and sensible mindset, had refused to work with anyone else, and Adam and Tarro had threatened to 'go on strike', they'd backed down and continued to keep a close watch on all their movements instead.

'Do you think my agreeing to see her again one day, will affect her life?' Shay asked.

'Not *again*, give it a rest,' Adam moaned. 'You're talking about her waiting around for seventy or eighty years, for a death bed appearance. Robyn's too full of life for that.'

Tarro collected the last specimen and looked around the mounting pile of carnage. 'Adam's right, she's not going to sit vigil in the wheatfield. If you're so concerned, you should have thought more at the beginning, when you chose to share a lot more than bodily fluids.'

Adam laughed out loud, then seeing Shay's stricken expression, reined himself back in. 'I suppose you could be the cause of her dedicating her life to discovering time travel, but I seriously doubt it.'

'Come on, let's get out of here, these magnetised fields give me the creeps.' Tarro glanced around uneasily, 'I hate the end of the twenty-eighth century.' The other two nodded in agreement. The researchers had done their jobs well. The area was safe, but knowing the tiniest magnetically charged explosion would wipe out every form of life within a twenty-mile radius made them uncomfortable.

The DNA samples from this time period would not be used in conjunction with their own. The scientists would tear them apart, comparing every fibre of every strand with samples from previous years. Quite what they hoped to identify, he wasn't sure, but if things didn't improve, if no breakthrough was discovered, it was quite likely the human race would be totally eliminated well within the next few hundred years.

Shay began to think about Robyn's request. It was three weeks since he'd last seen her and the promise was playing on his mind. He would do it... soon. One of the reasons his travelling activity had flagged up as a warning, was not only because he'd visited the same time period so frequently, but also because he hadn't gone through the scanners as often as he should. He'd thought by avoiding them he was maintaining some secrecy, but he should have known the likes of Christopher Channing would spot his error.

Even following a short visit to the past, every traveller was required to walk through one of the many body scanners. Any anomalies, even the weakest common cold virus, would show up immediately, and in most cases, were treated effectively, there and then.

Other problems, such as the ones that Tarro or Adam sometimes acquired, due to their love for nineteenth-century whorehouses, meant a visit to the lab. Regardless of the number of times they went for the simple but thorough eradication treatment, it didn't curtail their fondness or patronage of the Regency and Victorian brothels.

Condoms were a thing of the past; STDs had died out over nine hundred years back. Shay hadn't given it a thought when he'd been with Robyn, and it was one of the reasons she was now frantically working out dates in her head.

* * *

Shopping in the local supermarket for a decent bottle of wine and some chocolates to take to the housewarming, Robyn decided to stock up on toiletries. They were much cheaper here than the small local shop and offered more variety. She spotted Simone's favourite bubble bath, and pleased that her friend was more than a little excited about the party tonight, decided to treat her. It was only as she passed the rows of sanitary products and automatically reached for her usual brand that she froze.

I was due days ago. Robyn shook her head. *I'm never late.* Grabbing the box, she thrust it purposefully in the trolley with the other shopping, then hurried down the aisle to the checkout. Look, she felt like saying to the checkout girl, I'm buying tampons, that's because I can't possibly be pregnant. I'm on the pill for fuck's sake.

Putting the bags in the boot of the Audi, Robyn's head was swimming with dates and numbers. She turned around, went back inside the shop, marched to the aisle that housed the Paracetamol, grabbed two packets and a pregnancy testing kit, and made a beeline for the self-service checkout. The checkout girl didn't need to witness this purchase.

An hour later she sat on her bed, not quite daring to turn the stick over. *It's the stress of the new job or the upset of Shay going. I've hardly eaten anything since he left.* When she ran out of reasons for her period being late, she turned the stick and stared at the evidence. How could one tiny pink cross, mean so much? *I'm pregnant,* she thought matter-of-factly, amazed at herself for not going into a blind panic. She knew instinctively when it had happened. *The Northern Lights, it had to be then.* She wondered where the tiniest flicker of excitement had just come from. *I was so sick that day, after the BBQ, no wonder my pill didn't work.*

For a few minutes, she allowed herself the luxury of thinking only of Shay's child. Reality would hit soon enough, she hugged her arms around her body, imagining the life inside. *You did change the past Shay.* While she understood the impossibility of their continued relationship, the fact that he might have tried a little harder gnawed away. She loved him and now would have a constant reminder. 'Would it have made a difference?' she asked out loud.

* * *

'Not drinking Robyn?' Jack asked, a little surprised.

'Regretfully not, I'm driving,' she smiled back.

'Hmm, leave the car and get a taxi,' he suggested.

'Oh yes, do that Robz,' Simone urged. 'It's just what you need, a chance to let your hair down and go a bit wild.' If she felt awkward getting in and out of a taxi with crutches, so what, her friend needed cheering up.

'Not today, with my boss and his family. It's too far from here anyhow, it'll cost a fortune.' The excuses were lame, Jack's friends would think she was really boring, not to mention Jack himself.

'Ne'er push a lassie tae dram if she doesn't wantae,' Angus said, suddenly looming behind his grandson.

She gave him a grateful smile, perhaps he'd seen a sign of quiet desperation in her face. Jack shrugged, saying no more about it. Simone didn't accept things quite so readily. Robyn knew there'd be a reckoning later. Quite what she was going to share, wasn't certain at this point.

Where Angus went, Joey followed, and in turn Stephen and Andrew.

'Th' laddie haes made some freish mukkers.'

Simone's mouth fell open. She stared at Angus; he could have been speaking Chinese and she'd have had no more idea of what he'd just said.

'I think Joe's made friends with the twins,' Robyn explained sagely.

'Okay, good. Do they all speak like that at Frazer's?'

'God, *no*. Well, that's not true, Clem does a little I suppose and the odd '*bonnie lassie*' slips in here and there, even from Stella,' Robyn grinned. 'You haven't met her yet, she's really cool, did I tell you she has a baby.'

Simone nodded, not really that interested in the mention of an infant. 'I think that's it over there, the one crying.'

'*It*, is a girl, Annabel actually. I quite like babies,' she added.

'Since *when*? You wouldn't even consider that babysitting scheme I wanted us to look into a few years back.'

Shifting uncomfortably, Robyn threw herself back into the conversation with Jack and his uni friends. They seemed a nice bunch. Two girls, who had immediately wanted to know all the ins and outs of Simone's accident, and for once, Simone didn't mind reliving it all. It had made Robyn realise that she'd said nothing about the night Shay took her to watch the whole thing. If tonight was the chosen time for confessions, the least she could do was explain that the accident was all due to an errant fox.

Jack's other friends consisted of his long-term best mate and two other lads from his present course. As Robyn and Simone were the new 'single girls', they were both getting a lot of attention. Simone had mentioned Richard's name three times, but a 'sort of' boyfriend 600 miles away in Devon, was not considered a threat.

Jack looked anxiously at Robyn, eventually muscling in to stand next to her. 'I'm sorry about them, I did say you're just out of a relationship.'

'It's okay, they're harmless,' she smiled, thinking of her new precious secret. If they had any inclination about that, they'd run a mile.

'You know Robyn, my dad's been talking about you a lot the last couple of days. I think he's hoping we're going to get together.' He looked a little uncomfortable as he spoke.

She stifled a laugh. 'Well, you obviously don't feel the same way?'

'Christ, I didn't mean it like that, not like it sounded. It's not that I wouldn't... it's just that... aw hell.' He stopped, not knowing what to say.

'The last thing I want or need is another boyfriend, but another *friend* would be great. If you'd like us to do something together, some time, I'd be well up for it.'

Jack beamed. 'Good, that's great. In fact, I know you like historical sites and Beth,' he indicated to one of the girls talking to Simone, 'is doing a story involving druid stuff for her dissertation. We're going to visit a couple of places west of here tomorrow, Sunhoney and Tomnaverie stone circles, would you like to come?'

Robyn's interest lay more in proper structures, castles and old churches, but she appreciated the offer. 'Are you sure I won't be playing gooseberry?' she teased. Beth was constantly throwing glances at the two of them.

'Err definitely not. Been there done that.'

'Jack really, how disrespectful, that's no way to talk,' she giggled.

'No, I suppose you're right. Robyn, lass, you would be doing me a favour if you came. I'll ask Joanne as well, safety in numbers and all that. We could pick you up, I'll take Dad's car.'

'Go on then,' she agreed. 'Not too early, though.'

Robyn left Simone with Jack's group and walked over to spend some time with Stella. She almost felt a pull towards Annabel. Strange really, because Simone was absolutely correct, she'd had no interest in babies or toddlers whatsoever until today. The little girl was asleep at last. Just as well, asking to hold her might be one step too far. Simone would know for sure something wasn't right.

By the end of the evening, Robyn had spoken to everyone. She'd spent a long while chatting with Stuart and Moira, and as quickly as possible with Mr MacDonald, without being rude. She couldn't quite see herself calling him Mac, not that he'd invited it.

'I thought *'dour Scot'* was just an expression,' she whispered to Simone. 'Honestly, he didn't smile once. I'm going to stay well away from the office when he comes in to do the accounts next week.'

'He's a staunch Presbyterian.' Jack said, joining them. 'Very religious. He's okay really, just as you see him now, never any different. I've met him from time to time over the years and I can honestly say, I don't ever think I've heard that man laugh.' Jack turned to Simone, 'The Twins have asked your brother to stay the night. I can drop him back tomorrow when I pick Robyn up if that's okay?'

Pick Robyn up? She waggled her eyebrows at her friend, seeing the returned look of denial and slight frustration. *That's a shame, he'd be just right.* 'Yeah that's fine,' she nodded. 'I'll let my mum know.'

They sat together in the parked car a little way from the house and looked out at the night sky, as the moonlight dappled the dark ocean. 'I want to tell you a couple of things Sim.'

'Has Shay been in touch?' She would have kicked herself if only her legs moved more independently as she saw her friend's face immediately screw up with anguish. 'Oh shit, I'm sorry you just seemed a bit different tonight, almost happier.'

Robyn took a deep breath and related everything about the night that Simone was hit by a car and explained what led to her awful injury. 'So, you see Sim, it *was* an accident.'

'I feel *so* much better knowing. Dad's the one that really needs to hear it, though. If only there was some way to put his mind at rest.'

'That's impossible, unless'... Robyn hesitated and gave a quick smile. 'How about you have a revelation, an epiphany in the memory department.' She tapped Simone's head.

'*Ow*, what are talking about?'

'You start remembering stuff about that night. You saw the fox, right?'

'I... did? *Yes*, I did. I saw a fox dart out from the other side of the road, umm... the car stopped, someone got out and then everything went black. How's that?'

'It's a work in progress.' Robyn grinned. 'Once you can tell them like you're not reading it from a script, I think Babs and Clive, especially Clive, will be much more likely to finally put it all to rest.'

'Fancy Shay taking you to see that? It was really thoughtful of him. Umm, Robz, about... Jack?'

'I think he could become a close friend, maybe, which brings me on to the next thing. I only found out today, so don't have a go.' She paused for a moment, closed her eyes and blurted it out. 'I'm pregnant. I think it happened just after the BBQ.'

'Bloody *Hell*, I wasn't expecting *that*!' Simone looked at her friend thoughtfully. 'Hence the no alcohol and the fussing over Stella's kid. You don't exactly look upset?'

'I'm in shock actually, but no I don't think I'm upset at all.'

'It won't bring him back, Robz,' Simone said gently.

'I know. Not a word to Babs, or anyone else for that matter, not yet. I need to sort my head out first.' Before Simone could say anything else, Robyn slammed the Audi into reverse and pulled away from the cliff edge.

The girls remained silent for the rest of the journey home.

* * *

The afternoon with Jack, Joanne and Beth turned out to be good fun. Once Beth understood that Robyn had no interest in Jack, she couldn't have been nicer. 'Some people can feel vibrations.' She gushed excitedly, starting to hug all the stones in turn. 'You have to be 'one' with nature and all the forces.'

'What people?' Jack scoffed. 'You've been watching too much television lass.' He looked at Robyn and rolled his eyes. 'She was a crazy bitch when we were going out?' he murmured quietly. 'Always going on about alien abductions and stuff.'

'Strange things happen.' Robyn grinned.

'Yeah well, not *that* strange.'

The second stone circle visit didn't have the same impact in Robyn's opinion. She'd liked the wooded copse of trees by Sunhoney. Climbing the hill to reach these was exhausting, and although the weather was still reasonable, there was a cold wind that caught them by surprise at the top. She noticed, with some amusement, that Beth didn't bother to partake in anymore hugging that afternoon.

'Obviously, being '*one*' with nature is dependent on the climate,' she joked quietly to Jack.

'A fair-weather friend of the stones,' he laughed.

By the time she'd got home, had supper, spent some more time talking to Simone – who had been surfing birth sites and become a midwifery expert – Robyn was ready to collapse into bed. Her nightly ritual of holding herself still and waiting to see if any tingles started in her fingers, always had the same empty result. She watched the darkness, trying to see a slight movement of air, falling asleep long before Shay looked in on her. It was only the second time he'd done it. He only stayed for the briefest of moments, and told himself again, that apart from his promised deathbed visit, this had to be the last time.

* * *

Robyn opened a box housing some Tudor spoons. Her mind wandered back to Stratford-upon-Avon, and as always, to Shay. She'd spent many nights crying herself to sleep, thinking about what might have been. Places they could have visited together, famous people she might have seen from the hidden depths of a crowd. Who wouldn't be upset to have a carrot dangled and then watch as it was wrenched away?

She knew that wasn't the real reason she was still finding it so hard, the loss wasn't the time travelling, it was the time traveller. She'd fallen in love with Shay, the whole package just made it a bit more exciting.

Jack took her out sometimes to the cinema or sightseeing. By mutual consent, their relationship was strictly friends only, which suited them both. Jack had no hidden agenda, and his offer of friendship was a genuine one. The problem was, Robyn found that forgetting her troubles for brief interludes only made it worse when she was alone and had to confront them again.

Richard came for his promised visit and Simone positively blossomed. Only needing one stick, she was forging ahead stoically with total independence her goal. Neither Richard nor Robyn ever doubted she'd make it by Christmas.

Jack and Richard hit it off immediately, Stuart suggested Robyn take a week's leave and the four of them enjoyed a few days out together. Simone promised not to tell Richard about the pregnancy, but Robyn could see how difficult it was for her to remain silent. Soon, it wouldn't matter, she'd be showing, unless her choice of clothing made sure the tiny bump remained invisible.

Another month passed, and by Robyn's calculations, Shay's baby – as she always thought of it – was around twelve weeks' gestation. Evening walks to the beach, meant she could pass the barn on the way, climb the ladder, wrap a blanket around herself and sit quietly. Once or twice she felt sure her fingers started to twitch, but when nothing happened, she knew it was just wishful thinking.

The day she drove for five solid hours to the wheatfield to take one look at the ploughed rows of mounds and furrows convinced her, things had to change. Somewhere in the middle of all the mud was a portal, which she was unable to find and couldn't activate anyway, so why had she come?

'I'm going to have our baby, what do you think of that?' She shouted out across the desolate earth, willing the words to find their way to him, but only succeeding in frightening a few starlings. 'How do you like them apples?' she muttered, stumbling back to the lane and letting the cool wind dry the tears that were escaping down her cheeks.

She wouldn't allow herself to look in the direction of the barn when she got back. *I've got my friends. Stella has a young child and manages to work, I'll be okay...ish, with the help of Dad's money.* She thought briefly of her father, would he have been disappointed? Would he have liked Shay? Robyn couldn't allow herself to think of the negatives, there was time enough for that later. For now, getting some medical advice, which meant registering with a doctor, was the first thing to do. Something had happened that day, which finally helped her draw a line underneath the most wonderful summer that she'd most likely experience in the whole of her lifetime. Now she had to look forward, not back. Next summer she'd have a baby, what could be better than that?

Chapter Seventeen

'Everything we do alters history a tiny bit.'

Rebecca waited until Shay finally stopped pacing and sat down. Only then did she carefully lay the infant in his arms. 'So, what do you think, *Uncle*?' she asked, keen to hear his reply.

He studied the tiny features of the sleeping baby. Made up of joint DNA from his sister and her partner, plus a mix of whatever samples the lab had used from the past, he wondered if a higher percentage of this generation, his little nephew included, would grow strong and reach adulthood. 'He's a fine boy, perhaps some strong warrior genes course through him? Fascinating how one can see a likeness in such a small child. He favours you, I think.'

'I thought so too. I could just cuddle him to death, isn't he the most precious, wonderful thing?' Rebecca enthused.

He was momentarily taken aback by her emotional outburst. 'How does it work, between the two of you?' he said, and then paused. 'Sorry I shouldn't have asked that, forgive me.'

'Do you want some diagrams, Shay?' she laughed.

'No, I don't mean *that*.' Feeling acutely embarrassed, he saw the teasing glint in her eye. 'I meant with my sister being so stable and you being so...'

'Being so hypersensitive,' she cut in. 'Go on say it.' She studied him carefully and knew what this was really about. 'It's hardly unusual. In fact, I think mixed emotional couples do better. Mara keeps me on the straight and narrow, and I like to think I bring her joy and make life a little unpredictable at times. Buried emotions can be brought to the surface, you should know that better than most. You miss her, don't you?'

He blew out a breath and nodded. 'I do, it's like a pain that won't go away. The day they started to fix me in the lab made a difference. Just knocking me back down a few percent altered the way I felt. Still,' he mused, 'perhaps it was for the best, I don't know if I'd have had the strength to say goodbye otherwise.'

'The pain you're feeling is love.'

'It's strange, I'm aware of how much I felt, and it's kinda like it's still there... but not.' He gave a frown of frustration. 'I don't know how to describe it.'

She smiled at his use of the word 'kinda'. Unlike his two friends, Shay had never before adopted words or phrases from the past. 'Have you gone back yet?'

There was silence for a few moments before admitting he had. 'Only twice, just for a few minutes, both times when she's been asleep. Don't repeat it in front of Adam or Tarro, they don't know. It has come to an end, I've accepted that much.'

Rebecca took the sleeping baby and put him in the crib. 'It's for the best, even though I'm a huge advocate of true love. If you'd wanted to make the supreme sacrifice and live with her, it would never have been allowed. You'd be bound to alter the past somehow and you probably wouldn't survive, truth be told, too many germs and other nasty things. I'm sorry for you,' she took his hands in her own. 'I think you do still love her, desperately. It's just buried away like everything else you're not supposed to feel. Look inside yourself, Shay.'

'I can't, I *daren't*. I know what I'll find.'

Mara joined them, bringing a tray of hot drinks and biscuits. 'Did I miss much? You two seemed to be having a very *intimate* discussion!' She narrowed her eyes and scrutinised them as if waiting for one to confess to some misdemeanour.

'Your brother thinks our son, looks like me,' Rebecca said smugly. 'With a bit of Attila the Hun thrown in.'

'Attila the Hun! You'd better be *joking*,' she shrieked, rushing over to the crib to see if she could spot some telltale sign. 'What samples did they use? I shall demand to know.'

Rebecca started to giggle, 'An emotive outburst, I love it.' Mara couldn't help herself and started to laugh as well.

Shay got up as the two young women cooed over their baby and wondered if he would ever have a wife and family of his own. 'I should go,' he said quietly, hoping to slip away. He knew Mara had more to say and, he had so far managed to avoid another confrontation. Today, it wasn't to be.

'Hang on, not so fast. Have you thought any more about what I asked? Please Shay, at least consider it. Just a few more percent, you don't have to go all the way if you don't want to. I hate seeing you fight this constant battle with yourself and it would stop some of the misgivings.'

'Channing, you mean,' He spat the word out. 'I don't give a fuck what he thinks.'

Mara's lips tightened as she saw Rebecca silently applaud her brother's defiance. 'I don't like him either, but his popularity is growing and the council elections are due soon. It's almost certain he'll win. You have to be seen to maintain normality. Get rid of that silly bird on your wrist, it would go a long way to proving your stability is within normal parameters.'

'Give it a rest Mara,' he fought down the faint stirrings of anger at the mention of the tattoo. 'I know you mean well, but just don't interfere.'

'I'm worried sick if you must know, I can't bear the thought of them forcing you.' She burst into tears. 'Now look what you've made me do!'

Shay took a few steps towards his sister and folded her in his arms. 'I know you care about me, don't worry, okay. Now then, before I leave, what are you going to call my nephew?'

Mara had to accept that was the end of the conversation for now. Who'd have thought her little brother would fall in love so deeply with someone who was forever out of reach. For his sake, he needed to come to his senses.

Rebecca smiled, happy to follow Shay's lead and steer away from the controversial subject. 'Like everything else, we can't agree. I want a long meaningful name, like Gabriel or Alexander. Mara prefers short and to the point, Dan, Ben or Joe.'

He grimaced slightly at the mention of the name Joe, why did everything seem to link him back to Robyn? 'I rather like Gabriel,' he offered, swiftly.

* * *

Adam and Tarro had taken it upon themselves to research Robyn's date and hopefully her time of death. Shay had made no move to do it himself but was still adamant he was going to keep his word. They had come to the conclusion that he didn't want to face the finality of his relationship. The sooner Shay could be persuaded to fulfil his promise and visit her for the last time, the sooner it could be put to rest.

'Here,' Tarro handed his friend a couple of discs, 'there can't be that many Robyn Harleys alive in 2016. When was her date of birth?'

'How the hell should I know,' Adam growled. 'She had a birthday, didn't she? Shay gave her earrings.'

'You noticed them then,' Tarro smirked.

'Only because she nearly wore them to that blasted mediaeval visit.'

'Yeah well, your unwelcome appearance in her bedroom probably buggered up her preparation. I bet it wasn't only her *ears* you were checking out that day.' He cast a look of disgust.

'Stop glowering, you're asking for a thump.' They squared up to each other, a common occurrence between the two, often volatile, friends. It was only when one of the discs bleeped that their attention wavered.

'Twenty, she was twenty in... umm... August, which makes her date of birth sometime in...'

'1996,' they said in unison. 'And here she is,' Adam grinned, starting to read the information available. He recoiled, a look of horror spreading across his face. When Tarro asked, he shook his head and babbled something incoherently.

'What?' He pushed Adam away from the holoscreen and read the same words for himself. 'Holy *hell*, Shay's not going to like this.'

* * *

Robyn answered the Skype call with some trepidation. If her calculations were correct and it had been the night of the Northern Lights, she was sixteen weeks pregnant. So far only Simone knew. She'd registered with the Harmons' GP and made an appointment for the following week. After that, she'd promised her friend to come clean. Now all she needed, was to keep the news from her mother for one more week.

'Darling, how are you?' Josie asked, sounding a little jittery.

Robyn fixed a smile on her face and tried to get a word in between the barrage of questions and news from

263

home. In the end, she gave up, actually quite grateful to just listen.

'I need your measurements, remember.' Josie's one-sided conversation continued. 'You and Richard will be the witnesses, *obviously*. Have you got over the boyfriend thing yet? Are you still getting on well with Jack?'

Robyn could detect something in her mother's look. Amongst all the quick-fire chatter, a hint of anxiety perhaps? 'It's all good. Jack's great, he's just a friend, I told you that.'

'Umm, yes fine Robyn, I… have some news and it's rather wonderful. You must keep an open mind, though. You're almost the first to know, well after Steven and the Doctor,' she said, giving a nervous laugh.

'The *doctor*, you're worrying me now, what's wrong?'

'Nothing's wrong, I said it was wonderful. I-I'm pregnant, only just I think. Well, I'm not sure. I have a scan booked for next week. I thought it was the *change*.' She whispered the word as if she'd mentioned something sinister.

It took a few seconds for Robyn to comprehend what she'd just heard. This was meant to be *her* news; the conversation was around the wrong way. 'Oh, my God, that's… great. Are you sure you're okay?'

'Absolutely, and apparently, forty-three isn't so old these days.'

'No, I suppose it isn't.' This would have been a prime moment to slip her own pregnancy into the mix, but the words wouldn't come out. She'd stick to her plan and see the doctor first, it wasn't much longer to wait. Shutting her laptop, she went to share the latest gossip.

Simone was having a soak in the bath with bubbles, candles and a book. Robyn thought better of disturbing her, it could wait till later. Wrapped up with a scarf and hat, she headed outside, bumping into Joey as he hurried from Clive's car to get into the warm. Now Simone was so far on with her recovery, Clive had taken a step back and was giving his son the much-needed time he'd promised.

'Don't be too long dear,' Babs called after her. 'The weather's getting worse and it's already starting to get dark.' Her small figure stood in the welcoming light of the kitchen doorway.

Robyn gave them all a quick wave. 'Half an hour tops.' She let the wind carry her voice back.

The Mackay brothers climbed the cliff path with an armful of driftwood each. Robyn stood back to let them pass. Since the summer, she'd bumped into them frequently. Back then, it was gathering for early evening parties and BBQs. Now apparently, winter was the best time for beachcombing, or so they'd informed her.

'Alright, Robyn? You've left it a bit late, be careful the sea's rough as hell and the wind's a bitch. Perhaps you'd be best off giving it a miss.'

'You may be right, James,' she smiled. 'I'll just make it a quick one, ten minutes.'

They looked dubious. 'The tide's been running high, luckily this lot didn't get swept out in the backwash,' he looked with satisfaction at the pile of wood he carried, seeing each green damp piece as a unique object or sculpture.

'You'll transform that into something wonderful I bet.' The items in the shop window always drew customers in. 'Do you make furniture to order?'

'Yeah, all the time, coffee tables are very popular. Do you want to commission us?' he grinned.

'Could you make a baby's crib, do you think?' She looked at the smooth pieces of misshaped wood, trying to imagine the finished thing, complete with a peacefully sleeping infant.

'I don't see why not, I'll do some sketches. Come down to the shop next week and we'll talk about it.' They watched her descent anxiously for a few minutes, before continuing upwards to the car park.

With the tide going out, it didn't occur to Robyn that she'd be in any danger as long as she kept well back. The rock pools were uncovered, but for once looked dark and sinister under the stormy twilight sky. Climbing onto the first rock, she stood and watched the ocean. The waves were quite magnificent, much too far away to be of any concern, or so she thought. With care, a few more steps would take her to the larger pool. She slipped twice, cursing into the wind. The third time her ankle wrenched. *This really was a crap idea.*

An evening of sitting in the warm with Simone and listening to the wind howling outside sounded perfect. You had to do something like this first to really appreciate a huge mug of hot chocolate and marshmallows. She took her phone out to send Simone a text, '**get the milk on my luvver**'.

A selfie of her and Shay sitting behind a smoky fire and pointing at a cooked trout shone into the surrounding darkness. Not only had she not deleted it, she'd kept it as her locked screen picture. She burst into tears. Her ankle hurt, it had got dark a lot sooner than she'd expected and the last wave had crashed and sent angry looking foam all the way to her feet. The elation she'd felt in the first few minutes was fast changing to apprehension. What *had* she been thinking?

Struggling back over the last rock towards the sand, her ankle turned again and she dropped the phone. The picture of Shay faded. There was no way in hell was she going to lose that. Reaching down, the wash from another wave caused her to overbalance. Robyn gave a gasp of surprise and cried out. Just before she fell and everything went black, there was a sensation of being underwater.

James was about to get into his car when he heard a faint noise above the wind. His brother had already started back to the top of the cliff path.

* * *

Shay guarded himself the moment he saw his friends walking purposely toward him.

'You're not going to like what I'm about to tell you. Actually, I've been in two minds whether or not to even mention it, but you'll find out for yourself anyway,' Adam said.

Impatience was another reaction Shay often seemed to be dealing with these days. 'You're obviously going to say it, so come on.'

'I hate the way that you're suffering over Robyn, you don't seem to want to get over it, or maybe you don't know how? You were such good fun after you met her. You were a different person Shay, it seemed right somehow like that's how you were meant to be.'

'Look I miss her okay, and I am experiencing sadness, a lot if you must know. Just don't expect me to drown in my own tears. This is what I am, nothing you can do will change it. What *exactly* do the two of you want?'

'We've been checking out the longevity of our anchors for the early twenty-first-century time period.' Tarro gave a nervous smile, Shay wasn't looking at all pleased. 'Adam's found himself a thirty-year-old centenarian, who never leaves Inverness, so we've got a seventy-year window from that one. Oh, Christ,' he paused. 'I don't know how to tell you this, it's Robyn.'

Shay felt a chill spread through his body. 'You researched the date of her death, when I specifically asked you not to. Don't give me all the bullshit about anchors, this was what it was about all the time.'

'You know she's long dead anyway, so it makes no difference.' He shook his head, 'I'm sorry my friend.'

'What happens to her, and when?' Tarro didn't answer. 'I said *what* happens?' Shay started to shake, he grabbed hold of Tarro's arm.

'It's silly really, she drops her phone, slips on seaweed and falls into a rock pool.'

'*AND?*'

'And she doesn't get up again, and then, err.'

'WHAT THE HELL HAPPENS, TARRO?'

'A bloody big wave, that's what.'

'How come you know all that *detail*?' Shay took a step back. 'Those things wouldn't be recorded.' He studied the faces of his friends, they both looked way too guilty. 'You've seen it, you sons of bitches, you've gone ahead and watched her die.'

'We knew you'd ask,' Adam stopped to wipe his eyes. 'I've never wanted to help so much in all my life.'

'But instead, you watched it play to its final conclusion. How could you?'

'We can't... *you* can't change the past Shay. Robyn was there on her own. It was quick, she must have knocked herself out. If the wave hadn't come, she'd have drowned anyway.'

'What was she doing, before she slipped?'

'I don't know what you mean, she was just sort of pottering about, looking at her phone.'

'She was crying,' Tarro butted in, ignoring the warning look that Adam gave him.

Shay put his head in his hands and moaned, had she been crying because of him? It had to be so. His careful resolve to remain stable melted away the moment he pictured Robyn lying helpless. Those few percent he'd been knocked back three months ago, now surged forward, adding every suppressed emotion that he'd ever felt, plus more on top.

If that was the case, it was his fault. That was all the reason he needed to stop it happening. He raced to the research part of the library and didn't leave until he read every word for himself.

Newspaper headlines told of strong winds and high waves that day. Further up the coast, there were proper safety warnings. It was December, late in the afternoon, already dark.

'You *silly* girl,' he growled angrily and carried on reading. Two local men had seen Miss Harley walk down the beach to the water's edge, James and Colin Mackay of Mackay's Driftwood Emporium, thought they heard a shout, but when they went to look there was no sign of anyone. They alerted the emergency services, who in turn were hampered by the weather conditions. Her body was never recovered, but an iPhone was retrieved from a small crevasse in the rocks.

'You've been gone over two hours, Shay. There's not that much to read, what are you thinking? What are you going to do?' Tarro asked, sitting down beside him.

'Her body was never found, that's what it said. They called the search off after a week.' Shay's eyes were shining, whether, with excitement or unshed tears or both, Tarro wasn't sure.

'You're going there, aren't you? You *can't* prevent it, don't change history.'

Shay didn't answer. He stood, put a hand on his friend's shoulder and started to walk out. 'Whatever I do, I do alone, you and Adam can't be involved. Do you hear me, Tarro? You're *not* to come, not under *any* circumstances.'

* * *

'Now, what?' Adam asked as he watched Shay scoop Robyn from the rock pool.

'I can't just leave her to drown. She can have a life with... someone else.' His voice cracked with emotion.

'Like who? Any boy she's likely to meet now has already had his future mapped out. Think Shay, every breath she takes from this second will lead not only her, but possibly hundreds of other people, to a different outcome. Don't make things worse for yourself. Christopher Channing is just waiting for you to put another foot wrong.'

'Yep, changing the past should do it nicely,' Tarro added.

'Everything we do alters history a tiny bit. Have you ever considered while you're doing... whatever you do in the whorehouses, those women could potentially have been servicing different clients? If you weren't with them some aristocrat could have been. They'd most likely have died of the 'French Disease' as they called it then. Instead, you come back here, get treated and save them from their fate.'

'Don't be so bloody pedantic, we don't knowingly or *purposely* change things, there's a *massive* difference.'

'You knew when you told me, I wouldn't leave it,' Shay argued defensively. 'Why the hell did you even bring this to my attention?'

Tarro looked guilty. 'I didn't think you'd come charging back here like some kind of futuristic *saviour*. I just wanted you to get Robyn out of your system once and for all. Then we wanted you back to how you'd been during the summer, the real you. Maybe that was selfish.'

'We liked you better that way,' Adam added.

'Well, you succeeded, I'm back now and I have to make a decision.'

'There's nothing to decide Shay,' Adam said frantically. 'Put her *back*, if you can't do it, I will.'

'No!' His arms tightened automatically. 'I need to think.' He walked across the rocks and jumped down onto the sand, Robyn cocooned safely in his arms, every step taking them further from danger.

'Oh shit, stop bloody *thinking*,' Tarro recoiled, 'Here comes that wave.'

The three men looked in horror and automatically linked together, Shay holding his precious bundle between them, offering the best protection he could. Tarro couldn't stop the thrill of adrenaline that raced through his body. He gave a whoop as the icy water crashed over their heads.

'If we break apart,' Adam spluttered, 'head straight back to the portal.' The backwash was strong, but they kept each other firmly balanced.

'Whatever you're going to do, make it quick,' Tarro said. 'Two men are heading this way, they'll see us in just a moment.'

'I'll never be allowed to stay here. Anywhere I take her in our past could change things. But, what if it wasn't the *past*?'

'This isn't going to be good,' Adam muttered.

'I'll take her home, to our time? Nothing will be changed. Don't you see, whatever happens, it will be brand spanking new for all of us.'

'Take Robyn to the future?' Tarro began to smile. 'It could work, is it *possible* though? Will she be able to travel safely so far ahead?'

'Why not? It was only a problem for us because there is no future as such, not if the theory that we're at the forefront is true.'

'I guess if she doesn't make it, there's nothing to lose.' Adam looked sceptically at them both and then began to laugh. 'Nothing ventured.'

Robyn's head hurt and her ankle throbbed. She opened her eyes and everything was wrong. She was horizontal for a start. Her fingers tingled and voices, familiar voices were arguing? No... laughing. It was too dark. 'Am I dead?'

'No, Robyn, you've cheated death.'

'*Shay*?' I don't understand, is it really you?' She felt the lightest of kisses on her lips. 'Am I dreaming then, and if so, where are you taking me?'

'Home, my love, I'm taking you home.'

Chapter Eighteen

'I even believed in magic for a few years.'

'This is a long dream,' Robyn whispered softly, giving a groan as the pain in her ankle spread.

'It's not a dream, love,' Shay smiled. They were back in his time and she was safe. The portal activity may have flagged up an anomaly, or possibly, if they were very lucky, just recognised Robyn purely as a DNA sample.

'When I wake up, I want to remember you like this.'

'You're not dreaming, didn't you hear the man?' Adam loomed over giving her nose a pinch.

'Ow, that bloody hurt.'

'You stupid bastard,' Tarro pushed Adam out of the way. 'Look, Robyn, it's us. We're really here, it's all true, we came back to save you.'

Shay made an inarticulate sound. 'That's not what you wanted to do at all. *I* saved her, not you.'

'This really is happening. I couldn't possibly think up a pantomime like this, even in my sleep,' Robyn said, and as she glanced up at Shay, her heart swelled. *He came back.* 'Where am I exactly?'

'I'll explain everything soon. Right now, we're all soaking wet and you're freezing.' He looked questioningly at his friends. 'Mara and Rebecca's house?'

Adam grinned at the mention of Mara's name. 'Yeah, she'll probably kill us, but it's the best place for now.'

'Please tell me you've at least thought this through?' Mara glared at her brother. She'd shown Robyn to the bathroom, explained the controls for the water and dryer jets and left her with an insulating robe to change into.

'I'll think of something. I suppose I'll have to come clean, throw myself on the council's mercy. What can they do now she's here?'

Mara looked slightly mollified. 'If it's above board, she can stay.' A thought occurred. 'She's not contaminated, is she? I'm sorry Shayden, we have the baby to think of.'

'Mara, stop it.' Rebecca took her partner's hand gently but firmly. 'This is the girl your brother loves, she would have died. Of course, we have to help them.'

'Yes *alright*, I'm the only one of us thinking clearly, that's all,' she snapped.

'You're rather magnificent when you're so moody,' Adam smirked, not helping the situation.

Mara glared again, 'Are you still here? And Tarro for that matter, you two can clear off. Go and drip water… and seaweed in your own homes.' She plucked a long strand of something green from Adam's shoulder, allowing a smile as she heard him grumble something about 'charming hospitality'.

Tarro promised to make inquiries regarding any suspicions about their log entries. Yet again the three of them had travelled to the very time and place they were warned not to go.

'Thank you, both of you.' Shay grasped their arms as they left. 'I couldn't have done it alone.'

'That's what friends do,' Adam said matter-of-factly.

Mara sat next to Shay and felt him lean into her. 'My baby brother,' she smiled. 'Who knew you'd cause us all such turmoil?'

'What do you think will happen?' he asked. 'You work in the legal department.'

'I don't know, this is unprecedented. We need to plan carefully. Robyn's case has to be presented in a way that attracts sympathy if it's to be effective.'

'Let's not forget,' Rebecca began to smile. 'Robyn is a real living DNA source. The first one *ever*. Think how many samples spoil in the portals. If she's willing to help us, it could go a long way to gaining support.'

'I'll help.' Robyn pushed the door open and limped to the empty seat on the other side of Shay. 'As long as they don't try and bleed me dry.'

'Oh, your poor ankle,' Mara cried, jumping from the sofa to get the medical box. A small wrap around appliance showed there was no break. A hot pain relieving poultice followed, which started to work immediately.'

'Wow,' Robyn gasped, 'Impressive. Shay, I'll do what I can for your people while I'm here... when do you think I can go home?'

Silence descended, Mara and Rebecca, looked at the floor.

He took her hand. 'I-I thought you understood what had happened.'

'I do, but I'm okay now. You can take me back and I'll just say I had a fall or something.'

'No, Robyn, I can't. There is no going back, not ever.' He watched as she seemed to shrink into herself before his eyes.

'Not *ever*?' she repeated in a small voice. They all shook their heads.

'Would it be so bad to stay here, with me?'

'Of course, it wouldn't, but I need to say goodbye. Oh shit, this is awful. I do love you Shay, but my life is...'

'With me, your life is with me, you can't change the past Robyn, it won't be allowed. If you go back, then you go back to die. I can't, I *won't* let that happen.'

'I see.' She looked around the room helplessly.

'You're exhausted and you've a lot to think about. Let Shay show you to the spare room, we'll talk again about this tomorrow,' Rebecca said wisely.

She was taken to a comfortable if sparse room. Certain pieces of furniture, the bed for one, were familiar, the covers not so much. Gossamer light, they moulded to her body. Shay set the temperature controls. 'Your body heat will be monitored and regulated automatically, ensuring a good night's sleep.'

'You're doing that sales-rep thing again. What's wrong with a nice fat duvet?'

He chuckled and tucked her back under the cover. 'Go to sleep Robyn. I'll be back first thing in the morning.'

'Are you seriously leaving me alone?'

He flushed, the depths of longing in his eyes saying everything.

'Shay, come here.' She smiled and pulled him down onto the bed. 'I know I need to sleep, but I want you next to me.' Waiting until he was undressed and settled, she started to ask more questions. 'Will I be accepted here? Won't I look a bit freakish?'

'Why should you? Go back two thousand years from 2016, did people look freakish then? Did I look freakish that day in the field when you found me?'

'You looked wonderful, I think I fancied the pants off you that very first day.' She stared hard and noticed his eyes begin to dilate. 'You know what I mean, though, you have to admit there are differences.'

'Very subtle. We're maybe a few inches taller on average, live longer, have a little less body hair, well some of us.' He glanced down at his smattering of dark chest hair.

'I've missed this,' Robyn began to gently weave her fingers around his torso. 'I'm glad you're one of the hairier ones.' She snuggled against him and for the first time in three months fell into a deep and contented sleep.

Mara looked in a little later. Amazed how young and peaceful her brother's face looked, she crept away, thinking seriously of ways to help.

The next morning Shay found Robyn standing forlornly in the kitchen. She held an empty mug in her hand and looked completely overwhelmed. 'You should have woken me,' he smiled. 'Can I get you some breakfast?'

'I just wanted to make a cup of tea, you *do* have tea, don't you?' There was a slight tremor in her voice. She let him take the cup to some concealed switches on the wall. Pressing one caused a spout to drop, pressing a second and holding the mug in place, meant that her tea was ready in seconds.

'The preferences are set for my sister and Rebecca's tastes, it's easy enough to alter them, but we'll do that at mine.'

'Yours? Your house?'

'Mmm,' he nodded, taking a sip of his own drink.

'I'd like that, but I won't make you a very good girlfriend, not here.'

'You're the only girlfriend I want Robyn.' He grinned.

Frowning, she folded her arms. 'I don't recognise one tiny thing in this kitchen, there are no electrical sockets, no gadgets, well a few odd things in that cupboard,' she pointed, 'More like instruments of torture by the looks of them.' She brushed Shay's hand away, immediately feeling guilty. 'Don't you get it. People are going to say, 'Look, there's Shayden Lomax and his dumb-ass, ancient girlfriend'. I can't do that to you.'

'They most *certainly* won't,' Mara interrupted, joining them and putting some holodiscs on the side. 'Legal stuff, I need to study. Listen, Robyn, there's not one science worker that's isn't bursting with excitement to meet you. Even the stable ones are getting quite worked up.'

Shay's mouth fell open. 'You've already told them?'

'Yes, I have. We can't keep her a secret, this is far better. We're going to meet every challenge and negative comment head on.'

'Thanks, Mara,' he breathed a sigh of relief. 'With you on our side, things are looking up.'

She tutted. 'Right I've managed to get you a day's reprieve, told them Robyn needed to 'acclimatise' a little. That was the best I could do, be prepared for the onslaught tomorrow. There are also a lot of people not happy you're here, Robyn. We need to change their minds.'

Robyn nodded, not fully understanding how tentative her predicament was. 'Can I go outside, I'd like to look around a bit.'

Shay and Mara looked at each other and both gave a silent nod, obviously in agreement. 'I'll take you in covered transport,' Shay said. 'But not near the centres, not yet.'

'If I'm staying here with you forever, I have to say goodbye to Sim. I can't live with the thought of her being upset.'

'If my brother hadn't saved you, there would have been no choice. It's far too dangerous to go back, what if someone else should see you.' Mara didn't mean her words unkindly, but her limited emotion meant limited inflection. It was said straight and to the point.

Robyn nodded, the realisation that she would actually be dead had been playing on her mind. 'I'm sorry, but if I could get hold of a phone I'd make absolutely certain she was alone. Five minutes, that's all I'd need.'

Shay nodded. 'I'll do it, we don't think the portals recognise you, so no one will know. I can say I went to tidy some loose ends.'

'Don't take Adam, he's clearly unstable. Do you know he asked me to have sex with him last night? Dear God, even if I was interested in men, he'd be the last one I'd consider. And don't disturb Tarro, he's busy working on your behalf with his council friends. Ask Rebecca and use a different exit portal from this end.'

Shay huffed and threw Robyn a grin. 'My *very* bossy sister.' He watched Mara purse her lips. 'I only come here to see my new nephew.'

'Or hide strange women, sorry Robyn. It's true, we hardly saw him before Gabriel came home.'

Shay beamed. 'You did decide on Gabriel.'

'I didn't know there was a baby in the house, he must be very quiet.' Her hand went unconsciously to her stomach. *If things don't work out and I'm sent back, he can't know. I won't let him have that on his conscience as well.*

Mara smiled. 'My mother says they're nearly all quiet, until about thirty weeks.'

'Oh, he's premature, will he be okay?'

Shay sent his sister a warning to keep quiet. Robyn had likely forgotten a lot of what he'd told her a few months back. He didn't need to remind her again at this very moment.

'Don't think I'm not happy to be with you,' Robyn said, as they stepped onto the hard-frozen earth. 'I'd have moved mountains to live in your time, or anywhere come to that, as long as we were together. It's just when the choice is gone, it's harder somehow.'

'I understand and the circumstances could be better. I have to admit though, now we're together, I wouldn't change things.'

'This is where we met.' Robin closed her eyes and pictured the ripening wheat.

'Tarro's bad driving was the best thing that ever happened to me. Remind me to thank him when we see him next.'

'Right, you two lovebirds,' Rebecca handed over a phone. 'Make the call Robyn, I'll wait here for you both.'

* * *

Two days before the funeral/memorial service, Simone got a strange text. **'make sure u on ur own. R xxx'** Not recognising the number, she had a gut feeling, immediately texting back – **'5 mins. S x.'**

Feeling an unexpected yet familiar tingling, she broke down at the sight of her dearest friend. 'My God, how can this be? Come here, let me touch you.' The girls hugged each other, neither one could stop crying.

Robyn quietly explained everything and when she'd finished Simone gave a sad smile.

'Will I ever see you again, Robz?'

'I hope so if I'm allowed, but don't live your life waiting for me, enjoy every minute. Promise?'

'Maybe next time, I'll be married or have children.' Simone laughed. 'Oh, Robyn. Just knowing that you're living your life with Shay is enough, the alternative was so awful, it was worse than the despair I felt in the hospital after the accident.'

'I'm sorry we won't see our children grow up together Sim, I so wanted them to be friends.' As Robyn burst into a fresh flood of tears, Simone's arms went around her again and they were joined by Shay's.

'Time to go love.' He gave them both a sympathetic look, which turned to real sorrow as he heard the choked sobs.

'We're travelling to Devon tomorrow,' Simone managed to say between her tears. 'Stuart Frazer's flying down on the day.'

'My poor mum, I feel so bad,' Robyn sniffed.

'Don't feel guilty Robz, it's not as if you ran away and left us all to think the worst.'

'Goodbye Sim, be happy.'

Simone stared at the empty space. They were gone, her friend was over two thousand years away, but she was alive. Did Shay know he was going to be a father? she wondered.

* * *

The next few days, as Shay later described to Robyn, were like an iceberg. Everyone working tirelessly below the surface, whilst trying to shield her by just showing the tip. Lab technicians, Councillors, top Scientists from all the Capitals came to ask questions. Robyn, once again, made it very clear that she was prepared to help them in whatever way she was able. Shay also made it clear they would get no samples until a decision had been made as to whether or not she could stay.

Christopher Channing had been coldly charming to Robyn, wanting to talk to her alone. He was disappointed if not angry that his request was blatantly denied. Either Adam, Tarro or Shay were always in attendance. His demands, of which there were many, went unheard. No medicals, no scans, no probes, nothing at all, Shay informed him emphatically as he showed him from the house. A 'Go to hell, Channing, you're not the head of the council yet,' ringing in his ears.

* * *

Two weeks later, Robyn's future hung in the balance. The council called an extraordinary meeting to see if they could agree on an outcome. If not, Shay had been warned she would be sent back to her own time, at the point when her life, or in this case her death, had been altered.

Tarro waited with her outside the main hall. If he got the signal to go, he would take her straight to the portal and disappear into history. Shay would join them as soon as possible. Unaware of this latest escape plan, Robyn waited apprehensively, clutching at Tarro's arm every time a voice was raised behind the closed door.

'It's not looking good,' Adam stuck his head out to inform them. 'Jury's still out and Channing's got a lot in agreement. Be ready my friend.' He added quietly, seeing Tarro give a nod.

'What the hell's the matter with these people? I've offered to give everything I have. Blood, sweat, tears. Christ, whatever they want.'

'I'm going back in.' Adam gave her an awkward hug.

'What will happen if I can't stay? Have they come up with any other possible solutions?'

'Honestly, I don't have a clue,' Tarro said, knowing full well what her fate would be if he didn't intervene.

'They'll send me back, won't they? To just before the accident... I'll die then, I suppose.'

'It'll kill Shay if they do that. We're not going to let it happen, have faith in us, Robyn.'

'He'll be fixed again. Perhaps that's for the best. I couldn't bear to think of him sad.'

'It didn't work last time; I don't think that's an option anymore. Damn it! you're offering them so much; you're a continuing source of living DNA. If anything is going to sway them, that's what'll do it.' He scratched his head. 'If only we could spice it up a bit.'

'What do you mean?'

'We've played the blue-eyed card, that's raised the bar in our favour. You're also young and healthy, keen to continue a relationship here, so Mara's pushing that point. There could be children one day, she's reminding them all of that fact as well.' Tarro smiled at the thought. 'A generation of blue-eyed, strong children, who knows what that could do to the gene pool?'

Robyn gave a loud sigh; the time had come. 'There is something,' she said, chewing her lip. 'I wanted to protect Shay, in case... I couldn't stay. He doesn't know yet.'

Tarro listened and his amazement turned to pure satisfaction. A large grin broke across his face, and taking Robyn by the hand, he pushed past the council wardens and walked into the middle of the assembly hall.

'What do you think you're doing in here, Tarro Watson?' Channing sneered. 'You have no right to enter the hall, certainly not with... her. Still, as it's nearly time, you may as well stay for the final decision.'

'First,' Tarro said loudly, 'I think you all need to hear what Robyn has to say.' They looked up. A commotion in the crowd had caused a few council members to lose their footing and jostle the people standing close by.

Shay burst through and came to Robyn's side. 'Whatever happens, I won't stand by and do nothing.' He took her hand and faced Channing.

'Really, Shayden, what can the two of you do?' he asked sarcastically, so sure the outcome was going to go in his favour and supremely confident that it would ensure his rise to the head of the council the following month. He was surprised, however, to see Adam join them, who had been wondering what on earth Tarro was up to. 'Ah, your other partner in crime. What do the three of you hope to achieve here, we've heard all the arguments?'

'Five of us, actually,' Rebecca said, joining Mara and standing in a show of unity with Robyn.

A murmur went through the crowd. Rebecca was highly thought of, an expert in her field of horticulture. An area everyone was slightly obsessed with. If DNA replacement wasn't going to save their failing race, maybe some kind of super plant food would do it.

'Speak up Robyn,' Tarro whispered in her ear. 'Tell them what you just told me.'

'I'm pregnant,' she said hesitantly. 'If you send me back, the b... baby will die as well.' She heard Shay's sharp intake of breath and a few more from the assembly. Muttering started at one end and worked its way across the hall like a Mexican wave.

Channing was thrown momentarily, he could feel the immediate shift in mood. Compassion was rearing its ugly head. This was one issue he couldn't lose; it had become pivotal to his political career. If he wanted to remain in the running for the powerful position he craved, he had to win today. 'That's unfortunate Miss Harley, but, it must have been the case in 2016. You were pregnant and you died. Sad, but then so are many things.' The muttering started again and Channing began to think he was pulling it back.

'But this *isn't* just a twenty-first-century pregnancy, it's also a forty-fifth-century one. Shayden Lomax's baby to be exact.' Tarro walked forward appealing to the council leaders. 'Is that written in the legal holobase? It's not about our history changing, it's all about here, and *now*. Yes, we can send this young girl back to her death, *or* we can keep her here. Would you condemn an unborn child? And who knows, this untainted mix of DNA could be the founder of a new generation. He or she could be our salvation!'

The medics and scientists that made up a good part of the council were almost wetting themselves in near hysteria. Robyn's DNA was one thing, but a *placenta* and *umbilical cord*! The possibilities were endless. The Mexican wave went back in the other direction, by the time it reached its original starting point the outcome was crystal clear.

Tarro looked back and winked at Robyn. 'Was I good, or was I... good?'

'You were bloody amazing.' She ran and hugged him. 'Just think I thought you were such a moody old grizzly bear when we first met.' She turned to look at the one man that really mattered. 'I'm sorry I didn't tell you straight away.'

'I can't believe it.' He took her from Tarro and kissed her in front of the whole assembly, every emotion he possessed shining out for all to see. The crowd went wild, well the emotional half of them. The others clapped and smiled indulgently, a real hope for their future abundantly clear.

Knowing he'd lost, Christopher Channing scowled, threw his holopad down and stormed from the hall.

'How, *when*?' Shay asked, in a state of euphoric shock.

'I think it had to be the day I was sick when we went to see the Northern Lights. I haven't got around to getting checked properly. Didn't you notice?' She patted her stomach.

'I did actually, especially last night when you were on top and...' he stopped abruptly, as the council head approached them. 'I thought you'd just put on a bit of weight,' he whispered, grinning.

'Miss Harley, I'm Helen Manning, present head of the council and hopefully, thanks to you, I'll likely continue for another term.' She'd taken great delight seeing her nemesis, leave the building in such a fury. 'We'll arrange to take the foetus as soon as it's around sixteen weeks.'

Robyn looked into the smiling eyes of the older woman. 'I think I'm already seventeen and a half weeks actually, and in any case, you'll do no such thing,' she answered firmly. 'I've been told how you manage pregnancies here, no wonder all the wombs are too weak to hold a full-term baby. It appears it doesn't take that many generations to develop flaws. My womb, on the other hand, is as strong as an ox, or I have no reason to think otherwise. I shall keep my child exactly where it is, thanks. When it's good and ready it'll make an appearance and I'll probably scream the place down.' She glanced at Shay, who had gone a deathly white. 'You'll be right by my side.' She smiled and turned back to the Council Head. 'That doesn't mean I'll refuse your medical care or wonderful analgesia when the time comes.'

Helen laughed. 'It'll certainly be a first for us, we'll have to brush up on midwifery techniques. I'm sorry if I'm peering at you, your eyes are so beautiful.'

'I'm getting used to it, every conversation I have here seems rather *intimate*. I realised after a while it was because of the way everyone was staring so deeply at me.'

'Is there anything we can do for you today, Miss Harley?' she asked kindly.

'Not today, I just want to go and start my life properly with Shay, but I would like to be allowed to travel at some point.'

'I'm not sure about that,' the council leader replied, looking uncomfortable. She'd wanted to grant this young girl favours as she was giving them so much, but this just seemed one step too far. She looked thoughtful. 'I suppose there's no harm in recreational travel. You could never return to your own time, you would have to agree to that.'

Robyn explained briefly about Simone, the fact that her friend already knew everything, in detail.

Although she was sympathetic, anger flashed across Helen Manning's face when she heard the revelations of just what Shay had been part of. She gave him a look of disapproval which conveyed the strong reprimand that would soon follow. 'I don't like it, Miss Harley, to be honest. Perhaps in a few years' time, very quick and limited visits, with a travelling companion of the council's choice. You won't be having afternoon tea or days out together.'

Robyn nodded, she'd been hoping for more, but at least it was a start. Shay could hardly believe the concession. Robyn had no idea what a huge boon she'd just been granted.

'May I ask, Miss err Mrs Manning, why you haven't brought live people through the portals before? It kinda seems an obvious thing to try.'

'Please, call me Helen. For many reasons, contamination and morality being the top two. How would they explain it when we returned them?' She didn't add it was a rather barbaric and ancient way of thinking.

'I don't know, drug them or something, surely your mastermind race would stoop to that, wouldn't it?'

'Robyn, I can't believe you'd condone such a thing.' Adam stepped forward and bellowed with laughter. 'We've created a monster.' He winked at the council leader. 'Looking feisty today, Helen,' he leered.

'Adam Beaumont when did you last go for a health check? Make an appointment *immediately*,' she said firmly, allowing herself a small fond smile.

Everyone laughed, but it was a real issue, and as Shay took Robyn's hand and led her from the hall, Helen prayed that the young girl would somehow be their deliverance.

* * *

They were going to have a daughter in twenty-two weeks' time. Robyn had allowed a scan to get that information. She also wanted to know the baby was healthy, and the holodisc containing all the DNA information, including hair, eye colour, predicted growth patterns, lay on the side. 'I'd like to call her Aurora,' she said, but noticed Shay raising his brows. 'You don't like it, do you? I thought after the Aurora Borealis.'

'I do like it. It's just a bit of a mouthful. I can't promise I wouldn't call her Auri.'

'I can live with that,' she smiled.

* * *

Robyn made a conscious decision, not to research the whole of Simone's life, so she only ever looked a year ahead. That way she could try and visit each milestone in real-time. Their bodies would age simultaneously, and they could almost pretend nothing had changed.

The first time was just after three years, to attend Simone and Alec Frazer's wedding.

Richard and Simone had carried on seeing each other for a year after her recovery was complete. Eventually accepting the mutual realisation that it was their friendship keeping them together and the spark just wasn't there, however much they wanted it to be, Richard bowed out. They would continue to remain friends for the rest of their lives.

Joey's obsession with Angus Frazer, kept the relationship between the two families going. One day, when Alec returned from his adventuring and decided it was time to 'grow up', he was introduced to Simone.

Biding her time and remaining hidden at the rear of the church through the service, Robyn took a chance to slip into a photo at the back of the wedding group.

'I know you're here, Robz,' Simone said, a little later when she had a moment alone in the ladies. 'I felt Shay earlier.'

'Hello, my luvver, I've bought you a wedding present,' Robyn grinned, peering around the empty cubicle. 'Blimey, it's come to this, clandestine meetings in the toilets.' She handed her friend a small black disc and showed her how to activate it. A six-inch perfect copy of a blonde-haired toddler stood on the disc and waved. Simone's face was a picture, firstly because of the technology and secondly, this was actually a representation of Robyn's daughter.

'That's my little Aurora, she's nearly three.' They held hands for a few minutes, trying not to cry. A sob slipped out just as Shay arrived.

'We have to go, the council rep's waiting at the portal.'

Robyn nodded. 'Look for me in your group photo.' She gave her friend a kiss.

Every time Simone opened her laptop and looked at the screensaver, Robyn's face peeped out from between two of Alec's ginger-haired Aunts. It always made her smile.

* * *

There were one or two very quick visits over the next five years. One at the birth of Simone's first child, and another at Angus Frazer's funeral. That had been a pure coincidence and Robyn managed to see her old work colleagues from a well-hidden place behind a privet hedge. Simone had come to her, and if Alec thought she'd gone slightly insane talking to the greenery, he didn't comment.

After the birth of her son, a second blue-eyed healthy specimen, Helen Manning even conceded letting Robyn have her own implants so that she could activate the portals herself. Not that anyone was supposed to travel to the past alone; but in emergencies, she wouldn't have to worry about becoming lost or left behind.

Simone received two more holodiscs. One showed Auri, now eight, with her little brother Angus. The next had the two elder siblings standing by a driftwood crib singing to a baby.

'That's Simone, she's two months old,' Robyn beamed.

'Oh, Robz, how wonderful. I've got something for you, will you be allowed to take it back?' She handed over a book and a photo.

'My mum,' Robyn burst into tears, 'and that must be my... half-brother, he's the spitting image of Richard.'

'Simone nodded. 'He's eight, the same age as Aurora.'

'Of *course*, Mum was pregnant when I left. It seems like a world away. Is everyone okay?'

'Yeah, Rich keeps in touch. Josie took it very badly, your, umm death. They put the wedding off till the following summer.' She gave a sigh. 'Josie got a new child, Rich got a new half-sibling. I never got a new besty.' She gave a Robyn a sad smile.

'That's because you didn't lose the one you already had. What about Alec, he turned out to be a good substitute, are you happy Sim? Really happy?'

'I am and I adore him, as much as you adore Shay, our men are very lucky to have us,' she laughed. 'Did you see the second gift?'

'No I didn't,' Robyn picked up the book and read the title, *The Girl and The Wave*, by Jack Frazer. She gave a gasp and flicked through the first few pages.

'Don't worry it's not an autobiography, but you did inspire the title. Look at the dedication.'

'For Robyn, wherever you may be.'

'Oh wow, I'm so pleased he got published, is this his first book?'

'No, it's his fourth actually. He said it was always in his head. I told you on the last visit, he got married. Well, they've moved to Canada, the outdoors reminds him of home, he reckons.' Simone gave a giggle.

'And Joey, is he any more settled? I was a bit concerned after our last talk.'

'I think he may have a girlfriend. If so, he's keeping her under wraps. I worry about my little brother, he seems a bit... lost. Like Alec used to be before he met me, always searching for something.' Simone gave a shrug. 'What will be, will be. I've certainly learned that in my lifetime. Did you make a difference, Robz, to the future?'

'It's too early to tell, although the scientists are very positive. My DNA and the children's is being sent all around the world. Most of the new babies appear stronger, which is a huge step forward and they're left inside the womb until twenty weeks now.'

Simone nodded. There wasn't much Robyn hadn't told her about the forty-fifth century.

As they grew older it became easier to visit more often and stay longer, even having a proper catch up over a mug of hot chocolate with mini marshmallows and whipped cream. The council had long ceased keeping tabs.

Shay accompanied Robyn occasionally, but as Simone had been an anchor for her best friend for many years it wasn't imperative.

* * *

'Are you sure about this?' Shay asked, for the umpteenth time.

'Yes, my love, it's something I have to do.' Robyn gave herself a critical look in the mirror. The tiniest grey streaks of hair were well camouflaged by the blonde curls, which she wore at shoulder length. Not a vain creature by nature, Robyn felt a glow of pleasure when she caught a glimpse of her reflection. At eighty-six, she could easily pass for a woman in her mid-fifties in her own time. Shay looked distinguished, she thought, with the silver tips framing his face. They both took medication that slowed down the physical signs of ageing. It was her one concession to the many pills and potions on offer.

This last visit was the one Robyn had been dreading her whole life. During the funeral service, she sat quietly at the back with Shay. Babs and Clive were long dead, but she recognised, from photos, Simone's sons and grandsons all looking like the Frazer men they'd been destined to become.

Her breath hitched as a dark-haired woman caught her eye. It could have been Babs; the likeness was uncanny, she had her arm around an elderly man and called him Dad. It was *Joey*, she'd have known him anywhere. He was smartly suited but with a wildness about him, his grey hair holding the odd curl. It gave him the appearance of an old tomb raider or mountain explorer.

When everyone started to leave, he stopped in front of her, handing over a small package. 'Simone wanted you to have this, she thought you may be here today.'

Fighting back her astonishment, Robyn looked inside to find the three small holodiscs. She started to speak. Joey stopped her.

'I never knew where you used to go. I saw you and Shay disappear from the barn quite often, sometimes I'd watch and you came back again almost immediately. I even saw you go off from Simone's room in fancy dress once.' He gave a small laugh.' When you went missing, properly, my sister was in a terrible state, nothing we said or did gave her any comfort. Then a couple of days before your memorial service, things changed. She still missed you *dreadfully*, but she wasn't... *unhappy* anymore and so I knew you weren't dead. Wherever it was you used to go to, I figured you were there. I just never knew where '*there*' was. I even believed in magic for a few years.' He looked her up and down. 'Maybe it is magic, you're the youngest looking eighty-six-year-old, I've ever seen.'

Robyn smiled. 'Do you know how Richard is? Joey.'

He gave a small laugh. 'I haven't been called that for nearly sixty years. Richard's not well, which is why he isn't here. He lives with his eldest daughter, in Devon still. They kept in touch until... the end, it was some comfort after Alec died. Simone had a hard time getting over his death, she never embraced being widowed, but then who does? I told that stupid bastard not to go caving at his age. How many eighty-year-olds do you know that scramble through tunnels or dive in underwater pools?'

Robyn kept quiet. Most of the people she knew in their eighties were only just approaching middle age. She'd tried to see a lot more of Simone since Alec's death and knew how difficult it had been for her.

'She never told me the truth you know, whatever it was.'

'Oh Joey, I should have guessed you were watching, you were always far cleverer than we gave you credit for.' She leant forward and took him in her arms, trying to recapture a precious time with a cheeky mischievous boy so long ago.

'Are you sad, about the life you missed here?' Shay asked when they were finally alone.

'Of course, but I'd never have swapped it for the one I have with you. You were and still are the love of my life.'

'As you are to me. Now then we should get back to the portal, that service seemed to drag on, I thought it would *never* end. Sorry... I know it was for Simone.' He'd put his foot in it again.

Robyn thought of all the unknown yet familiar faces in the church, she could have studied them all day. 'I thought it flew by.' *How odd that the hands of a clock always move with the same speed, and yet for one person, time passes quickly and for another, far too slowly.* 'I never understood that,' she muttered.

'Never understood what?' Shay smiled.

'The passage of time.'

'Ah,' he squeezed her hand, 'me neither.'

Alison is one of two sisters who have both started to write novels now that their families have grown, left home and time is no longer the enemy.

A 35-year nursing career, most of it spent working night shifts, meant that, over the years, she got through a wide section of books from different genres. From YA fantasy and dystopian to historical romance, her choices have always been, and are still extremely varied.

From the Future with Love, is her first novel to be published. Imaginary worlds and situations that are realistic enough to create that ounce of belief that they could be real, is a common factor that can be found in all her stories.

Follow Alison on Facebook
https://www.facebook.com/plymouthauthor

Or visit her website
www.mckenziesisters.com

If you have enjoyed this book, please leave
Alison a review on Amazon.
She would love to know your thoughts.